SUNDERROOT

THREADS OF THE WORLD TREE

SUNDERROOT

CHRISTINA JUHLIN

Independently published in Sweden
www.christinajuhlin.se

ISBN: 978-91-990670-1-8 (ebook)
ISBN: 978-91-990670-0-1 (paperback)
ISBN: 978-91-990670-2-5 (hardcover)

Developmental editing by Nej Steer, Nej The Story Doctor
Copy and line editing by Nicole Evans, Thoughts Stained Editorial
Proofreading by Wren L. Helgren, Helgren Editing

For my son, the light of my life

May you find magic under every stone, in every crevice,
and within every ripple of water.

Content Warning

This story contains themes of bullying, classism, life in a children's home, panic and anxiety from the main character's point of view, the death of an animal and mention of other animal deaths, people fallen in comas, uncertainty surrounding the main character's parents, and a fantasy battle.

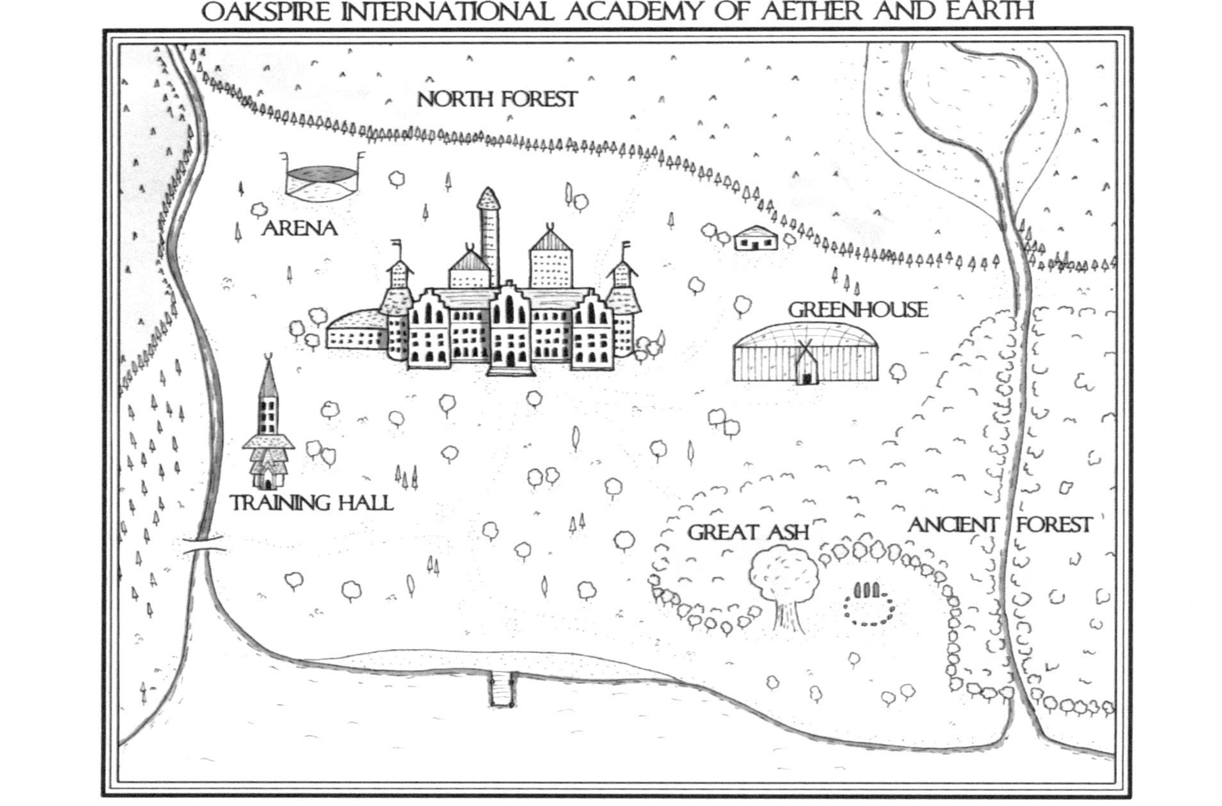
OAKSPIRE INTERNATIONAL ACADEMY OF AETHER AND EARTH
NORTH FOREST
ARENA
GREENHOUSE
TRAINING HALL
GREAT ASH
ANCIENT FOREST

Pronunciation Guide

This guide covers names and terms that may be unfamiliar or non-English. Capitalised syllables show where the stress falls.

Main Characters

Aria Renwood	AH-ree-uh REN-wood
Finn O'Heffernan	FIN oh-HEH-fer-nan
Taye Lundvik	TAY LOOND-vik

Other students

Carolina Valencia	kah-ro-LEE-nah vah-LEN-see-ah
Fraser Murphy-Mussa	FRAY-zer MUR-fee MOO-sah
Inaiê Kuaray	ee-nah-YEH koo-ah-rah-EE
Inessa Volkova	ee-NYEH-sah vol-KOH-vah
Jun Park	JOON PARK
Kaija Väinävirta	KAI-yah VAI-nah-veer-tah
Petra Nosenko	PEH-trah noh-SEN-koh
Suraya Clairmont-Ziadeh	soo-RAH-yah KLARE-mon zee-AH-deh
Tenzin Norbu	TEN-zin NOR-boo
Tove Bjørnstad	TOH-veh BYOHRN-stahd
Victoria Beauchamp	vik-TOR-ee-uh Bee-chum

Professors & Academy Staff

Alden Halvard	AHL-den HAL-vard
Astrid Frejd	AH-strid FREYD
Avery Kiran	AY-vree KEE-ran
K'amaye Haruki	kah-MAH-yeh HA-roo-kee
Klaus Grünwald	KLAUS GRUEN-valt
Lavinia Thistlecroft	luh-VIN-ee-uh THIS-uhl-kroft
Magnus Nordfell	MAHG-nus NOORD-fell
Nienke Vinke	NEEN-kuh VIN-kuh
Nkeiru Okezie	N-kih-REW oh-KEH-zee-eh
Rosemary Salvia	ROH-zmuh-ree SAL-vee-uh
Sigrid Vik	SIG-rid Veek
Torben Stormgaard	TOR-ben STORM-gahr

Creatures & Beings

Askafroa	AS-kah-froh-ah
Draugr	DROW-gr
Magifauna	MAH-ghee-FAW-nah
Sylvandir	SYL-van-dir
Vaesen	VEH-sem
Vavtrudner	VAHV-trud-ner
Völva	VURL-vah

Locations & Objects

Eldviken	ELD-vee-ken
Hnefatafl	NEF-ah-tah-full
Solkattring	SOOL-katt-ring

Prologue

Fog lingered above dark water, perfectly mirroring the towering, ghostly silhouettes of trees standing guard. The full moon shone above, its light diffused across the forest in a pale grey hush, like the world had been covered in a blanket, silenced.

Everything was impossibly still; no animal made a sound, no leaves rustled in the wind, and the water didn't break on the shore. The forest was waiting, watching in the darkness.

Until a cry stirred the stillness.

A strong, piercing sound echoed through the forest, signalling the start of a new cycle. A cry so raw and insistent, it rang out again and again, until at last, it stopped, and the forest exhaled.

The sound came from deep within, from a cottage made of stone tucked away in the woods. Its windows glowed with golden light, casting warmth on the wild yet lovingly kept garden outside. A hedgehog scrambled through the mowed grass, causing the patches of bluebells to wiggle slightly as it passed.

As the nature outside resettled in the stillness of the night, the gentle rhythmic breathing filled the bedroom on the second floor of the cottage. A newborn suckled in her mother's arms, wrinkly hands holding her mother's finger.

The mother's lavish red-brown hair was up in a knot, some strands glued by sweat on her forehead. She sat on a wooden-framed bed with soft flowered sheets, a white tunic covering her shoulders and arms, holding her newborn baby on her bare chest. She rested her head back on the bed frame, eyes closed.

Holding her hand was a man, sitting beside her on a leather chair, its surface dulled with age. He ran his hand through his dusky-blond hair, making it messier. His green eyes observed his daughter with a loving intensity.

They both sat quietly, taking in the intimate moment. The perfect little human slept, protected by the two that loved her the most.

A strong knock at the door downstairs broke their focus. The mother adjusted herself upright, her hazel eyes alert.

'She's here for her,' she said, biting her lip. 'Bring her in.'

'Right, I'll be back in a second,' the father said. He kissed his wife's head and walked out of the room.

He followed a corridor, the old floorboards creaking at every step. Landscape paintings on the white wall mirrored the fog outside; the painted trees and water moved slightly with an unseen breeze. The lamps lit up as he passed, each cradling a floating globe of golden light that flickered like fire yet held no flame.

At the bottom of the staircase was a green door, waiting to be opened. The man patted his white shirt and jeans flat and smoothed his hair back to receive the visitor.

He turned the lock and hesitantly opened the door.

Outside was a tall woman whose face was obscured under her moss green cloak, runes etched on the berm. She entered without looking at the man and went straight up the stairs. A scent of pine resin and anise lingered behind her.

The father closed the door, puzzled. He followed her calmly though, for he knew who she was, even though they had never met.

The fireplace crackled as the visitor entered the bedroom without direction. The father sneaked in behind her and hurried to his place next to his wife, holding her hand in both of his.

'Welcome,' said the mother. She looked down lovingly at the baby. 'This is Aria.'

Lowering her hood, the visitor exposed her long white-blonde hair. She looked young, but ancient at the same time. Her aquamarine eyes were stern, tingling with wisdom.

The visitor didn't reply, instead walked calmly to the side of the bed, and placed her long, slender fingers on the baby's forehead.

'Child of promise,' she said, her voice low and edged with authority, 'born from ashes, destroyer of worlds. A cycle to end all cycles.'

The mother gasped and the father frowned at the heavy words.

The visitor took back her hand, and turned, placidly heading towards the door.

'Surely, this can't be it,' said the mother, her tone hinting desperation. She held her baby tighter. 'There has to be more. This can't be it!'

The visitor said nothing and left the room.

'William! Stop her, this can't be it! She's a light elf norn, they bring good fates! This is bad!'

'Erm,' mumbled the father, stumbling from his chair. He hurried through the door after the visitor. 'Excuse me? Miss? Hello?'

His footsteps echoed in the corridor before he walked back into the bedroom.

'Tyra, she's gone. Didn't even leave through the front door. Just vanished.' He sat beside his wife. 'What does this mean?'

'I don't know,' Tyra replied, biting her lower lip. She ran her finger along the baby's hand. The baby wrapped her hand around it, holding tight. 'But we'll have to protect her. Whatever her fate holds.'

CHAPTER ONE

Acorn

Mornings were a battlefield. The smell of burnt toast lingered in the air, spoons clattered like swords, and the kettle screeched like a call to war. The only way to survive was to be invisible, and Aria Renwood did just that. She kept her head down, her auburn hair hiding most of her freckled face. Even though taller than most her age, she had mastered the art of disappearing in a room full of people.

Mrs Mabbott flapped around toast and mismatched mugs, trying to boss a kitchen full of children talking over one another. Her yellow cardigan was inside out again, her hair looked like it lost a fight, and the bags under her eyes were about as permanent as the damp patch in front of the leaky sink.

There were seven children crammed into a pastel-pink kitchen with bright green cupboards – a desperate attempt to cheer up the children who lived here. For Aria, it just added to the visual chaos of the house, now combined with the howling from under the table by the youngest: eight-year-old Johnny Layton.

'Aria, love – toast's on the table,' Mrs Mabbott said, nodding at the lopsided stack of bread as Aria entered the kitchen. 'Scrape off the burnt bits.'

Aria slid onto a wooden stool, visibly worn smooth, a reminder of the countless children who had come and gone before her. She picked up a handcrafted blue mug with rustic textures and the word "Jorvik" on it – surely a donation from the local museum. Aria poured hot water into her mug and in it, dipped a black tea bag. Beside her, Sara Davies, with foundation a shade too light, looked even paler in the morning light. Ironically, Sara was the complete opposite of that and buzzed with energy, bumping Aria's arm time and time again while Aria tried to spread strawberry jam on her toast. Instead, the jam got smeared across the table.

'Oh, nice one, Renwood,' said Oliver Sinclair, leaning against the counter. He was the oldest in the children's home, but not the wisest. He had a haircut so tragic, it looked like someone had put a bowl on his head and cut around it. 'You can't even spread jam on toast without mucking it up.'

Aria looked up, the golden flecks in her hazel eyes electrified with anger. 'Shut up, Oliver. No one asked your opinion.'

With a sharp flick of her wrist, jam flew from the butter knife, splattering on his white school shirt and yellow-and-black striped tie.

'Oi!' Oliver shouted furiously.

He pulled up his shirt from under his black trousers to rub the jam off. Instead, he smeared it more, making his shirt look like a crime scene.

'Smashed it!' Sara cackled, pointing at him. 'Looks way better now! Brings out your eyes!' She raised her hand at Aria for a high five, grinning wide.

Aria didn't move, hand still holding the butter knife, frozen mid-air. The laughter at the table exploded around her, but all she could hear was the rush of blood in her ears. Even though Oliver deserved this, and so much more, she knew she would pay for it.

Oliver looked over to Aria, his eyes narrowed. 'You're dead, Renwood! Just you wait!' he said, pointing his finger at her.

'Pack it in, the lot of you!' Mrs Mabbott barked. 'Oliver, go change – chuck that shirt in the laundry, I'll sort it. Aria, stop waving knives about. And for the love of all that is holy, Johnny, stop that friggin' howling!'

Oliver stomped towards the stairs, unbuttoning his shirt. Once out of sight behind her, Aria took a sip of her tea, hand trembling. As soon as warmth spread through her chest, something soft hit her on the back of her head. Aria jolted and knocked her tea onto her lap.

She jumped, the chair falling behind her. The burning sensation spread on her legs and rubbing it off did nothing. Her head snapped back to Oliver, who gave a smug grin, all crooked teeth and zero shame.

'Serves you right, muppet.'

'Eh! Pack it in, I said!' Mrs Mabbott shouted, slamming her palms down on the table. The room fell silent in an instant, the howling replaced by whimpering. 'Oliver, upstairs – now! Pick that shirt up from the floor, get changed, and head straight to school.'

She grabbed a towel and crouched by Aria, dabbing gently at her legs.

'Was it hot, love? Are you burnt?'

'It's fine,' Aria said, more embarrassed than injured.

Oliver's heavy footsteps could be heard upstairs. Mrs Mabbott leant in. 'Hold on a moment before you get changed.'

Aria nodded. It was common knowledge that when Oliver was hot-headed, it was better to leave him alone.

'Right.' Mrs Mabbott stood up and faced the other children. 'The rest of you, off you go – chop chop! Best not be late on your first day back!'

Aria stayed behind for a moment, clutching the now-damp towel on her lap. Her hands shook from Oliver's expression – his brown eyes burning, his crooked nose wrinkled, and his ears red with rage.

That morning set the tone for the first weeks back at school. School was continuously tedious and, at home, the tension hung in the air like smog. Oliver kept it low after Mrs Mabbott laid down the rules about no tolerance for violence in the children's home. Though it was clear a storm was brewing, making his silence more dangerous than shouting.

A few weeks later, one Wednesday morning, Aria stood in the kitchen, with her cream-coloured canvas backpack in hand, going through the pantry picking out the snacks for the day: ginger nut biscuits.

She had decided to take the day off and skip the history test she didn't study for. History was a bore, but that wasn't the reason she wanted to skip; she simply couldn't concentrate on studying. The thought of Oliver exploding at any moment made her stomach turn and her brain foggy. It'd been two weeks since the incident, and the pressure was reaching boiling point. Besides, sitting at her desk during the exam, staring at a blank piece of paper, would be deeply humiliating.

The test was on the Viking invasions into England and how they established Danelaw. A part of history that she found interesting, considering she lived in York – once Jórvík, the capital of Danelaw. Well, that's as much as she could remember. The rest was lost in a blur.

She picked up a red apple from the kitchen table and dropped it into her bag.

A part of her longed to be like them – a Viking. They didn't back down, showed no fear. If she'd been stronger, maybe Oliver would've stopped picking on her the moment he arrived, dragging his chaos from one children's home to the next. Of course, Aria was the one he enjoyed teasing the most, for reasons she didn't know.

Quietly and carefully, Aria stepped out of the house before the morning rush, hoping no one would notice her gone. The neighbourhood was quiet. The yellow-brick façades of the late-Victorian terraced houses caught the first rays of sun sneaking from behind the thick grey clouds. Warm asphalt with a hint of chocolate curled into the air, a combination Aria found curious even though she had lived here for as long as she could remember.

She headed to the Museum Gardens, where the trees and flowers helped clear her head. When her life was chaotic and unreliable, the cycles of nature gave her comfort: birds singing to find their mates; flowers turning to fruit; leaves bursting into colour before they fell; the stillness under the snow. She knew what to expect, and that expectation calmed her.

Her friends were also all here in the botanical garden, in the wilderness. They weren't exactly human friends, however. She took the time to learn the names of plants and animals, because naming them made them feel closer – almost like they were people, too. For it was clear from an early age that those around her were disturbed by the fact she had no parents or family, or that she lived in a children's home all her life. The loneliness was unbearable.

Aria jumped the closed gate and sneaked into her usual spot on the bench under the long branches of a willow-leaved ash. The scent of earth and flowers, and the way the leaves vibrated with the breeze, was exactly what she needed to unwind.

The Multangular Tower stood in front of her, a relic of forgotten worlds, a quiet monument to lives long past. Its presence gave her context, reminding her she was part of a bigger story. Even though she knew nothing of her past, she liked to think her ancestors roamed these lands, dating back centuries before. Surely, their ghosts wandered in this park, which made Aria feel less alone.

The grey clouds cleared and the bright sun brought back the heat to the garden. An odd late-summer heatwave plagued the UK still, and today was not the day it would go away.

Aria took off her grey hoodie, showing off an oversized purple T-shirt – a hand-me-down from a previous girl who lived at the home. Purple was not her favourite colour, but she didn't have a choice.

A woman passed by pushing a stroller. Her presence signalled the gates were now open for the public. She smiled at Aria, and an ache exploded in her chest – a wish to walk away with her, to be loved and cared for in a place she could call home.

Aria knew nothing about her parents. She didn't even know why she ended up in the children's home. The only thing she had from them was a pendant: a small blue sphere, cradled by a stainless-steel claw, hanging on a black leather thread around her neck.

Holding her pendant, she closed her eyes. The world went still while birds chirped around her and the tall branches swayed above.

Peace. Quiet. Solitude.

The last remnants of tension melted from her body, a calm spread within.

When she opened her eyes, a red squirrel stood in front of her, clutching an acorn near her feet. The tips of its ear tufts moved gently with the breeze.

'Hello there, little guy,' she said, bending down and tucking her auburn hair behind her ears. 'What have you got there?'

The squirrel's tail twitched as it hopped closer. It slowly

placed the acorn by her feet.

'For me? Why thank you, that's too kind.'

The squirrel nodded and stared up at her with deep, bright eyes. It was strange behaviour, Aria noted – she'd never seen this before. The squirrel had something to say, she was sure of it, but the message stayed just beyond her grasp.

A loud whisper broke the moment. Heart hammering, Aria turned to search for the source but found nothing. It lingered for a moment and then subsided. Surprised and confused, a shiver crept up her spine. She tried to brush it off. It must have been her imagination.

When Aria looked back, the squirrel darted to the willow-leaved ash. It scrambled up the trunk and vanished among the leaves.

The acorn was left behind, resting on the concrete path before her. She reached down and picked it up. Its smooth surface caught the light as she turned it between her fingers.

A smile tugged at her lips while she closed her palm over it. It was as if Nature had sent her a gift just when she needed it most.

For a brief moment, the acorn began to vibrate. The subtle vibration tickled her palm, which led to a strange tingling sensation in her chest – sharp and electric.

Something had awoken within her.

The air became thicker, colours more vibrant, and the air reflected invisible threads in the air.

And that's when she heard it again, louder, and more insistent. Multiple whispers surrounding her, in a language she did not comprehend.

Oh, absolutely not, she thought as she threw away the acorn into the bushes.

She got up slowly, stuffed her hoodie into her backpack, and slammed it against her left shoulder. She hurried towards the exit, avoiding making a scene.

Yet the whispers followed her, louder by the second.

I've gone mad, she thought. She ran, her feet heavy on the concrete path. Past the flower beds, bushes, tourists, and the woman with the stroller. Through the gates. Up the street. Cars. People. Motion everywhere.

It was a welcome noise, so welcome she no longer heard the whispers.

Aria sighed with relief and slowed her pace. There had to be an explanation. Acorns don't whisper. Acorns don't *vibrate.* It's impossible.

Oliver would have a field day with it if he ever found out. Which he never would, of course, because Aria would never speak of it. Not to him, not to anyone. It would make her life more complicated, and she was not willing to abdicate the little freedom she had.

Still, as she glanced back over her shoulder, the hairs on her arms stood up. The world carried on, indifferent to the strange secret she now bore alone.

CHAPTER TWO

Rowan

Aria stepped into the front garden of the children's home, sent back early from school on Friday morning. The teachers had just announced classes were cancelled because of a wildfire that broke out near the school. Most of her peers went straight to the coffee shop in the city centre to enjoy yet another hot day, but Aria headed home. It had been a couple of days since she'd heard the whispers, and she was afraid to have it happen again – being in her room was the safest option.

By the bright red door of the children's home, a pot of purple Michaelmas daisies turned their flowers to her. All of them, at once; dozens of tiny star-shaped flowers faced her, their yellow centres like eyes.

One lifted slightly higher and blinked. It looked like a blink, because it closed and opened all its petals.

Aria stopped cold. That was not *normal.*

Another flower swirled back and forth, side by side, dancing, and the whole cluster shivered with a sound of soft giggling.

Flowers don't laugh.

She leant in closer, an eyebrow arched.

'Chatting to the flowers now, are we?'

Startled, Aria looked up. Oliver was leaning out of the window, a cigarette dangling from his thin lips.

'That your thing now, forest rat?' He smirked down at her. 'Proper nutter. No wonder your mum and dad ditched you. Thick as two short planks, you are.'

'Shut it!' she snapped.

'Oh, touchy, are we?' Oliver said, blowing a lazy stream of smoke into the air.

'Like you're any better. Your parents didn't want you either.'

'Yeah? Well, my parents are dead, not like I had a choice in that.' He flicked the cigarette butt away, landing onto the grass in front of her. 'You, though? You were abandoned.'

Aria flinched, her stomach twisting at his words. 'Shut your face! You don't know anything about me.'

'Oh, I know enough. You're just a forest rat who talks to flowers, innit? Probably lost your marbles out there somewhere, surrounded by dirt and weeds.' He gave a nod at the wild path behind the house. 'Might be better off living out there, eh? I could always take your room and actually use it for something useful, instead of having it full of... well, *you*.'

Aria tightened her jaw, the blood rushed up to her face, her knuckles clenched white at her side. He always did this – picked and picked, to break her. Two years of it, every day.

She'd had enough.

'I'm not—' she started, but her voice cracked.

The air stilled. The garden quieted. The birds paused their morning chatter.

The leaves of the rowan tree in front of the house moved. The branches quivered, and one of them twisted sharply, bending in a way no wind could shape.

SMACK!

A branch whipped against the window, making Oliver tumble back into the room with a loud thud.

'What the—?!' he shouted in a high pitch.

His head popped out of the window, hand rubbing the side where he'd been hit. His eyes turned red as they locked on Aria's and pointed at the tree. 'How?! HOW did you...?'

'I didn't!' she shouted back. But even as she said it, part of her wasn't so sure.

The rowan tree stood perfectly still now, leaves swaying lazily.

'I know you did, you witch!'

Aria blinked. Her heart thudded in her chest like a warning drum.

'That's it! You're dead meat!' Oliver shouted and disappeared from the window.

Panic erupted in her. She backed away from the house, eyes at the door. Once at the gate, she turned and sprinted down the road, her backpack jumping erratically with every step.

Behind her, she heard the front door slam open. 'You'll wish you were never born!' Oliver's voice rang out.

Aria's shoes slapped the pavement as she bolted past garden gates and bins, breath coming fast and ragged.

Once at the main road, she dashed straight across without thinking. A car screeched to a stop metres from her. She flinched but didn't stop, weaving between cars.

'Oi! Watch where you're going!' a driver shouted.

As she ran past a Victorian house hidden under vines, the leaves shifted dramatically with her presence, attempting to reach and cover her. She didn't care. At this point, she just hoped it would dart towards Oliver and make him trip.

A horn blared behind her and Oliver's pounding footsteps got closer and closer every second.

'ARGH!'

She glanced over her shoulder just in time to see him trip, vines catching his foot. He went down hard, face-first.

Aria slowed for a half second. *Did I...?* But the thumping of her heart drowned the thought.

She sprinted down the street, her black school blazer moving with the wind. She turned under the railway and down a narrow path as her lungs burned. Being older and slightly taller than her, Oliver was not far behind, catching up with every step.

'Stop running, you freak!' he called.

Aria sprinted across the bridge over the River Ouse, dodging tourists and commuters as they scrambled to get out of her way.

The massive curved roof of York Railway Station came into view.

Hope.

Maybe she could hop onto a train and escape this hell.

She stumbled with the thought, her legs trembling from exhaustion. Oliver's voice shouted from behind, barking at people to move.

SPLASH!

Aria whipped her head around. The water shot back down into the River Ouse, giving her the impression the river itself had risen to hit Oliver.

He froze mid-step, drenched from head to toe, water pouring off him in a cascade. His eyes were wide with shock, his mouth opening and closing in disbelief.

People stopped and watched. A young girl pointed and laughed. An elderly man looked over the rail to the river, confused, while a businesswoman stepped away from Oliver with disgust, like he was plagued by leprosy.

Aria turned back to the station. Her legs ached, but she forced herself to run faster.

'I'll kill you!' Oliver shouted, voice hoarse.

The station's arched roof loomed over her. She halted in

front of the platform signs, her mind jumbled trying to figure out where to go next. No plan, no ticket, and no clue where they would lead her. But something pulled her – not reason, not fear, but a feeling in her chest – to the train on Platform Four.

She couldn't explain it and she didn't take the time to explore it. Her feet echoed through the station as she ran to the blue bullet train waiting on Platform Four.

Once faced with the open doors, she faltered only for a heartbeat. The soft blue carpet was a welcome sight, and Aria wanted to collapse on it. As she drew in a breath to step inside, a raven landed on the top of the train.

A raven? Here? In the middle of the city? It made no sense. She had no time to dwell on it. Surely exhaustion led to this hallucination.

As soon as the train conductor blew the whistle, she jumped in and the doors slid shut behind her.

The train jolted into motion, and Aria pressed a hand to her chest, lungs burning. Oliver emerged on the platform, his school uniform dripping.

He scanned the train until he saw her and shouted something, throwing his fist around, but it was lost behind glass and the rising noise of the train.

Aria waved attentively and stepped backwards from the doors. The other passengers on the train watched her with curiosity as she passed by them to head to the back of the carriage.

Her pendant rose and fell with her chest as she held it. Once seated on the grey-blue seats, she gave a loud sigh and loosened her yellow-and-black striped tie, finally able to relax.

The station disappeared from view, and York became a blur of motion. Where the train was going, she did not know, but that would be a problem for later. She found solace in watching the landscape move outside, her eyes heavy. Her body was exhausted from the run, her feet swollen in pain.

Aria closed her eyes. For now, she would rest.

CHAPTER THREE

Raven

'Wake up, love. We're in Scarborough. End of the line and we need to turn the train around.'

Lifting her head from the window, Aria's eyes blinked open. A large man with shoulder-length dirty blond hair and a beard full of breadcrumbs peered down at her. He wore a blue tie and vest over a short-sleeved, uniform white shirt which showed off tattoos winding down his. arms – runes she recognised from a museum back in York. The badge on his chest read Jeremy Hopper.

'Bit young to wander around here alone, no?' he asked, his bushy eyebrows frowning as he took a bite off his sandwich, adding more crumbs onto his beard.

'I—uh—' Alert, Aria tried to come up with an excuse to stop him from handing her to the police. Going back to the children's home would be the end of her, she could see it in Oliver's eyes.

Before she could come up with an excuse, a large raven landed on the exterior frame of the window and tapped insistently with its beak. The conductor's light brown eyes widened.

'Ah, I see.' He turned back to Aria with a broad smile. 'How exciting! Sounds like someone has a journey farther North! Late to start at the Academy, if you ask me, but who am I to question the messenger?'

'Wait, what?'

Aria was taken aback by the sudden redirection of the conversation. She turned to the raven, which flew off, and back at the man, trying to decipher their silent exchange.

Jeremy gestured down the empty corridor. 'Go on – the bus is outside, 'bout to leave. You'd better hurry.'

The carriage was eerily quiet and empty, only a low rumble beneath her feet. She got up, adjusted her blazer, flattened her black trousers, and picked up her canvas bag. As she walked slowly towards the door, she glanced over to the windows, unsure what kind of bus could possibly be waiting – or why she was meant to catch it.

'Great Academy,' Jeremy said behind her. 'Been there mi'sen – learned loads. But I've always loved trains. Travelling through the countryside, meeting new people every day. Sometimes, I meet others like us. Help guide 'em to the magical biodiversity hotspots up on the moors... Or lead 'em to the stones, if they're travelling farther.'

Aria turned to stare at him. 'Like us?'

'Magifolk!' Jeremy said brightly. His face changed with recognition. 'Oh dear, you're green as moss, aren't you? You vardbarn have a lot to relearn. Commonfolk know so little of the actual world around them. I find it so odd how confident they are in their ignorance.'

Aria tilted her head. *Magical what? Stones? Vardbarn?* None of it made any sense.

She opened her mouth to ask, but words got tangled behind her confusion. She turned forward, hoping to get away from him as soon as possible because he clearly was not thinking right.

'Mary!' Jeremy called once they stepped outside. 'This one's off for the stones!'

Above, the raven circled and landed on the blue bus, where a woman with a remarkably round face, fussy grey hair, and vivid red lipstick sat on the driver's seat.

'Go on, lass, we ain't got all day!' Mary shouted back.

'Off you go!' Jeremy said, beckoning Aria forward. 'Hurry and you'll surely get there in time for a feast.'

Hesitantly, she walked up to the bus, her eyes drawn to the raven. Its dark stare was fixated on her with a strange intensity.

She shook her head.

'I don't have any money,' Aria said to Mary, one foot on the bus's steps.

Mary snorted. 'Ticket or not, you're meant to be on this bus. Otherwise, the raven won't stop pestering me. Sit, before I change my mind.'

'Good luck, lass!' Jeremy shouted from the train.

Aria waved reluctantly at the stranger and stepped inside. The doors hissed shut behind her, and the engine gave a wheezy groan as the bus lurched forward.

It was essentially empty, with just a couple at the back: two men in their 50s dressed for a hike, binoculars around their necks. They smiled as Aria sank into a seat near the front, clutching her backpack in front of her like a life jacket.

'Hot all through the morning, it was,' Mary said as she drove the bus down winding roads, fields and hedgerows blurring past. 'Not a breath of air to be had. You could fry an egg on the causeway. My nephew tried it. Idiot.'

Aria remained silent, holding her backpack tighter.

'And yesterday – hotter still! Like July boiled over. It's the kind of heat that dings you right up. You wouldn't expect it in The Moors, but here we are, as if we're in the Sahara.'

Mary cackled at that. Aria forced a small, confused smile.

'I said to Derek – my neighbour, useless man – I said, "Don't open all your windows, Derek, it'll trap the heat." Did he listen? Course not. He started roaring about the heat and how he couldn't sleep. If only he listened.'

This conversation was getting too personal. Aria smiled politely.

'And tomorrow – thunder, maybe! September is fool's summer. Can't trust the weather, not this time of year. Feel it in the knees, I do.' She glanced at Aria through the mirror. 'You feel it yet, lass? No? You will. Age is not something to joke 'bout.'

Aria tried not to look alarmed. She had no idea where the bus was going, or why no one had asked her any proper questions, yet knew where she was headed while *she* had no idea. But Mary was utterly confident Aria belonged here.

Outside, the landscape went from houses, farms, and parks to forests and meadows without a sign of civilisation. Trees grew thicker, the road darker.

The bus stopped to a halt. The front door hissed open.

'Here we are! Just follow the path, lass, and you'll get there.'

'What? Where?'

'The stones, love! Trees will give you shade from the heat. You'll be there in a jiffy!'

Aria stood slowly, placed her backpack on her back, and went down the steps. She turned back to Mary holding its straps.

'Gotta go.' Mary nodded her head to the back of the bus with a smile showing her teeth smudged with red lipstick. 'These gentlemen are off to Whitby. There have been reports of azure robins in the area! I might go check it out mi'sen during my break, actually. I love birds!'

'Azure robins?' Aria said. She was sure there was no such thing as azure robins. Maybe Mary misspoke.

'Tarra, lass!' Mary waved as the doors closed.

The bus took off, leaving Aria stranded on a road that went through the forest. Thick tree trunks stood on either side, green leaves dangling softly. Behind her was a dirt path, arched by the branches above, creating a tunnel into the forest.

The sun stood high in the sky, its rays filtered through the leafy canopy, painting shifting patterns on the forest floor as unease set. The air was fresh, with hints of resin and moss, with the sweetness of decaying leaves coming from the dirt path itself.

What have I done? she thought, still by the road, clutching her pendant like it might answer her.

A raven gronked from a twisted wych elm nearby, perched on a branch. It stared at her with acute curiosity.

Ravens are scavengers, which made the whole situation unsettling. Was it waiting for her demise? And what was up with the ravens today, that kept following her? Or was it all her imagination? Though Jeremy had seen it too. And so did Mary.

She did her best to ignore the bird.

After a few minutes walking down the dirt path, she sat on the thick raised roots of a large, broad oak that stood behind her like a guardian. She shuffled through her canvas backpack, its edges darkened by use. With her hands shaking, she took out an apple and took a bite, its sweetness welcoming on her tongue.

She twisted the leather straps of her pendant with her other hand. *This is bad*, she thought as she looked around the forest. She had no idea where she was, no idea why absolute strangers led her here and, worst still, she was stuck with no way back.

Running away was not one of her finest moments, but Oliver's threats and torments were escalating, and the staff did little about it.

A soft gronk broke through her thoughts, sharp and deliberate. Aria's head snapped up. The raven was back, now perched on the oak's branch, its piercing eyes fixed on her as though it could see straight into her soul. Its feathers glistened in the sunlight, a deep iridescent sheen, alive with shifting light.

She shivered. A strange feeling in her chest, faint but insistent. It wasn't fear, exactly; it was a yearning she couldn't grasp, yet with a deep sense of familiarity. It was the same sensation she felt in the train station, though only now did she take notice.

The bird tilted its head, and, for the briefest moment, Aria was certain it knew. Knew her in a way she didn't fully understand. She was intrigued by this behaviour as she stared back at the strange bird.

Without warning, the raven spread its wings, leapt from the branch, and dove straight towards her.

Aria gasped. She threw her arms up to shield her face and ducked. The apple flew from her hand and landed in the bushes. A rush of wind swept through her hair as the bird streaked past, so close she could hear the whispers from its feathers. Heart pounding, she turned to watch it soar, its sleek form cutting through the air like an arrow.

Was she meant to follow? The thought came unbidden, yet it clung to her, refusing to let go. Despite the uncertainty growing in her mind, a flicker of intrigue sparked to life. With newfound determination, Aria slung her backpack over her shoulders and began pursuing the raven.

Aria ran along the narrow path through the woods of North York Moors, her shoes thudding against the earth. Dry twigs snapped beneath her feet, their sharp cracks breaking the silence of the forest as the air vibrated with a quiet, electric charge – the tense stillness before a thunderstorm.

Around her, ferns shifted in unexplainable ways, leaning aside to clear her path, while some brushed against her legs tentatively to urge her onward. The forest was ancient, where moss crept up trees, and pale lichen clung on the weathered branches. Fallen logs lay scattered across the forest floor; not dead but filled with life. One twitched as a forest mouse scurried across it, collecting seeds and nuts for the winter ahead.

The deeper she went, the darker it became.

Unnerved by the way the forest moved around her, she remained focused on the raven that darted through the trees. The pull was incredible, a power just beyond her understanding, growing stronger with every step.

At last, the raven stopped and landed on a stretched-out branch of an ash. Its leaves fluttered, acknowledging the bird's presence.

Aria stopped too, leaning on her knees to catch her breath. *Water would be nice,* she thought. While she spent most of her days outside, she had never ventured in a forest so vast, where trees were rugged with age and the forest floor alive and wild.

She straightened herself up at the edge of a grassy clearing, scattered with the season's first fallen leaves in shades of amber, gold, and scarlet. It was small, bathed in the warm light of the sun overhead, a spotlight broken through the leaves. Tiny insects drifted lazily in the light while around her, tall trees stood still, their thick branches casting shadows that made the forest beyond seem darker. Older.

At the centre of the clearing stood a tall, weathered stone, moss crawling up from its base, and orange, grey, and light green lichen clinging to its surface. The stone was carved with runes worn by centuries of exposure to the elements, emitting a low steady hum that filled the air.

The fine hairs of her arm rose to the magical scene before

her. Never had she seen anything like this – here time stood still, connected to the past, rooted in the present, and tugging at the edges of unspoken possibilities of the future.

A soft crack of a twig snapped her attention to the tree line. A red deer emerged, its antlers outlined by the sun, giving it an otherworldly aura. It stood still, watching her with an almost human intensity. With a small dip of its head, it turned and melted back into the trees, gentle and certain.

Aria closed her gaping mouth as the stag disappeared through the darkness of the forest. She let out a breath she hadn't noticed she was holding. The encounter was unreal. Too quiet, too purposeful. Aria couldn't explain why, but she knew the stag approved of her presence in this mystical location, satisfied with what it had seen.

The humming from the runestone grew louder, like a swarm of bees flying around her, bringing her attention back to it. The runes shimmered, pulsing with a cold light. Aria stepped closer, drawn to the light. With each step, the runes glowed brighter, the buzzing louder, calling to her like a salmon swimming upstream – driven by a primal urge, compelled by instinct to return to where it began.

Entranced, Aria reached out. Just as her fingers grazed the warm surface, she stumbled, tumbling face-first into the cool, damp earth.

Everything went still.

CHAPTER FOUR

Pine

Pushing herself up, Aria was momentarily disoriented. The forest floor was no longer covered in grass and golden leaves. Instead, it was blanketed with a layer of pine needles and earth. She picked up her backpack from the ground and removed the dirt from her black trousers.

The scent of pine resin awakened her senses, its sweet and round aroma grounding her wandering mind, triggering a sweet memory she could not place.

The forest was silent, the air motionless.

She lifted her head and took in the strange sight before her: a woman with deep red hair braided over her shoulder, dressed in a flowing dusky purple robe adorned with intricate gold embroidery. Sitting gracefully on the woman's shoulder was a raven, its beady eyes locked onto Aria's.

'Wh-where am I?' Aria asked, her hand instinctively finding the comforting edges of her pendant.

The woman smiled, her features emanating quiet warmth: high cheekbones, sharp yet kind eyes, and a smile that hinted at a restraint amusement. 'You've come further than you know, Aria Renwood.'

Aria took a step back, trying to process the weight of the

words. 'What? How do you know my name?'

The raven gronked.

'This raven tells me a great deal,' the woman said. 'You must be hungry.' She reached into the leather pouch at her belt and pulled out a small bundle wrapped in parchment. 'Here – rye bread, cheese, and a few vegetables from my garden.'

Hit by the scent of fresh herbs as she opened the bundle, Aria took a bite almost instantly. The last time she'd eaten was breakfast, and judging by the angle of the sun, it had to be well past noon. She hoped it wasn't poisoned, but at this stage, hunger was stronger than any reasonable argument.

Even as she chewed, her eyes never left the raven.

'The raven... It tells you things?' Aria asked, reminded by the strange encounter with the train's conductor.

The raven's head tilted, eyes glowing like the night sky.

'Ravens are messengers that slip between space and time. This one guided you here – to the old forests of the North. Whispered your coming before you arrived.'

'The North?' Aria asked as the difference in temperature caused her to shiver, when moments ago, she was struggling against sweating on a hot summer's day.

Her mouth went dry as she scanned the unfamiliar pine forest. Moss and blueberry bushes took over the forest floor. Pine trees were thick; their trunks were covered with green-silver lichen.

'Farther north than you imagine. Beyond your British Isles, across the sea, to the old lands of the Norse.'

'Norse – you mean Denmark?' Her memory went back to the test she skipped, and now she wished she had learned her Viking history.

'Sweden.'

The woman's smile was genuine, friendly even, but the raven – that impossible raven – was incredibly odd. None of this made sense.

'My name is Astrid Frejd,' she added. 'I'm the groundskeeper and herbalist at Oakspire Academy.'

Aria's brow furrowed in bewilderment. 'I honestly do not understand... Why has that' – she gestured wildly at the raven, which ruffled its feathers in response – 'creature brought me here?'

The woman took a step forward, silent on the soft forest floor. 'For you to learn to harness your magic,' she said, and nodded to the raven. 'I've been told your magic has manifested, and Oakspire Academy trains mages and wizards, like yourself, in the intricate workings of our magical system.'

'I think there has been a mistake, Ms—'

'Please, call me Astrid.'

'Erm... Astrid. How can I even be a wizard? It's impossible.' The declaration sounded ridiculous out loud. She might as well have announced she was a dragon slayer.

'A mage.'

Astrid lifted her hands, summoning the pine needles scattered on the ground, raising them into mid-air. With a slow, sweeping gesture, she drew a wide circle, and the needles surged through the trees, like a murmuration of birds, hissing while branches swayed and creaked in protest. As soon as she lowered her arms, the needles unhurriedly descended onto the earth.

'Your magic flows from within, tied to the natural world. Surely you have felt it by now?'

Aria's mind drifted to the peculiar incidents that happened the past week: the squirrel that left her an acorn that vibrated in her hand; the Michaelmas daisies that danced and giggled; the rowan tree slapping Oliver in the face; the vines that tripped him and the river that drenched him. And the most unsettling: the loud whispers in unknown tongues that echoed through the Museum Gardens.

A nervous laugh escaped Aria's mouth. 'Nice trick with the timing, but that was just the wind...' Even as she said it, she doubted her own words.

Distraught by what she had witnessed, Aria's legs buckled beneath her weight. *Is this really happening?* She reached out, her fingers stretching towards a nearby tree trunk, which leant slightly to help her steady herself.

'I fell through a glowing rock into magic school? Just like that?'

'I understand this may be difficult to believe. Nature has recognised your power and brought you here to guide you.'

Aria wrapped her arms around herself. 'Sorry, but this makes no sense. I'm just an orphan. A nobody.'

'You are far more than what others have labelled you.'

Aria swallowed hard.

Astrid looked up at the sun, her fair skin glowing with warmth. 'The sun is starting to descend. We must hurry to make it in time for the evening feast.' She gestured towards the dirt path through the forest, worn down by countless footsteps, uneven with embedded stones pushing through the dirt. 'Please, follow me.'

Aria glanced back at the runestone, the runes still pulsating. The thought of turning back was tempting; back to the familiar, to the town she had called home all her life. But the thought made her stomach turn. *I can't. I can't go back.*

She turned to the narrow path through the pine forest, an earthen trail carved through moss and blueberry patches. It was a path to the unknown.

'It's a big decision, I know,' Astrid said. 'I'll bring you back here in a flash if you feel like this is not for you, and you can go back home to your friends. The children's home considers you adopted, now that you've passed through the stone and became a ward of the Academy. But we can fix that and help you reclaim your life in York.'

Life? Friends? Her mind snapped into a decision. There was nothing left for her in England. She squared her shoulders, held the straps of her backpack, and followed Astrid into the dense forest. The birds chirped for the first time since she arrived, as if they had held their breaths until now.

They walked in silence. The tall pines with thick, sprawling branches stretched out to one another like old friends. Woodpeckers drummed in the distance and a great tit trilled from a low branch. No cars. No voices. Just nature.

As they drew closer to the edge of the forest, the canopy thinned, and light began to spill between the trunks. The murmur of water led them to a wooden bridge arched over a serpentine river. It ran merrily through a glade, leading towards a vast lake just beyond the tree line, visible now as the woods cleared.

Pausing midway across the bridge, Aria faced the lake, surrounded by an endless landscape of trees. Despite being in a strange place, there was excitement bubbling inside her. Being among the trees is where she felt most happy. She breathed in the fresh air and stepped on the other side of the bridge.

Mesmerised, Aria stopped. Before her was a vast park, trimmed and pruned, but wild and free, more spacious than any she had seen in York. Majestic deciduous trees were scattered throughout, leaves orange and yellow. Their trunks were wide and weathered, some with large cavities where animals could surely nest. Each tree was a guardian of the land, standing there for centuries. Some stretched for the sky, others had wide spreading branches, casting shadows on the low grass covered with golden leaves and large patches of dried-out meadows.

They followed the dirt path through the park. Mists gathered near trees and bushes, moving with a quiet life of their own. Some coalesced into something more recognisable, like an animal – from large to small, but all of them different. They flowed in place, like smoke moving in a container.

Was she imagining this? *Morning mist, perhaps... in the afternoon. Sure. That made sense.*

Farther down the path, a massive bull moose, translucent with its proud antlers catching impossible light, stood near a young birch tree. It lowered its ghostly head to nibble at the golden leaves, only to have its mouth pass right through them. The creature hardly seemed to mind, continuing to chew its lunch with all the time in the world.

Breaking through her shock at seeing an actual ghost in broad daylight, a burst of laughter drew Aria's attention to a game. Young people, like herself, dashed about in robes with elbow-length sleeves, and hems that swished around their knees as they ran. Their robes were forest green, ocean blue and ember red – each one edged with repeating knotwork in gold, tightened by a leather belt at the waist. Underneath the robes, they wore casual clothes; someone had layered it over a tweed vest and crisp shirt, while another wore theirs with jeans and a long-sleeved top. Somehow, it all worked.

They darted between trees and mossy rocks, wielding long wooden staves that emitted strange silver threads through the air. They were chasing a small flag, which flapped merrily above their heads, dancing through the wind, from one side of the field to the other.

It all looked so magical and unbelievable.

More people lounged on the grass, reading books, or laughing and talking with one another. All utterly at ease and carefree.

Aria's chest tightened. It was like standing out in the cold, watching through a window, aching for warmth. She had always been an outsider. Neither was she used to stability – not at thirteen, not with people coming and going, not with herself moving between children's homes. She only wanted what everyone had: a place at the table, a voice, be someone's person, have *her* person. Could this be it? She held the hope carefully, like a fragile spark refusing to die.

'Come,' Astrid said, placing a hand on Aria's shoulder. 'You'll have time to explore and take it all in later.'

They continued down the winding dirt path. Rising above the trees was a castle of stone. Lichen and moss clung to its weathered walls, merging it seamlessly with the surrounding nature. Towering windows caught the bright light from the sun above.

Aria's neck bent as she looked up in awe. The castle loomed above them, its three towers stretched against the endless blue sky, a testament of power and permanence.

'Welcome to Oakspire International Academy of Aether and Earth,' Astrid said, the words spoken with a reverence that made the castle feel like so much more than just a place.

Aria climbed up the steps leading to the massive arched wooden doors. She reached out tentatively, her fingers brushing against the rough wooden surface.

Real. This was all so wonderfully, undeniably real.

'The Front Hall,' Astrid said as they stepped inside. 'The name's older than these walls. It goes back to the Norse days.'

Too busy taking it all in, Aria didn't answer. Calling it an entrance didn't do it justice.

The Front Hall was striking without being immodest, daring without being pretentious. Above them, beams stretched across the ceiling, carved with complex patterns. A majestic circular iron chandelier hung from chains, its flickering flames casting a warm glow across the stone floor, uneven and worn by centuries of use.

Beyond was a Grand Staircase, its wide, heavy steps made of smooth, dark wood. Along the wall, beside the staircase, hung round shields, each with an iron boss at its centre, eyes watching anyone who dared enter. Their paint faded, their edges torn or splintered.

The air was alive, humming with the weight of time, making the fine hairs on the back of her neck stand up.

The ghost of a wolf appeared through the right wall in front of them. Aria jumped. It padded silently, body low and steady, eyes fixed ahead. It didn't react to their presence, and neither did Astrid react to it. It soon vanished through the left wall.

Aria swallowed dry. Animal ghosts were clearly normal in this place.

Their footsteps echoed floor as they walked towards the portraits that lined the dark panelled walls. Beneath the gilded frames, brass nameplates shimmered in the sunlight that peered through the floor-to-ceiling arched windows. She half-recognised the names in the nameplates: Carl Linnaeus, Anders Celsius, and Alfred Nobel.

'Some of Sweden's greatest minds passed through here,' Astrid said, gesturing to the oil paintings. 'Mages who had great influence in science and magic.' She shook her head with a smile. 'What always impresses me is how they lived two lives – one among the commonfolk, and one among the magifolk. Then, like now, magic and science were tangled up together. Commonfolk tried to explain everything with science, but magifolk knew exactly what was going on. They saw magic for what it truly was, while the commonfolk just couldn't – or didn't – understand.'

'What do you mean? We – I mean, normal people – can't see magic?'

'Commonfolk,' Astrid corrected gently. '"Normal" makes it

sound like *we're* the strange ones. Humanity has lived with magic for millennia, until some people were born without it. That's when the rise of the commonfolk began.'

'How come?'

'No one knows exactly, but there are theories. Some say the rise in use of iron changed something in the body, constraining people's connection to magic somehow. Others believe it's a disease that spread and damaged the part of the soul that links to magic.'

'Oh.'

'The most popular theory is genetics. A sad, random event in our biology.'

Astrid looked up at the scholars, her green eyes thoughtful. 'Whatever the cause, it changed everything. For a while, we lived side by side, but soon after, the world split. Magifolk went into hiding, and commonfolk built a world without magic. This Academy was built in 1100 as a sanctuary for Norse mages when their livelihood was threatened. Similar academies exist around the world to guide the next generation with knowledge of magical systems. It's the only way our knowledge survives.'

Aria's mind raced. If everything she'd known was wrong, what else in history had been false?

She shifted uncomfortably as the eyes of the Swedish scholars followed her every move with an unsettling intensity. She held her pendant, trying to focus on Astrid's words, but these revelations were too big, too strange. Magic. Mages. Scholars who could see things she couldn't even begin to understand.

'What about wizards? You mentioned wizards before,' Aria asked.

'There's a bit of a difference between us mages, and wizards. We channel magic instinctively. Wizards, on the other hand, need tools, like wands and spells. Their approach is more technical.' She leant in slightly, voice lowering in a conspiratorial tone. 'Between you and me, they do like to think of themselves as the elite among magifolk. Maybe it's because they are a minority, so they might have an inferiority complex.'

Aria nodded slowly, still trying to wrap her head around it all.

'Right. Wizards. Tools. Technical. Elitist.' She swallowed. 'This is a lot.'

'I can imagine. Take your time adjusting, you'll see soon enough this is where you belong.'

That would be nice, she thought. *Wait, did he just...?* Aria could have sworn Linnaeus's painted lips curved into an imperceptible smile. Aria turned with unease and looked up at the majestic chandelier, walking away cautiously, desperate to escape the piercing looks. Astrid followed.

On the opposite wall, niches with glass domes displayed an assortment of curious artefacts: a polished drinking horn; a golden arm ring with funnel-shaped ends; a small axe with a dark, worn handle; a wooden bowl with amber beads; a blue-smoked stone inside of what looked like a compass. Beside them was a statue made of wood of a man holding an axe and a staff. "Eiríkr the Stormbringer" was written at the bottom.

'Objects from the founders,' Astrid said as Aria reached out to touch them. 'It's all thanks to them that we have this sacred space for knowledge. These objects are a reminder of what they had to fight for us to live.'

The objects didn't look like much, just old things worn with time. But she wondered if they were mere objects or if they had magic in them too.

'Astrid, is this the newcomer?'

An older girl with long chestnut-brown hair walked down the Grand Staircase, her deep blue robe flowing as she hurried to meet them. She had two brooches on her chest, connected by a chain of light blue and white glass beads. Students bustled past on either side with ember red robes, boots clattering as they rushed down the stairs into the side corridor, barely sparing a glance at Aria.

Beside the girl was a younger boy, radiating with warm confidence. He had a wide smile, his rich black curls bounced as he strode towards them, his almond skin glowing under the sunlight that flooded the Front Hall.

'Aria Renwood,' Astrid said. 'Just arrived from England.'

'Pleasure to meet you! I'm Carolina Valencia,' the girl said, holding out her hand with conviction, her robe swaying drastically. Her hand was slender with well-groomed nails, her smooth, olive-toned skin standing out from her crisp white shirt.

Aria shook it, surprised by the firm hold.

'I'm in my last year at Oakspire, and Head of Fossheim Krets,' she added, her big brown eyes bright with interest. 'A Krets is like your family away from home. One of three, each with their own dorms, common rooms and robe colour, so you always know who's who. Ours is obviously the best Krets, and blue is by far the most beautiful colour,' she said with a wink.

The boy let out a delighted gasp. 'Obviously! Where else would all the fabulous people go?'

He stepped forward with theatrical flair and extended his hand. 'Taye Lundvik. First-year. Fossheim. And you must be the mysterious newcomer everyone's been whispering about!'

'Everyone?' Aria whispered as she took his hand. Blood rushed up to her cheeks.

'Secrets are never secret in this Academy,' Taye said with a smirk, his dark brown eyes glittering with amusement. 'Which is why everyone knows I'm descended from Björn Järnsida. Yes, *that* Viking king.'

Taye rolled his eyes, half-laughing. 'I prefer to be known for my personality. Or my eyebrows. I mean, look at them – perfection doesn't happen by accident.' He traced a finger dramatically over one brow.

'Right. No idea who that is,' Aria said, distracted by Astrid and Carolina, who had stepped away and were deep in conversation. 'But wait, I just arrived. How could everyone know? Not even *I* knew.'

'First of all – refreshing! Björn Järnsida is the son of legendary Ragnar Lodbrok. He raided the coasts of the Mediterranean and built an empire,' Taye continued with a shrug. 'Just because I come from an old Norse mage lineage doesn't mean I have to live up to the same old legends, you know?' He raised his perfectly shaped eyebrows. 'I mean, don't get me wrong, I admire the man! He was smart and pushed boundaries. But it's just too much to live up to.

'And to your second question,' he continued, 'they announced it at the Stone Ceremony a month ago. Halvard said Nature had chosen someone to join us this year, but no one knew when you'd show up.'

'What? *Chosen?* And what do you mean, a month ago? Weird things only started happening to me this week!'

'Maybe it was waiting for you to be, like, emotionally aligned or spiritually open or something?' He leant in closer, his voice a mix of awe and admiration. 'But do you know how rare this is? Most of us had to apply, go through all sorts of tests and interviews, the whole shebang. But you were handpicked by Nature itself. What an incredible honour!'

'It doesn't happen often,' Carolina chipped in as she and Astrid rejoined them. 'When Nature chooses someone, it's because there's something special about them. A sort of destiny that is to be fulfilled. It's the deepest honour our world can give.'

'Like them.' Taye jerked his chin up to the portraits. 'They basically changed the world.' He turned to Carolina. 'Destiny, though? A bit dramatic, don't you think? The girl is already hyperventilating at the thought of being chosen.'

'Right,' Aria managed to say as her throat threatened to choke her. 'No pressure or anything. I was just fine minding my own business, contemplating my life choices without needing a *destiny*.' She looked up at the portraits, her stomach flipped with the thought of filling those shoes. 'I don't want to change the world. I can barely...' Her fingers found her pendant. *I can barely stand up for myself*, she thought.

'Everything will come at its own time, don't you worry,' Astrid said, her voice reassuring. 'It's not so much of a destiny, but a potential. Nature already sees the truth inside you. It means you belong here more deeply than any test could prove.' She placed a hand on Aria's shoulder. 'So, first-years take part in the Stone Ceremony at the start of term. Considering you arrived later, yours will be a little different.'

Taye gasped. 'Wait – she gets the Wild Claiming?' His voice dropped, almost reverent, before bursting into a grin. 'That hasn't happened in forever! I've always wanted to see it!' He rubbed his hands together, his golden bracelet sneaking out from under his coral-coloured sleeves, giving a grand contrast with his deep blue robes.

'The what now? The Wild Claiming?' The words got caught in Aria's throat. 'That sounds like I'm about to get dragged by a troll into the forest.'

Astrid laughed. 'Nothing like that. When someone is chosen by Nature itself, the stones respond directly. No formal ceremony. Just you and them.'

Carolina nodded. 'If you'd arrived with the others, you would've stepped forward and chosen the Krets you want to be part of. But now the stones will choose it for you instead. It will place you where you belong, or where you can find the most growth.'

'Another destiny thing?' Aria asked, crossing her arms. 'Did I just lose my right to free will?'

'Not destiny,' Astrid said. 'More like the stones already see a piece of you. A part you might not even see yet.'

The late-afternoon sun spilled across the stone floor. Astrid placed her hands on her hips. 'We'll go to the stones at dusk,' she said. 'That's when the veil between realms is thinnest.'

Carolina clapped her hands, the glass beads on her chest swaying in response. 'Taye and I will be your guides for the evening. After the Wild Claiming, it will be the Head of your Krets that will help you further. But of course, we'll be here if you ever need anything.'

With an elaborate snap of his wrist, Taye swept Aria's arm into his. 'Come, chosen one,' he declared, leading her down the dim corridor.

The light blue drawings in the ceiling and dark panelling on the wall were lit by lamps with flowing orbs inside, acting like flames. At the far end of the corridor were two great wooden doors.

Behind them waited her future.

CHAPTER FIVE

The Great Ash

A low rumble grew louder with every step, like the sound of a storm coming in. Laughter and chatter filled the air as they drew nearer. Anticipation bubbled in Aria's chest, mixed with dread with what lay ahead.

Taye pushed open the heavy doors with both hands.

'Welcome to the heart of the Academy: the Mead Hall,' he said with a theatrical bow.

Aria stepped in and stopped short.

Towering arches stretched overhead like a cathedral, making the Mead Hall spacious. Along the wooden walls were more worn and discoloured Viking shields like those in the Front Hall, adding weight to history – a reminder of the warriors who came before.

Above them hung banners in ocean blue, forest green, and ember red, each shaped like a long rectangle with a curved bottom edge. A circle with a tree and branching roots marked the centre of every flag.

Sunlight flooded the Hall, highlighting the steaming platters on various tables. Among them were roasted root vegetables with herbs, stacks of warm flatbread, and a rainbow of berries. The smell of fresh bread and raspberries was welcomed by her senses, yet her stomach growled silently in protest of being deprived of real food all day.

At the tables were students, her age and older. Some wore deep blue robes like Carolina and Taye, while others were in forest green or ember red. Knowing each colour represented each of the three Krets, she found it odd that the seating wasn't divided by Krets at all. Instead, students mingled freely, sitting wherever they liked.

The laughter and chatter switched to murmurs as faces turned to the newcomer. Taye walked in with a sense of importance, his chin up, smiling wide showing off his dimples. Aria walked behind him, trying to make herself smaller, though being as tall as him was not doing her any favours.

A burst of footsteps behind them made her glance back, as more students ran through the doors into the Hall. Even though they were late to the feast, Aria still stood out with her English school uniform – no one else was wearing a tie or blazer.

'I'll be up there,' Astrid said quietly behind her, pointing at the long table ahead, where the staff sat facing the students. 'I'll meet you at the Great Ash at dusk.'

'Right. The Wild Claiming,' Aria responded, convinced it was probably the worst name for a ceremony she'd ever heard.

With a light squeeze of her shoulder, Astrid offered her a reassuring smile and walked past them towards the high table.

Taye led Aria and Carolina down the Hall until they reached an empty bench space near the front.

'Gentlefolk,' Taye said, turning to a group of Aria's age and gesturing towards her. 'May I present Aria Renwood. Make sure she feels *very* welcome!'

'She's just arrived from England,' Carolina added. 'She'll be under our care this evening.'

The group stared at her with curiosity – some leant

forward, others pretended not to look while sneaking glances.

Taye motioned Aria to take a seat on the bench. She slipped off her backpack and set it down beside her. Carolina and Taye sat on either side of her like bodyguards, their presence oddly reassuring.

Murmurs continued to echo through the Hall, many whispering behind their hands to their neighbours. Those farther away stood on their benches to have a better look, plainly staring like she was a creature in a zoo.

'Settle down, everyone,' a voice rang out, clear and commanding. Silence spread in the Hall.

At the centre of the high table, a man stood – tall with an air of gentle authority.

'That's the headmaster,' Taye whispered, clutching Aria's arm. 'He is THE Professor Alden Halvard. I spent my childhood playing his Echodusts, especially the ones where he spent hours sitting with frost giants. And look at him! The way he just stands there, all silver-fox distinguished. He's a national treasure, if you ask anyone with sense.'

'Echodusts?' Aria asked back in a low whisper.

'Oh, you poor thing! You've never lived life to the fullest, have you? You'll love Echodusts! I'll explain later!'

Professor Halvard's long robes were twilight-hued, the silver runes on the berm twinkling like stars. A Viking brooch, smoothed by time, fastened his robes on the side. Something about him felt timeless, belonging equally to the past and present, like the stones of Oakspire itself.

Under his white, bushy eyebrows, Professor Halvard's blue eyes swept the Hall, pausing on Aria.

'We are not in the habit of interrupting meals, but some things are worth noting.' A warm smile spread across his weathered face, partly hidden under his semi-long beard with a bronze bead gathering at the tip. He offered her a wink before facing all the curious and eager faces in the Hall.

'For over 900 years, Nature has, in its incredible wisdom, revealed chosen peers for this Academy. Nature does not rush. It moves with purpose, guided by rhythms far older than we can grasp. It is conscious in ways we can only begin to understand.'

Susurration of agreements could be heard throughout the Hall.

'This process is rare. So imagine the gift of having a new soul join our humble community today.'

His eyes swept over the Hall with encouraging warmth, his arms wide and welcoming. Every face was turned to him, taking in every word. It was clear he knew how to entrance an audience, his voice deep and calm.

'History reminds us Nature is never mistaken. It shapes the world with great complexity and purpose. For in nature, as in magic, true purpose unfolds through challenge, not design.'

He raised his drinking horn high, its polished surface reflecting the evening sun.

'Let us offer our newest member the courtesy Oakspire is known for: curiosity, respect, and kindness.'

Everyone raised their wooden cups.

Aria raised hers hesitantly, avoiding eye contact, even though those closest to her were trying to catch her eye.

'That is all. Enjoy the feast.' Professor Halvard sat back down.

The Mead Hall immediately filled with noise, and Aria let out her held breath.

'Hi!' A girl with long black hair leant forward, hand outstretched, her golden-brown complexion striking against the ember red robe. 'I'm Inaiê Kuaray.'

Her grip was confident and warm, like she was genuinely glad to meet her.

'Aria,' she said, unsure whether to reintroduce herself or not.

Inaiê smiled, scrunching her nose slightly, causing her septum piercing to tingle.

'Don't worry, we're mostly friendly,' she said, looking from under her fringe as she gathered her hair into a ponytail, exposing both shaved sides of her head. 'All of us here are first-years, so you'll spend a lot of time with us.'

'Could be a gift or a curse,' said a boy with curly blond hair, wearing a forest green robe. 'Depends how you handle chaos before noon.' He chuckled. 'Finn O'Heffernan, at your service.'

'Well, chaos before noon is how I've survived for years,' Aria said, attempting a smirk.

'Survive Taye before breakfast, and the rest of the day's a breeze,' Finn added as a flush of amusement coloured his pale cheeks, his green eyes bright.

Taye took her plate and filled it with food with an easy smile. If Taye was the chaotic one in the group, she counted her blessings.

'*Rude*,' Taye said. 'I'm a delight in the morning!' He placed her plate with an assortment of different foods in front of her. 'Here! I figured you weren't going to pick anything, considering the awkwardness. See it as the best Sweden has to offer. A gastronomic experience, if you will.'

'Thanks,' Aria said, feeling warmth in her chest – never did she get this kind of kindness.

She picked up her knife and fork, curiously exploring foods like meatballs, root vegetables, a cheese tart, and whatever the red berry jam was. It was a welcome sight, and her belly was enjoying the experience as well.

'Oh, by the way, Taye,' Carolina jumped in, a piece of potato stuck on her fork. 'I saw a firedrake this summer back home in Spain.' She nudged Aria slightly. 'Touchy creatures.

One tried to set my hair on fire.'

'Wait, you've actually seen one?' Next to Inaiê was a boy with rich brown skin and tight coils of copper hair, who perked up from behind a large book entitled *A Comprehensive Encyclopaedia of Magifauna.* At least two dozen sticky notes stuck out from its edges, each one glowing faintly whenever he touched them.

He moved his plate aside, his ember red sleeves dipping into the red berry jam. He placed the book on the table with a thump, pushed his circular glasses up his nose, and frantically moved pages back and forth. 'I just read about them! Where was it...? Ah!' he shouted, making everyone jump. 'Found it! According to this, firedrakes are one tenth of the size of a dragon, but like dragons, they don't actually *breathe* fire. It's a chemical reaction, see? Glands in the throat mix two compounds that combust on contact with air. Like a biological flamethrower!'

'That's Fraser Murphy-Mussa,' Inaiê said to Aria with a smile. 'His mums have a bookshop in Edinburgh, so he grew up with books all his life. You can always count on him to turn our meals into lectures.' She turned to Fraser, frowning slightly. 'Honestly, these names are so unimaginative. In my village, we call them fireleaf serpents, which is a lot more poetic!'

'Actually—' Fraser began, rifling through the pages once more, but froze, his charcoal dark eyes widening for a moment. 'Sorry, taxonomy and classification are in another book. Intriguing, though, how these names are chosen! I can go get it right now, if you want,' he added, already positioning to stand.

Inaiê placed her hand on his shoulder to sit back down. 'That's fine, leave it for another day.'

'Firedrakes would be in Siberia during the summer,' Taye said, waving his fork. 'What Carolina saw was probably an emberwing. Common mistake.' He winked at Aria, smiling wide, making it impossible not to smile back.

'One has feathers,' Finn chimed in, 'and the other is more like a winged reptile. Not exactly easy to mistake. Unless, of course, Carolina is in desperate need of glasses.'

'No, no,' Carolina shot back, shaking her head. 'It definitely didn't have feathers. I'm sure of it!'

A thoughtful expression crossed Taye's face. 'Maybe it was a local subspecies? That makes your finding so much more interesting!'

'Did I miss anything?' asked a voice behind them.

A boy with buzzed black hair and a green fringe slid into the seat beside Finn like he belonged there, which, apparently, he did.

'Oh, hi, Aria!' He beamed.

'Hi...?' Aria said, knowing they had never met before.

'For a timeweaver, your sense of timing is *tragic!*' Taye said, laughing.

'This is Aria Renwood,' Inaiê said. 'She just arrived *today*. From England.'

'I know,' the boy replied between mouthfuls of flatbread. His dark eyes sparkled with joy as he took another bite, the ocean blue of his robe set off the warm olive of his skin. 'Hm! I can never get enough of these flatbreads. These are so good!'

The table stared. Inaiê raised an eyebrow while holding her chin; Finn observed him with curiosity; Taye was grinning ear to ear with amusement; Carolina frowned in quiet judgement; and Fraser peeked from behind his book, goggle-eyed.

'Tenzin,' Finn said, patting his back. 'This is the first time you've met Aria.'

Tenzin blinked at Aria, confusion in his eyes. He swallowed hard. 'That's right! First day! Have you done the Wild Claiming yet? That's a fun one.'

'No, not yet,' Aria said. 'But how...?'

'Tenzin Norbu,' Finn introduced. 'They're a timeweaver, but sometimes they behave like a seer when they have glimpses of the near future.'

'Being a timeweaver makes things interesting,' Tenzin said, laughing, their eyes warm and endearing.

'Timeweaver?' Aria asked.

'It's like a fabulous superpower each mage is born with,' Taye said, twirling his fork. 'For some of us, it can take its sweet time for it to manifest clearly. I don't even know what I am yet!'

'It's not known how these are triggered or manifested,' Finn said, 'but every mage has a certain magical predisposition that they excel at and master faster than others.' He paused, looking at Aria, who frowned trying to take it all in. 'We're all mages here,' Finn added with a reassuring smile. 'Except, well... Carolina.'

'We don't get that kind of gift,' Carolina said with a shrug, 'but us wizards can train into any specialty we want.'

'What's your specialty?' Aria asked.

'Still figuring it out. I'm in my last year, so... decision time soon. No pressure, right?' Carolina said with a faint smile.

'Guess not.'

An ethereal sound filled the Hall, prompting voices to fade. It was unlike anything Aria had ever heard: sharp and clear, yet soft. The notes pierced the air, rising and falling with a haunting melody, echoing through the walls. The wild call stirred a weight in her chest, an empty cup waiting to be filled.

'The kulning. It's time! Let's head to the Great Ash.' Carolina stood, her eyes tingling with excitement.

'Wild Claiming!' Taye shook Aria's shoulders. 'I've wanted to witness this since my sister told me about Oakspire history. This will be incredible. Hah! Chosen by Nature, an absolute dream.' He stopped in his tracks and turned to Carolina. 'We *can* witness it, right?'

'I don't see why not. Though maybe just the six of us?'

'We should definitely be there,' Finn said, his voice softer. 'Moral support. But also so Aria doesn't feel like she's being thrown to the wolves.' He gave a cheeky nod.

Wolves? A tinge of panic spurred in her full stomach.

Curious faces turned as they walked past towards the exit. Aria could feel every eye on her, piercing the back of her skull as they exited the Mead Hall.

Aria followed them to the main doors but stopped before stepping outside, her jaw tensed. She held her pendant. What was she getting herself into? Was it dangerous? Would it be humiliating?

'Okay,' Taye said as he peeked in from the outside. 'This is definitely giving me main character energy! The mysterious new student, dramatically hesitating at the threshold? Such protagonist behaviour.'

'I'm just—'

'Nervous? Listen, if I had Nature itself in my corner, I'd be strutting through that door like I owned it. But also, totally valid to need a minute.'

Finn sneaked back in and stood by Aria. 'We're with you all the way; through the Wild Claiming, catching up with the classes, guiding you through this world. Whatever Krets you end up in.'

'Exactly!' Taye said with a grin. 'Come on, let's see what other dramatic protagonist moments await!' he added, locking his arms with Finn's and Aria's and gently pushing them forward.

Aria focused on the ethereal sound, allowing it to calm her thoughts. Her shoulders dropped after realising they were tight with tension. She let go of the pendant and went through the threshold, her backpack thumping on her back with every step.

They walked down the dirt path towards the lake reflecting the purple and pink sky. The call pierced the air, growing stronger and more insistent with every breath, sending shivers through her core.

The water mirrored perfectly the surrounding forest and softening skies. Standing on the edge was a woman. Her long blonde hair swung softly over a flowing white gown. Her lips parted as she sang the haunting melody. The song wrapped around Aria like a spell, meant only for her.

Taye pulled Aria back, breaking her trance. They gathered in front of the biggest tree Aria had ever seen, in a clearing by the lake, surrounded by an old deciduous forest. The tree's broad branches stretched far and wide, some dipping low on the ground while others reached high into the sky. The leaves glowed like fire in the westering sun.

This must be the Great Ash.

Instead of feeling small beneath it, she felt... held. Protected. Like this immemorial giant recognised her. The nervous energy buzzing through her all day melted away, replaced by a calm she'd never remembered feeling.

She closed her eyes.

This was home. She knew it in her bones.

A single leaf, golden and perfect, drifted down and landed on her shoulder, like the gentlest of welcomes.

CHAPTER SIX

The Wild Claiming

The woman stopped singing. Silence spread in the clearing and surrounding forest. Slowly, Aria opened her eyes. Professor Halvard walked towards her from behind the Great Ash with a dark wooden staff, with Astrid by his side.

'Welcome Aria,' Professor Halvard said, he held her hand in his. He studied her for a moment with an expression of recognition in his weathered face and warmth in his blue eyes.

A strange feeling lingered in the back of her mind. Surely, they hadn't met before this day? Though he did look like any old wizard in the stories she had read. Yet, unlike them, he appeared to have spent the day in the woods; his silver-white hair cascaded down his shoulders, and his beard had small leaves sticking out of it.

Professor Halvard released her hand and bowed his head slightly with a soft smile.

He gave a small knowing nod to the Great Ash. Aria followed his gaze and caught sight of the raven. *Again.* And it was as though she had arrived in the middle of a conversation about her, but she didn't have a say in it.

Just as the weight of it all settled on her shoulders, Professor Halvard's tone lifted the mood without forcing it.

'I see you've already drawn around you a circle of companions.' He nodded to the group behind her, who straightened with pride.

Taye had his arm slung around Finn like they'd been long-time friends, while Fraser let out a squeal of nervousness and fidgeted on the spot. Inaiê sat on a rock, legs crossed, with one ankle resting on her knee like she owned the place. Tenzin was completely zoned out, looking around the forest. Carolina stood by Astrid, hands clenched in front of her robes, smiling with pride.

'Thank you, Professor,' Aria said, scratching her head, reassured she was not alone in whatever she was about to face.

'After such an eventful day, I expect you'll want to rest, so we'll go straight into the Wild Claiming and call it a weekend. What do you think?' He gestured to the stone circle by the Great Ash.

Three tall stones stood with runic inscriptions, each with their own engravings etched in golden light. Beside them were smaller stones making a complete circle. The stones were weathered, with lichen covering their surfaces.

'Over the years, students have gathered in this sacred circle,' Professor Halvard said as he walked towards the stones, his twilight-hued robe dragging fallen red leaves on the ground. 'There are three paths: Fossheim, where waters hold both wisdom and transformative power; Lundgard, steady as a forest, where knowledge and roots grow deep; and Stenvald, mysterious as the meeting of stone and earth, where hidden routes lead to understanding.'

Aria rubbed her arm and looked up at Astrid, who gave her a reassuring smile.

'The magic flowing through our veins is intertwined with the natural world and the remarkable thing about the natural world is it evolves innately, gradually. Our students, guided by instinct, chose their Krets through these stones. Yet for you,' Professor Halvard paused, looking at Aria with an expression suggesting he was choosing his words carefully, 'a Krets will be chosen, one that will nurture and help you unlock your fullest potential.'

Butterflies took form and wrestled inside her. It was a relief she didn't have to choose anything when she hardly knew who she was in her world, or this one. And, at the same time, she was annoyed to not have a choice, trapped in a cycle she could not break.

'When you step into the circle, the stones will show you possibilities, echoes of paths you might walk. Inevitably, the stones will tell you the Krets you belong to.'

A black Raven landed on Professor Halvard's shoulder, its feathers moving like smoke underwater, slow and unnatural, with watchful amber eyes. The bird looked half real. Professor Halvard raised his wooden staff and the runes carved into the Great Ash began to shimmer in a golden light.

The runestones responded, their own engravings shining brighter in conversation with the tree. Torches burst into flame around them, flickering bright, marking this sacred space. A deep, raw, primal drum played through the grounds, its steady rhythmic base thumping on Aria's chest. Where did it come from? Aria could not find its source.

'Please, step into the stone circle, Miss Renwood. Touch each runestone. Take your time. Let them read your soul and speak to you.'

Aria swallowed hard, her pendant heavy on her neck. She took off her backpack and laid it next to a fallen tree trunk.

The moment her foot stepped into the centre of the stone circle, the fire flicked dramatically and the Great Ash let out a low, deep creak. Within the forest edge, misty forms gathered on branches, others half-hidden behind trees. Their presence was eerie – the land itself was watching her, judging her. Were they good or influencing her demise? Somehow, she knew Professor Halvard would stop them if they were to attack.

Aria shifted uncomfortably. She tried to ignore them, to focus on the stones, but the sensation clawed on her skin with the whole forest watching, waiting, impossibly aware.

Her fingers twitched at her sides, her breathing shallow. She wasn't ready for this, whatever *this* was. What would happen once she touched the stones? Would they test her? Transport her to a quest? Show her the future? The past? A mirror? The unknown devoured her whole.

She took a deep breath. Then another. And another. Each breath calmed her nerves; each breath brought her to the present. And as a gift, warmth radiated from the stones. Oddly comforting, like a blanket in the evening after spending the day in the sun.

Everything went still, quiet. Time slowed. The drum grew farther away, muffled by the ecstatic energy in the air.

It was now or never.

Aria approached the first stone. The runes traced the border, sunken with golden light emanating from it, pulsing like a heartbeat. In its centre was the depiction of storm waves – a moment frozen in time, of waves crashing onto the sea.

Tentatively, her fingers touched its surface, tingling from the contact. It was warm to the touch, like a living creature and not a dead, cold rock.

Her hand blurred and multiplied, like a ghostly echo of countless hands layered above hers. The stone reacted, light flickering uncontrollably, to the point Aria thought it would go dark completely. But it didn't – it stabilised.

Adrenaline rushed through her body; well aware she wouldn't be able to stop whatever was coming.

Her whole palm made contact and a rush of images crashed

over her with the power of waterfalls, overwhelming and unescapable. Glaciers elbowed their way through mountains, rivers pushed and eroded the soil, waves collapsed on cliffs. A clear vision of her hands cupping clear water from a stream in a place she did not recognise. A voice she knew called her name, echoing across a vast lake. The endless cycles that shaped and reshaped the earth. Aria tried to catch her breath, but her body thought she was drowning.

Gasping, she pulled her hand back.

The engravings on the stone went even brighter, like the sun had descended from the night sky. She raised her arms, squinting through the light, trying to understand what she'd done.

Aria turned to her companions.

Shadows danced across their stunned faces, equal parts awe and alarm. Their expressions were not reassuring. It only confirmed what she already knew: this wasn't normal.

For a moment, she was sure the stone would explode. But instead, the light subsided – almost reluctantly – until it settled into its original glow.

'Remarkable,' Professor Halvard finally said. 'You're doing wonderfully.' He extended his hand, prompting her to continue.

Rubbing her trembling hands on her black blazer, she approached the second stone. It was slightly broader than the first one, with moss covering the top of it. This time, engraved was a tree, its roots forming a band with runes etched on the border of the stone.

As she reached for the stone, her hand blurred again into a thousand hands. As soon as she touched it, she could hear the roots creaking through the soil, deeper and deeper into the Earth's core, fragments of conversations she'd never had. She saw her feet bare on the earth, dirt under her toenails, tired from walking for days. Forests moved in silence, whispering secrets to the darkness as the moon watched. Leaves turning, trees growing, flowers sprouting through the snow, the smell of decay.

When Aria took back her hand, the stone went dark.

Immediately, the air exploded. A shockwave burst outward in every direction, hitting her hard on the chest. She fell backward, hitting the floor as the trees were rustled by the sudden storm; her auburn hair tangled with dirt and leaves on the ground.

Fraser stumbled as well, and Taye yelled, 'Woah!'

She looked up to Professor Halvard for direction, but he stood motionless, watching. His shoulders were tense, both hands gripping the staff as if to hold himself steady. She couldn't read the man. Was he stopping himself from intervening? Was there *something* to intervene against?

Aria pushed herself up, brushed the dirt from her palms and tried to untangle the leaves from her hair. She decided to push through her growing anxiety, her pendant rising and lowering rapidly with her chest. One more, and then she would be done.

The last stone was the tallest and the leanest. In the middle was a serpent eating its own tail, runes etched around it. In contrast to the other two, the stone was cold to the touch, like ice.

As soon as her palm touched it, shadows danced between hidden realms in her mind, light pierced through the void. Countless moments of her last breath, over and over, in ways she couldn't grasp, followed by awakenings, a cry at the end of the tunnel. Just beyond her reach, voices echoed, coming from nowhere and everywhere at once, growing louder, like a beehive ready to swarm.

Aria let go at once, feeling dizzy. The voices continued,

however, louder and louder. It was no longer in her mind but emanating from the stone itself. Birds flew from the trees to escape the loud whispers, while those present pressed their hands over their ears.

All except Professor Halvard, who stepped forward and raised his hand. The noise subdued almost instantly, leaving Aria with a high-pitched tone ringing in her ears.

In the newfound silence, the three runestones pulsed with their golden light, all at different rhythms, adding chaos to the clearing. The torches' flames around them moved erratically on their own accord. Vibrations spread beneath her skin, into her bones. It was difficult to endure, but she stood her ground.

The play of light and shadow continued until, one by one, the flames died – a countdown to the finale.

The stones dimmed. Darkness fell.

As Aria's eyes adjusted to the lack of light, various sets of amber eyes were clearly visible in the forest line. The misty creatures were watching her.

What just happened? She didn't understand what she just experienced. Why did her hands multiply? Who called her name? And who were the voices that shouted at her?

Her thoughts were interrupted as the runes of the first stone began to glow again, adding light to the clearing.

'Fossheim it is,' Professor Halvard said, stepping into the circle. 'Miss Valencia,' he added, 'guide Aria to the Fossheim Tower. She could use some rest.'

Taye clapped excitedly.

Taking it as a cue, Aria hurried back to the group.

'We're in the same Krets!' Taye shouted while hugging her.

Aria flinched. Hesitantly, she hugged back. Trembling from head to toe, this was exactly what she needed.

Finn gave her a shoulder squeeze and a reassuring smile. 'That was a lot,' he said, 'and you did brilliantly.'

Tenzin gave her two thumbs up, their wide smile accentuating their sun-kissed red cheeks. Inaiê got up from the stone and patted her on the back, while Fraser was still gawping at the stones.

'Glad you're staying with us,' Carolina said with a smile. 'You'll learn a lot with us, and I am sure we will learn a lot from you too.'

A golden eagle landed on a branch beside Carolina. Aria took a step back, alarmed. Its sharp yellow eyes fixed on her with eerie intensity. What's up with these birds lately?

'Don't mind her, it's just my familiar, Esmeralda,' Carolina said. The golden eagle closed her eyes as Carolina petted her head. 'A gift from my father when I came of age.' She sighed and gave it a smile.

Carolina clapped her hands. 'Okay, let's go back.' The golden eagle jumped from the branch and glided ahead through the trees. She fell in step beside Aria as they walked. 'You did really well.'

Taye swooped in on Aria's other side, threw an arm around her neck, and gave her a playful shake. 'That was iconic! Those stones went full theatre for you. I'm obsessed.'

Aria managed a shaky smile.

'Wait—' She stopped in her tracks. 'My backpack.' She turned. 'I'll catch up!' Aria called as she darted back to the clearing. The others kept walking, their voices fading.

Aria picked up her backpack that rested by the fallen trunk and glanced back at the forest, now hidden in darkness. Whatever those creatures with amber eyes were, they were gone now.

Professor Halvard walked slowly towards the stone circle, tapping the staff on the ground with each step. He placed his hand on the Fossheim runestone, deep in contemplation.

Clearly, the Wild Claiming did not go as it was expected.

Based on her friends' reactions, it sure wasn't normal. And what were the images she saw? Were they possible futures? Aria gulped with the images of her dying.

'Don't be fooled by the golden ones that shine bright,' a voice said beside her, undulating like waves and oddly disjointed from the present. 'We forgot to look in their shadows...' The voice caught, like time itself had snagged.

Aria turned to find Tenzin, swaying slightly, steadying themselves against the nearby aspen, its trunk white with a hundred eyes.

'Whew,' they said, attention snapping back. 'This spot is like a temporal hurricane. You know what I mean?'

'Right,' Aria said slowly. 'What did you mean with "don't be fooled by the golden ones?"'

'I said that?' Tenzin scratched their head. 'Oh, this has never happened before. Maybe chanterelles? They say it's the forest's gold?'

'Chanterelles? What's that? Mushrooms? Are they poisonous?'

'No... Hm, maybe that's not it.'

Aria raised an eyebrow and turned back to the castle, frowning at that weird moment. Tenzin merrily walked along.

They joined the others. Lanterns floated above them, darting and dancing around each other like playful fireflies.

'Do rest, Aria. And have a lovely weekend,' Astrid said as she came to a halt by the steps of the castle. 'I live in the red cottage by the Greenhouse, if you ever need anything.'

'Thank you,' Aria said. 'You too! I mean... Have a good weekend.'

Astrid smiled and turned down the path next to the castle walls, a floating lantern above her, casting long shadows of the large trees.

One by one, they entered the Front Hall.

'See you at breakfast tomorrow, then,' Finn said. 'Lundgard Longhouse is here on the ground floor.'

'Oh right. You're in another Krets,' Aria said.

'It doesn't make us rivals. It's just another lifestyle, in a way.'

'Of course it does!' Taye said, clutching his chest like he'd insulted his honour. 'If I ever call my Krets a lifestyle, please dunk me in a fjord.'

Finn gave an eyeroll with a soft smile. He didn't argue, just turned left into the Hall.

'Come, we're going up the Grand Staircase. Think of it like levelling up.' Taye chuckled at his own joke.

Fraser and Inaiê turned right to the Stenvald Stone Halls, while Carolina, Taye, Tenzin and Aria turned left to the Fossheim Tower.

In the western wing of the castle, they climbed a narrow spiral staircase, winding up like a nautilus shell. As they climbed, Aria was in awe as stones on the wall transformed like water flowing through sand.

At the top, heavy doors swung open, their surfaces carved with intricate patterns of waves, dancing in the torchlight. Beyond lay Fossheim's common room, with the fire burning as moonlight pushed through the windows. Below was the lake, reflecting thousands of stars of the night sky. *This is incredible,* she thought.

Above them, lamps with balls of light moved like flames, illuminating shelves filled with books. Captivating art pieces moved and changed whenever you looked away. Comfortable leather armchairs and sofas were scattered around the room, many occupied by her peers reading, studying, or talking. Aria didn't know what time it was, but some already had their pyjamas on.

The chatter diminished as many faces turned to her; some curious, others happy, a few suspicious. Their heads followed as Aria walked through the common room to the staircase.

'Your room is on the left,' Carolina said once they stepped on the platform.

'That means goodnight to you, chosen one!' Taye said. 'I will plan this weekend accordingly, and I'll let you copy all my homework so you can catch up.'

'Good night!' Tenzin said, waving their hand as they followed Taye down the corridor.

'Thanks,' Aria said.

'Here's your bedroom,' Carolina said when they faced an empty bedroom. 'If you need anything, just shout for me. I'm down the corridor.' She tilted her head and gave her a smile before leaving her alone in the room.

Two wooden box beds stood on either side of the room, one of them unused, while the other had beautiful sketches of landscapes, people, and animals pinned on it. Aria sat on the empty bed on the left, tracing her finger through the carvings highlighted by the moonlight. Was it a Viking ship battling a storm or a sea serpent?

'Aria, right?' said a voice. 'The girl chosen by Nature?'

A girl with large round glasses low on her nose and dark curls escaping from her messy bun tumbled into the room. On top of her head was a chameleon, changing through a rainbow of colours. Aria couldn't take her eyes away from the animal, whose one eye rested on her, while the other on the moon.

'I'm Suraya Clairmont-Ziadeh. And this' – she pointed to her chameleon who changed colours with every word, matching her enthusiastic energy – 'is Louis. He's been with me since forever. My pet initially, but once I got my acceptance letter, we got help to turn him into a familiar. I couldn't pick any other one. Of course, Louis would come here with me. Gave my parents quite a shock – the whole thing. They thought the acceptance letter was an elaborate prank, at first!

They are scientists, not magifolk in any way. A genetic anomaly, they think. Anyway, did you get a familiar yet?' She looked around the room, her dark brown eyes sparkling with excitement.

'Eh... no?'

'Oh sorry, you must be a mage! I can't tell. Some people can tell right away, but being new to this world myself, I guess my radar is not in tune or something. I still don't understand how you mages can do big magic rituals without familiars. The books don't go into much detail about it, either. All a mystery! But wow! Chosen by Nature. What an honour that is!'

Aria wanted to reply but felt utterly lost with it all. Suraya spoke so fast, she had a hard time following.

Suraya approached the window. 'Have you seen our view? I've never seen so many stars until I started at Oakspire.' She turned to Aria and paused. 'Oh *purée*, sorry, I get a bit intense sometimes. But isn't it all so magical?'

'It really is,' Aria said, admiring Suraya's genuine wonder. She glanced around the room, taking in the candles that cast warmth against the white panelled walls, the light curtains with Fossheim's ocean blue, the simple desks beneath the large window.

'Though I have to admit, I don't even know where to start,' Aria confessed. 'I didn't exactly pack for this magical boarding school situation.' Aria placed her backpack down, which looked out of place in this room.

'Oh! Check the wardrobe!' Suraya said, pinning more sketches on the wall beside her bed. 'Everything we need should be in there. My mum told me Oakspire provides the basics for those who can't bring their own. Something about everyone has the right to an education.'

Aria bit her lip. She opened the wardrobe, and her jaw fell to the floor. Everything inside was new, from crisp shirts, tops, elegant blazers, and sweaters, to perfectly tailored blue robes, cloaks, boots, and shoes.

'This can't be real...' she whispered as she ran her fingers over the luxurious fabric, hardly believing they were hers. Everything she has ever owned had been second-hand, worn thin by previous owners. Never had she touched anything so fine.

'It absolutely is!' Suraya said. 'Though I still can't figure out how they get the measurements right... No one ever asked!'

Suraya got dressed into her deep blue pyjamas, with a white line around the rim. She sat on the bed and took a notebook from a pile at her bedside table, her dark brown hair falling over her shoulders. 'Mum and dad asked me to document every magical thing I encountered. It's a bit impossible now, of course. This is my fifth notebook in a month. They're completely fascinated by it all. It's a whole new world to study.'

Aria got dressed into her own pyjamas and glanced at her own backpack, packed with school notes, books and pens – a memory of a life that was no longer hers. Her hand reached her pendant, the only real thing she owned, which had been hers since as long as she remembered.

As they drifted off to sleep, the sounds of the Academy settled around her: distant laughter from the common room; the window's metal handle tapping slightly on the white wooden frame by the wind; Louis's gentle snores, now in his natural greenish brown. They lulled her into sleep, and the night carried her away.

CHAPTER SEVEN

The Elusive Barkfox

The nights were wonderfully uneventful, and the weekend unfolded like a holiday. Aria had never been this relaxed, in a place where she got treated like an equal.

Each day, Aria woke up to unfamiliar silence. She often lay still, looking up at the wooden panels of her box bed, letting the memories come back to her: the arrival to Oakspire; the ghost animals that roamed the corridors and outside on the grounds; the food that was always on point; the refreshing camaraderie; even the cold weather was cosy.

This still wasn't a dream.

Watching Taye and Finn doing homework was not an experience she expected. They tried to explain as much as possible about what she had missed, but one thing was clear: there was no way she would be able to immediately manipulate water with her bare hands or mix potions that could heal a burned wound. Worst still, she was way behind, and who knows, maybe her magic doesn't even work?

On Monday morning, Suraya's bed was empty, yet Louis sleepily watched Aria as she got dressed. Familiars did not always stick with their wizards, and she was grateful for it. The past few days, encountering some of these familiars, had made her uncomfortable. These were animals she had read about in books and seen in documentaries, but they didn't behave animalistically. They had a human intensity in their eyes and were clearly domesticated, influenced under a spell.

Aria got dressed in a loose off-white, long-sleeved top and brown trousers. On top of that, she wore her blue robe, which went down to her knees, its wide sleeves up to her elbows – a practical robe for the occasional field work, as Taye had told her. She tightened the leather belt around her waist.

Looking in the mirror, she did not recognise the girl opposite her. The golden flecks of her hazel eyes illuminated as she looked back at herself, mesmerised with unknown joy. She had her auburn hair down to her shoulders, accentuating the freckles on her face, and smiled broadly. The clothes fit her perfectly, no longer an armour for battle, but an extension of herself.

The common room buzzed with energy when she walked downstairs. It looked different in the morning light, as the folk drawings on the bookcase doors along the wall gave it life. While at night, the space was intimate with the fireplace and warm candles, during the day it was alive with possibilities as the sunlight flooded the room through the high windows, making it light and vibrant.

'Good morning!' Taye said, perched on an armrest. 'Are you ecstatic to indulge yourself in knowledge?'

'Yes and no? I'm eager but terrified at the same time.'

'You'll blend in in no time! Come on – breakfast!'

They joined Finn in the Mead Hall, who looked up from a large book on the table as they approached. 'Morning!'

Across from him was an older girl with short platinum hair wearing Fossheim's ocean blue robes and a black turtleneck top underneath. She was writing and drawing technical diagrams in her notebook. Methodically, she added honey to her porridge while occasionally glancing at Finn's book with patient amusement.

'Anything interesting in there?' Aria asked, intrigued as she settled on the bench beside him.

'Oh yeah, I'm reading about narwhals. Did you know they can bridge our world to the spirit realm?' He leant in, clearly excited to share. 'Their tusks hold magical properties. They can change currents, heal, and even communicate with other species.'

The platinum-haired girl looked up. 'The book's got it partially right,' she said. 'My mum studies them off the coast of Svalbard. Narwhals don't just communicate with other species; they maintain song lines beneath the ice. Something she just recently discovered.' She lifted her chin slightly. 'Still to be published!'

The girl turned to Aria. 'I'm Petra Nosenko, by the way. I'm a third-year.'

'Nice to meet you. I'm Aria.'

'I know. I've seen you in the Fossheim common room.'

'Excuse you a minute – *song lines*?' Taye leant in like she'd just revealed state secrets, his forgotten spoon sinking into his blueberry porridge without protest.

Petra turned to him, brown eyes glittering with the thrill of having piqued someone's interest.

'They're like underwater ley lines but made of sound. Their tusks act as tuning forks, keeping magical frequencies stable. Without them, the whole Arctic magical ecosystem would fall out of harmony.'

'Incredible!' Aria said. 'I've heard about narwhals but never knew about the magic part.'

'Speechless!' Taye declared, his head dropping into his hand, elbow on the table, eyes on Petra for a few seconds. He turned to Aria with pedagogic flair. 'There are so many magical creatures hiding in plain sight!' He went on, gesturing dramatically. 'Take the waxwing, for example. They shine like flames in the night, helping lost travellers find their way on winter nights. They're life saviours!'

'Wait, what?'

'Exactly! They've been helping common and magifolk alike survive winters for centuries.'

'It's wild when you think about it,' Finn said. 'So many animals have magical abilities, and commonfolk who study them don't even realise what they are dealing with.'

'That's why magical conservation is so important,' Petra said, her voice turning serious. 'Shipping routes are disrupting the song lines with sonar pollution, and when that happens, it's like drilling into the ocean's veins and the whole system starts to collapse.'

The words were heavy. Aria had grown up worrying about endangered species, but the same threats reached this hidden world in plain sight. She never imagined whales could sing magic, or that birds could emit fire; let alone that they, too, were threatened. A whole secret world was starting to open up to her... and it was already slipping away.

'Oh, you wait until Professor Klaus Grünwald gets started on Arctic phoenixes in Magifauna Studies. Now *those* are incredible,' Petra said.

The Magifauna Studies classroom was on the ground floor, deep in the eastern wing, facing the North Forest. Sunlight illuminated rows of jars where fantastical specimens floated in glistering liquids: an amphibian with fur; a mouse with scales; a fish with wings; and something she could only describe as a mushroom with eyes. Some specimens twitched and turned, though given where they were, Aria suspected magic was at work.

'Did that just blink at me?!' Taye whispered loudly as they

descended the stairs of the auditorium. 'That mushroom totally just winked!'

She glided into the seat near the front, next to Taye and Finn, processing the room and everything she learned about narwhals and waxwings. She opened her notebook, ready for whatever else this class might reveal.

The door swung open dramatically, and in walked Professor Klaus Grünwald, a tall man with wild grey hair with a life of its own, contrasted by a tight groomed beard. The multiple pockets in his vest were filled with all sorts of curious objects. His blue eyes sparkled, inquisitively looking around the auditorium.

He clapped his hands together, drawing all eyes to him.

'Good day, my young friends!' His German accent rang through the room.

Aria leant forward, curious to see what this professor was all about.

'Now,' Professor Grünwald continued as he strode to the side door, 'why waste such a beautiful day inside? Come! The best specimens are not in jars!'

There was a burst of movement as the first-years scrambled to gather their things. Taye nearly knocked over his chair. Finn managed to pack his bag without taking his eyes off the professor and Aria bumped into Fraser, who was choosing which field guide to take with him.

They poured out through the doors onto a stone terrace, the sunlight blinding them as Professor Grünwald marched across the grounds towards the Northern coniferous forest, his wild hair bouncing with each step and his jiggling tools in his vest adding noise to his movement.

The whole class hurried after him.

'Okay,' Professor Grünwald said as he stopped on the edge of the forest. 'Before we dive into specific creatures, tell me, what is the most important animal in an ecosystem? Anyone?'

Everyone exchanged nervous looks.

Fraser's hand went up cautiously. 'A predator? Like a maned wolf? According to Stanley's research—'

'Ja! The predator could be one!' Professor Grünwald exclaimed, pointing at Fraser with passion, cutting off what Aria was sure it would have been a fascinating citation.

Inaiê leant back against a pine, arms crossed. 'I disagree. Every creature is important, not just the big predators.'

'Ah!' Professor Grünwald's eyes lit up. 'Indeed, it is so! In fact, what if I told you some creatures, even the smallest, tiniest creatures, can hold the fabric of life and magic together?' He added a dramatic pause. 'Without them, the magical world would collapse! Poof! Gone!' He mimed an explosion, causing a few to giggle. 'These are called keystone species.'

'You mean, like wolves in Yellowstone?' Aria asked, recalling her biology lessons.

Taking the courage to speak up led to a flow of whispers around her.

Professor Grünwald beamed at her. 'Ja! When they returned, the ecosystem healed. Wolves controlled the deer population, and the forest regrew.' He spread his arms. 'The balance of the magical system is even more delicate and keystone magifauna stabilises it. Let me give you another example.'

He waved his hands and conjured an illusion of a small slender creature with short legs, its fur black with sparkling tips that made it look like it fell into a bucket of glitter.

'This,' he said, pointing at the creature moving around, curious about its surroundings, 'is the spell badger, often hidden in the forests near civilisation. They break down used magic, preventing it from accumulating and becoming toxic.'

The spell badger sniffed Tenzin's shoes. Tenzin tried to pet it and gasped when their hand went through its head.

'This way, they convert it back to its pure essence that goes back into the system,' Professor Grünwald continued.

He paced in front of the class, now completely absorbed in his own lecture. 'Some creatures are masters in ways we don't yet fully comprehend. Take the antler bear.'

The spell badger dissolved in mid-air, and with a simple movement, an antler bear appeared: a large lumbering creature with moss-covered fur and glowing orange eyes, its antlers imprinted with runes.

'The antler bear roams the northern mountains and is what we call a magical catalyst.'

The bear pawed the ground, and small sparks of electricity danced between its antlers.

'Its antlers act as conduits, drawing raw magical energy from the atmosphere and converting into forms other magifauna can use. Without the antler bear, many species would be unable to access the magic they need to survive. Neither could we.'

Aria's skin tingled with excitement. So many new species to learn.

'We might be studying magifauna, but remember, they are the real teachers. They show us Nature is not about dominance, but about balance. Now!' He clapped his large hands. 'Let's see what we can discover in our own North Forest! I spotted some barkfox specimens earlier.'

They walked a few minutes into the North Forest, their collective footsteps crunching dry needles and twigs on the path. The forest was dominated by large spruce and pine trees, the air was fresh and the sun above illuminated the uneven forest floor of a green carpet of moss that covered large rocks.

'Trolls threw those at churches, annoyed by the tolling of

church bells,' Taye said as Aria paused to study how a massive stone balanced oddly atop a smaller one. 'Total drama queens. But let's be honest, there are no churches around here, so... what exactly were they aiming for? Questions, questions.'

'Maybe mosquitos?' Aria laughed and squinted at the stone. 'I'd throw a boulder if I could. Higher the chances of hitting it.'

'Oh yes! The real menace. Forget church bells.'

'Not that it would work,' Finn said. 'Troll skin is basically rock. Pretty sure their blood is half mud as well.'

Finn glanced around at the scattered stones with a half-smile.

'Maybe they just had terrible aiming skills. Or really, really hated pinecones.'

'Aha!' Taye exclaimed. 'Maybe they were targeting pinecones but hit churches by mistake. Bad aim and rage issues.'

The three of them laughed, catching up with the rest of the group.

They spent the rest of the morning scouring the North Forest for the elusive barkfox. Based on Fraser's field book, the barkfox was small, its fur blending seamlessly with the bark of the trees, shifting in texture and colour to mimic its surroundings like a chameleon.

Aria crunched low, her fingers pushing through blueberry bushes, focusing on the rough bark of the trees ahead. It was like trying to find a shadow in the dark, she realised.

After what felt like an eternity, there it was. A flicker of movement, almost imperceptible. The small barkfox watched her with its big black eyes. It was much smaller than a red fox, with short legs and large ears, and fur that gave the illusion of being made of bark.

It took a step towards her.

Her heart swelled with a quiet sense of understanding – the

creature and she were part of the same. Her hand reached out, slowly crawling closer, a soft smile tugging at her lips.

A high-pitched dissonant sound pierced her ear drums, its rhythm deeply wrong. Before Aria could process what or why it was, a screech made her whip back.

'Ah! It's trying to eat me!'

Taye was flailing under the attack of a large territorial dragonfly with dazzling, crystal-like wings. The sunlight refracted off its wings, sending mesmerising patterns of light across the forest.

The class burst into laughter.

Professor Grünwald rushed over, shooing the dragonfly away with exaggerated gestures.

'No need to panic! The crystalwing is just curious!' he said with a chuckle. 'Though perhaps a bit too curious. Let me just...'

He raised his hand, and a soft blue glow emanated from his palm. He took cautious steps towards the dragonfly with the careful patience of taming a tiger. But the glow flickered with uncertainty, like a candle in a draft, before fading completely.

'Peculiar,' he muttered. 'No matter! Sometimes even we mages have our off moments!' He stretched both hands this time, and the blue light soared stronger. The dragonfly reacted, slowed its pace. It buzzed around Taye a couple more times, before finally flying up into the canopy.

'Well,' Professor Grünwald said, clapping his hands and turning back to the class with a grin. 'Eventful, yes? Shall we return to our search for the barkfox?'

Aria turned back at the barkfox, but it was gone. The sensation of their connection lingered – it was more significant than just watching a magical creature.

'I'm definitely going to dream about that crystalwing.' Taye laughed as he brushed dirt from his blue robes, the curls in his hair accentuated by the sun. 'You think the light show was a warning or a challenge?'

The morning breeze carried the earthy scent from the forest as the first-years made their way back to the castle.

'I'd say both,' Finn grinned.

Taye gasped, clutching his chest in mock outrage. 'I don't know if I should be honoured or offended!'

'Actually!' Fraser thrusted his small *Magifauna Field Guide* forward. 'That was mating behaviour, see? But' – he squinted at the page and then up at the sky – 'that can't be right. They're supposed to only display in spring when—'

'Fraser, darling, are you suggesting I've got that special something something that makes magical insects want to put on a show?' Taye struck an exaggerated pose. 'I mean, I know I'm fabulous, but this is next level!'

They all laughed, though Aria's mind snapped back to the barkfox. She always had a bond with animals. Birds settled outside her window without fear, stray cats rubbed against her ankles as one of their own. Yet, this was deeper, primal. She couldn't shake the feeling there had been more in those eyes. A plea? The thought settled uncomfortably on her shoulders.

'Earth to Aria!' Taye waved his hand in front of her face. 'We were talking about the next class, History Through the Ages.' He groaned dramatically. 'It's such a whiplash, going from exploring magifauna in the wild to sitting in a stuffy classroom learning about has-beens.'

'Tell me about it. I could do Magifauna Studies all day,' Aria said, looking back at the forest as they entered the castle.

'And I honestly detest having classes with wizards. They make everything so... square.'

Aria's eyebrows shot up. 'Square?'

'Rigid. Boring. Everything-must-have-its-place people.'

'Oh? It's not only us... mages?' These words still felt foreign in her tongue.

'For some classes, it's only us,' Finn said. 'Others, we share.' He turned to Taye. 'I actually think it's interesting to learn with them. They give another perspective in class.'

'I know *you* would think so!' Taye rolled his eyes with a wide grin. 'You're such a diplomatic soul. And I love you for it.'

By the time they slid into their seats for History Through the Ages on the third floor of the western wing, the wild spark from being outside dimmed in her chest. The classroom looked like an old library, complete with ceiling-high shelves filled with dusty books and old scrolls.

With it came a bad feeling. Maybe it was the coldness of the stone floor and the gloom of the dark wooden panels. Or maybe it was being in a room filled with history she knew nothing about, surrounded by people who knew a lot more. Or worst still, the palpable tension in the air with wizards seated on the opposite side of the atrium, like the British parliament.

She was dreading this already.

'*You're* what Nature has chosen?'

A sharp energetic voice made Aria's head snap back as she was about to sit.

A girl with regal and commanding posture stood behind them, her dark brown hair falling in natural waves just past her shoulders. She had Fossheim robes, though Aria didn't remember seeing her in the common room during the weekend. Her porcelain-perfect face looked like it had never known doubt, while a smirk played on her lips. Behind her were two Stenvald girls, who looked down at everybody with superiority.

Aria shifted uncomfortably on the spot.

'Kaija, darling,' Taye said with a loud sigh. 'Must we? No

one summoned your royal presence.'

'What, we can't say hi to the Academy's new prodigy?' Kaija tilted her head, voice condescending. 'We've just been away on a hunting weekend at my family estate in Finland, so we're dying to see what all the fuss is about.' She looked at Aria from head to toe. 'Hm, you'd think Nature itself would've sent someone a little more... seasoned,' she added with a smile that did not reach her cold blue eyes.

Aria didn't respond, her jaw muscles tense.

'Kaija Väinävirta,' the girl said with a cool cocky arrogance. 'My family runs Finland's world renowned magibio labs. If it's cutting-edge and actually works, it's probably ours.' She smirked, eyes gleaming.

'That's Victoria Beauchamp,' she continued, nodding at one of the girls behind her, with immaculate makeup, her golden-brown hair perfectly shaping her face. 'Her family has been advisors of the British Crown for generations. Old money, older magic, all class.'

Victoria tilted her head back, and even though slightly shorter than Aria, she mastered the art of looking down at her from below.

'And Inessa Volkova,' she gestured to the other girl, with soft pink bob hair, a bland contrast to her pale skin, whose expression was deep boredom. 'Her family owns half the ancient magical sites in Eastern Europe.'

Inessa's large brown eyes watched Aria with an uncomfortable intensity.

'You've probably heard of us. Noble wizarding families don't usually go unnoticed. I mean, we essentially rule the world. No offence.' She shrugged and gave pointed looks at the mages who were finding their seats nearby.

Aria had never heard of such names. Probably a good thing.

'I—' Aria started.

'Renwood, is it?' Victoria asked, looking down at a red leather notebook with excessive interest, her British accent clipping each syllable. 'Curious. No magical lines to speak of.' She *tsked*, the corner of her mouth turning down in a pout of disapproval. 'Pray tell, have you been somewhat misplaced?'

Aria blinked, caught off guard by the blatant hostility. For a small moment, she thought she had left this kind of cruelty behind, but no. It had followed her here, like a curse.

She opened her mouth to respond, but the words got stuck in her throat.

Taye straightened to his full height, making him tower over everyone else. 'You know what's *really* curious? How some people with so much class find themselves with this gross bullying behaviour. Must be exhausting keeping track of your superiority complex.'

Kaija rolled her eyes dramatically. 'Spare me the heroics. You have to wonder whether she can keep up. I mean, does anyone believe someone plucked from obscurity can handle the pressure here?' Her gaze settled on Aria, a playful but cutting challenge in her tone. 'I hope you're ready for reality. This is not a fairy tale.'

The rest of the class went silent, watching the exchange. Some stood and moved closer.

Inaiê's easy smile had vanished as she watched Kaija twirl her ornate silver wand between her fingers.

'Typical,' Inaiê said, lifting her head in defiance. 'All flash, no substance.'

Victoria wrote in her notebook with a black and golden fountain pen, her lips pursed in a thin line. 'So quiet, like a little forest mouse. Dreadfully provincial. First day reactions are so telling, don't you think?'

A heat of anger rose in Aria's chest.

She met Kaija's blue eyes, her own hardening with

determination. 'You know what? You're right about one thing: this is not a fairy tale. If it was, you three would be way better at the whole "evil witch" routine. Honestly, I have seen so much worse.'

The words tumbled out before she could stop them, each one carrying the same fire she'd have wanted to use on Oliver Sinclair, though now, she was not alone.

'Look, sure,' she continued. 'I don't know why Nature chose me, or if I believe in this whole destiny thing. Maybe it was all a mistake. But I'm here now and' – she swallowed hard, wiping her sweaty hands on her robe – 'I'm staying.'

A ripple went through the room, many circling them. Someone whispered, 'Whoa.' Fraser let out a low whistle, which dissolved into an unconvincing cough when Inessa's glare snapped in his direction.

Kaija laughed. 'Absolutely adorable. Let's be honest, the Academy's not kind to those who can't keep up. You're in over your head, sweetheart. You'll figure that out soon enough.'

'That's enough!' Taye said as he raised his chin up with a sharp look. 'Don't go throwing shade just because you're terrified someone else might actually sparkle brighter than you. Your fancy wizard bloodline doesn't give you rights to treat people like this.'

'How refreshingly... Swedish,' Victoria said, examining her nails. 'Believing talent alone trumps centuries of magical refinement. Only a mage would think everyone deserves a chance to shine. Some of us have standards.'

Three taps against wood silenced the room.

A petite woman stood in the doorway, surveying the scene with an expression of a person reading gossip magazines: curiosity and judgement mixed with poorly disguised amusement. Her silver-streaked black hair was pulled into an immaculate chignon, her gold-rimmed glasses on her nose tip.

Everyone scrambled to their seats. Amid the chaos, Aria spotted Suraya on the opposite end of the atrium, looking down into her notebook, colourful pencils at hand. Aria tried to wave at her, but she never looked up.

Kaija and her friends took their time, moving with deliberate slowness to their seats. The woman tracked their movement without comment.

'Miss Väinävirta,' she finally said as Kaija settled into her seat. 'I presume your hunting weekend was productive? Your father's approach to magifauna conservation remains... consistent, I see.'

Kaija's cheeks flushed pink before she composed herself.

'Yes, Professor,' she answered, her confidence slightly diminished.

'Splendid.'

The professor made her way to the front, each step measured and precise. She turned in a graceful pirouette to face the class, clicking her shiny black shoes together with theatrical precision. She wore a high-collared button-down black gown with a fitted waist, austere yet elegant.

'For our newest addition—' She looked at Aria from under her glasses. Aria sank lower in her seat. 'I am Professor Lavinia Thistlecroft. In this classroom, we examine not just what happened, but why it still matters. Possibly one of the most important subjects you will encounter.'

With a flick of her wand, a piece of white chalk flew to the large blackboard behind her, bouncing mid-air, like an eager dog waiting for commands.

'Today, we continue our exploration of the scandalous chapter of the rise of wizards in the late medieval period, when knowledge became as intoxicating as power.'

Everyone pulled out their notebooks with practised ease, writing down the notes the chalk was writing on the board as

Professor Thistlecroft dictated. Aria fumbled her pencil, feeling increasingly out of place.

'Before the Great Systemisation of 1479, magic was primarily an oral tradition. Spells passed from mentor to apprentice, knowledge held close like family secrets. Then came the obsession with documentation.'

Taye slouched, looking up at the ceiling. It was clear this was not his favourite subject. Aria's mind wandered as well. Was magical history so different from the history she learned, like a parallel world, or was it shared with more nuance? What other secrets were waiting for her outside, in the forest, in the wild? Could she potentially have the power to speak with animals? The red squirrel in the Museum Gardens was clearly trying to talk to her. Maybe it sensed something? If she could only ask the barkfox—

'Miss Renwood,' Professor Thistlecroft said, her tone as cool as frost, tapping her wand on Aria's desk. 'Perhaps you'd enlighten us on the Great Systemisation of 1479 and its consequences?'

'I... well...' Aria's mouth went dry. Scattered laughter rippled through the room, Kaija particularly loud. Aria's cheeks burned.

'Quite,' Professor Thistlecroft said. 'I'd suggest a little less daydreaming and a little more attention to actual history. On your first day, no less.'

She walked over Taye's table and tapped her wand on it, making him jerk awake.

Aria sank lower in her seat, feeling the weight of every smirk in the room. Finn shot her a sympathetic shrug, while Taye looked grossly disoriented.

On the corner of the black board, the chalk drew two stick figures – one slouched with droopy eyes, the other snapping upright with a startled look. The animation repeated this movement over and over again. A clear, cheeky caricature of Aria and Taye, a moment immortalised for the rest of the class to relive.

'As I was saying' – Professor Thistlecroft looked around the room – 'can anyone explain why wizards rose to prominence?'

Victoria's hand shot up. 'They documented spells and made them more accessible, Professor. Unlike certain... others.' She shot a meaningful look at the mages.

'Correct, Miss Beauchamp, though I didn't ask for commentary,' Professor Thistlecroft replied. 'Wizards did systematise magic, founded universities, and created structure. But' – her lips curved slightly – 'does order necessarily equal improvement?'

Inaiê raised her hand, her expression sceptical. 'But isn't that limiting? Forcing magic into structures and rules? It's part of the land, river, and trees. You can't exactly contain that.'

Professor Thistlecroft's eyes gleamed, a flicker of approval crossing her face. 'An excellent point, Miss Kuaray. Many mages indeed share that belief: magic's strength lies in its freedom and fluidity, learned through experience. Yet, many wizards believed magical knowledge would otherwise be lost without its categorisation.'

'Bingo!' a boy exclaimed, raising his eyebrows and shooting finger guns at the professor while glancing around the classroom with an approving nod. 'That's what I say! Wizards end up being superior to mages in every way.'

'I couldn't have put it better myself,' Victoria said, pulling on the tips of her golden-brown hair. 'I'm with Jun on this one.'

The boy smiled confidently, tilting his head just enough to seem casual, letting his black fringe fall across his thick eyebrows.

Inaiê pouted in disagreement, rolling her eyes.

'Not quite, Mr Park,' Professor Thistlecroft said. 'One

might suggest scholars got a bit carried away. Seventy-three volumes on proper ritual circle alignment alone... Clearly, they had ample free time.'

She moved around the classroom, wand tapping thoughtfully against her arm as she spoke. 'Centuries of tension followed, as wizards imposed their "superior" methods on all magical communities. The results were' – she paused for dramatic effect – 'well, mixed.'

Everyone shifted, chuckling nervously.

The rest of the class passed in a blur of dates and diplomatic disasters. When the bell finally rang, Aria's stomach was growling louder than her embarrassment was making her sick, for she stared at the animated caricature far too long.

The smell of food lingered in the corridors as they headed downstairs from the third floor, along with the whole student body that came out from every direction.

To add to the confusion, ghostly animals walked among them: a large wolverine ran between people's legs, dodging them, and a ghostly cat played with Fraser's loose shoelaces, making him stumble not once but three times.

'Oh, Renwood!' Kaija called mockingly behind them.

Aria's stomach dropped at the sound of her voice. She stood midway down the Grand Staircase and turned to see Kaija gliding down, Victoria and Inessa flanking her, proud like peacocks. The crowd naturally parted around them, giving the trio plenty of space – and an audience. Aria looked up at the honourable Viking shields on the wall, wishing she could grab one and hide behind it.

'We simply *had* to catch you before lunch,' Kaija said. 'I've been thinking about your performance in History.' She paused dramatically a couple of steps above Aria, using the stair's height to her advantage, now only slightly taller than Aria. 'Or should I say, your lack thereof.'

Taye moved closer to Aria's side. 'I don't think my head can tackle this just before lunch. Find someone else to pester.'

'Oh no, this is educational!' Kaija's eyes sparkled with malicious delight. 'I mean, Professor Thistlecroft practically had to remind you to focus in class. Like that isn't the bare minimum in school.' She let the words linger in the air, looking around at the crowd they attracted, resting their arms on the rails from the landing. 'You know, I am just concerned about our academic reputation. I mean, what kind of message does it send when someone misses a month of lessons and doesn't have the decency to pay attention in class? It's disrespectful to the professor, to us, to the whole Academy. Makes one wonder if Nature made a terrible mistake.'

Heat crept up Aria's neck, her eyes darted to the people around them. She couldn't escape. She was out of her depth, disappointed in how she handled herself in history class, without any magical lineage to speak of, confused in this new world she wasn't born into, and chosen for whatever reason she never asked for.

A glint broke her thoughts, leading her attention to Victoria, who held up her wand, wooden and polished, from below her waistline. She pointed it at Aria and muttered something she couldn't hear.

A flash of light shot from her wand, landing straight into Aria's hair. In horror, she felt her hair move, twist and turn, taking shapes she never thought possible.

The bystanders in the Great Staircase burst into laughter as her hair stood up like a porcupine. Aria tried to push it down, but it wouldn't. It moved under her hand like a cat.

Finn stood beside her, hovering his hands over her hair, light emanating from it. 'I don't—' Finn said, focusing. 'I don't know how—'

'Oh my, oh my,' Kaija said, 'even your hair wants to escape

your body. How unfortunate.'

Victoria and Inessa joined in the laughter, echoing louder than the rest.

'Fix it!' Taye shouted. 'You can't do this, it's against the rules.'

'Watch me, darling,' Victoria said, leaning closer with a sly smile.

'That's– That's not nice,' said a soft voice.

Suraya stood on the landing behind them, clutching her books to her chest, looking terrified but determined. Her fingers were etched with yellow and green paint, holding a reddish-brown wand.

Kaija's eyebrows shot up in surprise. 'And you are?'

'Suraya Clairmont-Ziadeh. We've met a few times, but you don't... It doesn't matter. Aria's been nothing but kind, and you're being horrible for no reason.'

'Ah yes. *Un artiste!* Sure, of course you vardbarns would stick together. Commonfolk tend to do that. Love living in ignorance.'

'Well... Um... One thing we have that you don't have is perspective.' Suraya lifted her wand and pointed at Kaija. 'Which you desperately need more of.'

'Put your wand down, sweetheart. You'll take someone's eye out.'

'*Orð snúa aptr*,' Suraya said, moving her wand in a circular pattern.

A white light shot out from her wand into Kaija's chest.

Kaija looked alarmed, but once nothing had happened, she settled. 'Cute. How predictable, can't even do a spell right. I'm in over my head and have no idea what I'm doing.'

Kaija froze and looked around in confusion.

'No, what I mean was... You're clearly not ready for real magic. My father would disown me if he saw how badly I'm handling it all.'

Victoria exchanged a worried look with Inessa.

'Kaija, darling, are you alright?' Victoria asked.

'Of course I'm fine! This imbecile couldn't possibly affect someone of my calibre. I'm just a scared little girl pretending to be important.'

The hall went dead silent.

'Don't say another word! We need to find the counterspell. Come on.'

Victoria placed her hand on Kaija's back and guided her down the stairs. Kaija's cheeks were red with embarrassment, her eyes wide in shock.

'You will pay, little girl,' Inessa said to Suraya as she followed Victoria and Kaija. Her eyes lingered a long second on Aria's as she passed.

Once out of sight, the crowd dispersed, whispering to one another.

'How did you do that?' Aria asked Suraya, half in shock at what she had witnessed, half amused.

'They walk around saying horrible things to people. And you know when you shower and come up with all the best comebacks? I've been looking for spells that could be useful. This one, in particular, stayed in my mind. I had to try.'

'Genius!' Taye exclaimed, shaking Suraya's shoulders. 'I wonder how long your spell will take to wear off.'

'A few days. Unless they figure out the counterspell.'

'I bet we won't see more of them today,' Finn said with a shrug.

'Odin's eye, I hope you're right!' Taye said. His stomach made a loud rumble. 'Food. I need food. Too much to handle on an empty stomach.'

'You didn't have to do that,' Aria said to Suraya as they walked down the Grand Staircase. 'I could handle it.'

‘Says the girl whose hair is still up,’ Suraya giggled. ‘We should go find a remedy for that.’

‘Let’s go to Sigrid, she probably will have something for this,’ Finn said.

‘Oh, are we saying goodbye to this fabulous hairstyle?’ Taye said as he hovered his hand over Aria’s hair, which moved, avoiding his touch. ‘It could start a trend.’

‘No, I’m good, thank you,’ Aria said. ‘Where is this Sigrid?’

‘Healing Hall,’ Finn said. ‘Come on, let’s get your hair more domesticated.’

They headed down the corridor into the eastern wing, while Aria’s hair moved slowly like an animal playing with the wind.

What did she do to deserve all of this? She just wanted to be ordinary, boring even. She was not an academic, and Kaija was probably right – maybe she would be a disappointment to the Academy.

CHAPTER NINE

Fire

Water spray with chamomile and lavender was all they needed to fix the porcupine hair, which left her hair shiny and smelling divine for days. It even looked better than before. A simple solution to a simple spell.

Suraya told Aria she wasn't too sure her spell would be as simple.

Kaija had not shown her face for a few days, while Victoria and Inessa silently fumed whenever they saw Aria. Since the incident, it had now been told and retold through the Academy so many times, the "truth" claimed Aria's hair grew so much, she was covered from head to toe. Not only did the professors come to realise she was not a magic adept, the whole student body now labelled her as a joke too.

By the end of her first week, the first-years climbed the twisted staircase to the Fundamentals of Magic laboratory, where multicoloured smoke danced in geometric patterns across the ceiling. Streams of blue and green smoke flowed in separate layers, never mixing.

As she did in every class, Aria hoped the next one would be different. Maybe Fundamentals of Magic was a time to redeem herself, show that she had potential, had the focus, and the interest.

Ten minutes into class, grains exploded in every direction, causing everyone to scream and duck. Aria looked down at her lab station, horrified to realise they were hers.

'How intriguing!' Professor Kamaye Haruki appeared beside her, making her jump. He scribbled across his notebook with gusto. 'The grains respond to your subconscious instead of conscious direction. Not the intended outcome, but...' He beamed at her scattered grains. 'Sometimes magic has its own ideas of organisation.'

Professor Haruki seemed to live for the chaos, yet his pastel robes were immaculately pressed and adorned with geometric patterns, and not a single strand of his long black hair was out of place. His classroom was dimmed by the multicoloured smoke, with no clear source, which made Aria suspect Professor Haruki created it for ambiance.

'*Koma atpr*,' Professor Haruki said as he flicked his wand, and all her grains flew back into her vial. 'Try again! Sense the pull through the energy fields and guide the grains!' He turned to Taye next to her, who guided the enchanted grains to find their proper partners. 'Watch how he hovers his hands over the vials and concentrates? Magic will naturally seek connection, like magnets. Others prefer to separate, like oil and water, if you will. Your job is to guide them.'

Another explosion made Professor Haruki move quickly and precisely to Jun Park, who scattered the grains throughout the room with perfect precision.

'Wonderful! You've just found out what happens when you use the incantation *dreifa*, but today, we are focusing on *skipa*.'

Professor Haruki traced a pattern in the air with his wand and uttered *skipa*. The grains rose from every corner of the room, made an impossible dance in the air, and slowly settled on the table in impeccable rows sorted by colour.

'See? Simple.' With a flick of his wand, the grains mixed up in the vial. 'Now try again.'

'Erm, Professor?' Fraser squealed across the room, his glasses crooked on his nose, panicking as his grains swirled higher and higher in the air.

Professor Haruki laughed as he hurried to help him, writing in his notebook.

By the end of class, Aria's documentation page had become a jumble of words, exclamations and diagrams. Professor Haruki's enthusiasm never wavered. If anything, each mishap delighted him more, but she couldn't share his joy in the chaos. Her magic was clearly speaking a different language entirely.

'Remember,' he called out as they packed, 'precision isn't about control. It's about waltzing with the unexpected!'

Aria's shoulders were up to her ears as they headed downstairs to Elementals for her last class of the week. Maybe Elemental magic would be different. It had to be. Aria desperately needed a win.

'Don't worry. Haruki doesn't actually fail anyone.' Finn gave her a reassuring smile as they descended to the Elementals classroom on the western wing. 'He says mistakes are just part of the process. The more that goes wrong, the better the learning.'

'Yeah, sure. Oh—!' Aria said as her fingers brushed the wall. It was warm to the touch and the air itself was thick, hitting the scent of bark, smoke, and sap. 'Is this normal? It's like entering a furnace.'

'Only on fire days,' Taye said. 'Professor Kiran believes in environmental immersion. Says it helps attune our senses to the elements.'

'Wonderful,' Aria muttered. Of all the elements to start with – fire. The one element she never felt at ease with.

From chaos to sleek organisation, the Elementals classroom

was arranged in a semi-circular pattern of individual stations facing inwards to the front of the room. Each station had two unlit candles.

Aria paused at the threshold, hesitant. Something about this room hinted at being more demanding, less forgiving than Professor Haruki's chaotic laboratory. No space for error.

'Move it or lose it, prodigy,' Kaija's voice came from behind. 'Some of us have actual talent to showcase.'

Kaija, Victoria, and Inessa stood at the doorway, smirking and looking all superior with their accomplishment of finding a counterspell to Suraya's. Kaija looked at Aria from head to toe with indifference.

Before Aria could respond, a voice cut through the room.

'I presume there's a profound academic discussion occurring at my doorway?'

At the centre of the room was a woman half-seated on the desk, palms flat on the surface. She radiated casual confidence, almost electric. Her short chocolate-brown hair sharpened the angles of her fair cheekbones, giving her a commanding presence. The oversized tweed blazer only accentuated her authority, while the pushed-up sleeves shouted her no-nonsense, practical nature.

Kaija and her friends slid past Aria into the room, as did everyone else, finding their designated stations. Momentarily confused, Aria looked down and made eye contact with Professor Kiran who looked straight at her – dark, observant. A peculiar sensation in the back of her neck, like being sized up by a predator who hadn't yet decided whether she was prey or irrelevant.

'Miss Renwood, I presume,' Professor Kiran said, her voice neutral, but her eyes intensely curious. 'Welcome to Elementals. Where we deal in consequences, not theories. I'm Professor Avery Kiran.'

Professor Kiran gestured to an empty station near the front.

A gentle hand touched her back, bringing her back to reality. Finn helped her down to her station.

'I trust you have all read Chapter Thirty-Three on the characteristics of fire?' Professor Kiran said once everyone was seated.

There was a murmur of agreement, and Aria's stomach twisted. She read Chapter Thirty-Three and understood nothing. Taye and Finn tried to explain it, but it was like explaining three-dimensional space to someone who's only ever known a straight line.

Professor Kiran straightened and waved her hand, conjuring a flame on one of the candles on every station. Aria gasped, but she was the only one. Everyone else was clearly used to this.

'Elemental magic requires a connection,' she said as she walked up to the blackboard at the front, where she wrote "eldr" with white chalk. 'You must listen, feel, and allow the elements to speak to you.'

'I want each of you to summon a flame on the second candle, by connecting with the first,' she continued. 'Wizards, point your wand at the unlit candle, focus, and use the incantation *eldr* with intent. That will focus your power. And mages, the key is to focus on the energy flowing through you, creating a connection with the flame in front of you.'

Aria looked at the flame on her candle, mocking her by waggling merrily. She stared at it, her jaw tensed. Those instructions weren't instructions at all. They were vague, useless.

Professor Kiran moved around the room, her hands in her trouser pockets. A few tables from Aria, Suraya flicked her wand erratically at the candle. Professor Kiran placed her hand on her wand, lowering it.

'Make sure to point your wand at the candle to avoid catching someone else on fire,' Professor Kiran said, loud enough for everyone to hear. Kaija chuckled.

One by one, flames sparked to life around the room. Aria sighed and straightened in her seat, determined. She was going to make this work.

She closed her eyes, searching for that same wild energy she felt with the barkfox. The deep connection with nature, the yearning for something she couldn't place, the happiness of being out in the wilderness. A feeling now dissolving into nothingness, burned by the flame in front of her.

She opened her eyes. No. This wasn't working. She had to clear her mind.

Aria stared at the flame again. *Connect! Connect!*

Instead of conjuring a flame, she conjured a knot in her stomach. The little confidence she had in her crumbled to ash.

'Whoa, whoa!' Taye yelped while flames climbed up his sleeve. 'Is it supposed to be this... enthusiastic?'

Professor Kiran sped up towards Taye, moving her hands in synchronicity and grace, extinguishing the fire. Smoke filled the room.

'Breathe,' Finn said behind Aria, who gripped her station with a white-knuckled grip.

'I'm trying!' she blurted out, her voice cracking.

Just as she said it, many in the class turned to watch her, giving stares that pressed heavy on her skin.

Kaija leant back in her chair, perfectly poised. 'Oh honey,' she said with a patronising tone. 'Are you sure you're in the right class? Elemental magic is for those who can actually connect with their magic, not just' – she waved her wand dismissively – 'wish really hard.'

Victoria and Inessa tittered, and Aria's cheeks burned

hotter than the flame in front of her.

'That's enough,' Professor Kiran's voice sliced through the room. She approached Aria's station. 'You're struggling,' she said, more to herself. She reached for Aria's hand but paused. Her fingers hovered above it to assess the situation. She looked Aria in the eyes, her own narrowing slightly. She blinked and turned to the class, her tone shifting to a more direct one.

'Control is essential. Maybe a demonstration may prove useful. Please gather around.'

Aria's stomach twisted some more. *No, not this.*

As instructed, the class gathered around her desk. Wide-eyed, Aria's lips trembled and her heart beat so strong, it could have escaped her chest.

'Now, Miss Renwood,' Professor Kiran said. 'Focus on the flame. Feel its warmth. Analyse its movement. Connect with its essence.' She placed the candles closer to her.

Aria stared at the candle with the whole class watching, waiting for her to succeed or fail miserably. She squeezed her eyes shut. Her hand shook as she hovered it over the unlit candle.

Please, please work.

Nothing. The candle remained stubbornly unlit. The silence in the room pressed in, a lump grew in her throat as she suffocated under the watchful eyes of the whole class.

'Perhaps,' Professor Kiran's voice cut through the tension, 'additional instruction may be needed.' She gave a small nod and walked away, addressing the whole class as they moved back to their places.

The whispers began immediately:

'Can't even light a candle...'

'How did she even get in...'

'Probably a mistake...'

Aria stared at the flame, wanting to melt into the shadows.

Taye tried to help by dramatically setting his own sleeve on fire again, but it only emphasised her failure.

Professor Kiran ignored the whispers while waving her hand to extinguish the fire on Taye's sleeve. 'The elements respond best when you truly embrace your core and have the ability to follow proper methods.'

Kaija's hand shot up. 'Professor, should I demonstrate the proper technique? Since some of us actually understand the principles of elemental magic?'

'That won't be necessary, Miss Väinävirta. Though your enthusiasm is noted.'

When the bell finally rang, Aria couldn't get her things packed fast enough. It was clear she didn't have magic at all.

'Better luck in your next life, Renwood,' Kaija said as she passed by in the corridor. 'Maybe you'll actually have magic in that one.'

'Oi!' Taye said as he stepped between them, trying to look intimidating, despite his burned robe sleeve. 'You know what, Kaija? Some of us are here to learn, not just to be...' He fumbled for the right words. 'Not just to be pretentious snobs who peaked in preschool.'

'Leave it,' Aria whispered, tugging his robe. 'Please.'

Finn stepped up beside them, his calm presence diffusing the tension like a breeze.

'No one wins from this. Let it go,' he said to Kaija.

Kaija paused, caught off guard by the low tone.

Finn turned to Aria and Taye. 'We could use some fresh air.'

They found a quiet spot under the shade of an old rowan tree near the lake, its red berries and many deep red and orange leaves welcoming the change of the season.

'How you manage to diffuse Kaija is beyond me,' Taye said as he flopped onto the grass.

'My dad runs a healing centre,' Finn said with a small smile.

'I picked up a thing or two on how to keep calm in turbulent situations. People usually respond to calmness.'

Taye smirked downward, half-impressed.

Aria lay down beside them on the dry mossy ground, arms stretched out, eyes on the leaves.

'You know what,' Taye said to Aria. 'Don't be so hard on yourself. It's literally your first week. You've not grown up around magic like we have. I mean, Suraya's a vardbarn too, and Fraser grew up as a vardbarn, even though he's technically a halfling – his mage mum didn't even tell him until he started showing signs – and they struggle too.'

'Absolute failure, that's what it is in my book,' Aria muttered, watching the leaves now dancing to a gust of wind. She paused and sat up. 'And what *is* a vardbarn? I've been called that a few times.'

'Magifolk born to commonfolk,' Taye said. 'You've also got halflings, who have one magifolk parent. And arfbarn, like me and Finn – both parents from magical lineages.'

'That feels... kinda messed up, honestly.'

She hated labels. Being put in a box – orphan, *girl* – all of them came with assumptions. And now *vardbarn*, which meant more like she was magically challenged. Could life ever be easy for her? Or did she need to struggle with every single thing?

Finn remained quiet, observing Aria with curiosity.

'You haven't been exposed to magic all your life,' Finn said with a nudge. 'You can't expect to excel directly. It takes time to get attuned. Give yourself a break.'

Aria sighed loudly.

In the distance, first-years were practicing with fire, and every flicker mocked her own failure. A wave of frustration threatened to swallow her whole. On Monday, there was clarity and wonder. And now, it all slipped away, and now resembled a chase for a fading dream.

‘You okay?’ Finn asked, his voice pulling her back.

Aria nodded, her lips quivering involuntarily. ‘I think I’m just... overwhelmed. Like I don’t belong.’

‘Absolutely not!’ Taye said, holding her face with both his hands. ‘You will not have this kind of talk, not on my watch.’ He let go. ‘You’ll find your rhythm. So, honey, give it time.’

Aria looked at them, a burning sensation behind her eyes. The thought that maybe this wasn’t her world after all came crashing down. Their looks only made it worse.

She turned away, wishing she could shake this sense of displacement.

From the corner of her eyes, something shifted. She glanced down, half-expecting to see a trick of the light from the lake, but instead, a mist curled around her feet, thickening and swirling purposefully with a life of its own.

Her breath caught as it began to take the shape of an animal, but she couldn’t be sure. And yet, it felt like something she knew, or something that had known her for aeons.

It just stayed there, curled beside her. Its head turned, and its amber eyes locked with hers.

She swallowed hard, caught between wonder and fear, frozen in the spot. She felt the same tingling sensation in her chest she felt before, with the raven in the Moors, a deep calling to the unknown beyond.

‘Aria?’ Taye’s voice broke through her trance.

Just as quickly as it had appeared, it dissolved, leaving nothing behind but the faintest memory of its presence. Aria’s heart clenched by the sudden emptiness.

CHAPTER TEN

Winddrift

Aria was curled up in one of the armchairs in Fossheim's common room, observing the fog lingering over the lake's perfectly still surface. The forest on the far shore stood dark, its treetops gradually taking shape as night gave way to day.

Her first month at Oakspire cemented her disastrous attempt at magic. Not only did she continue to struggle in Fundamentals of Magic and Elementals, the other practical classes were just as bad. Vitality and Combat Arts became a constant humiliation. Every spell sent her way was unchallenged by her, to the point that she got to know the healer Sigrid Vik on a personal level. The woman's arnica salves healed her purple bruises, and her life stories were a welcome distraction.

Crafting Enchantment with Professor Nienke Vinke proved equally mortifying. Objects remained mundane under her touch while, around her, quills wrote without hands and cups filled themselves with water. Such a disappointment – having the skill to enchant a cup that fills itself with water would have been useful when doing homework late at night. It would be a way to avoid going to Fossheim's kitchen.

At this stage, she just wanted to run, hide – or better yet, disappear, never to be seen again. The embarrassment was too big, the pressure of being picked by Nature too heavy. What kept her here were the friends she made and the greener classes of Magifauna Studies, Herbology, and Magical Ecology – which, coincidentally, were also the classes they didn't share with wizards.

'Found a good spot?' asked a cheerful voice. Aria's head snapped up to see Carolina descending the staircase. Her golden eagle familiar Esmeralda swooped past her and settled on a nearby bookshelf, causing the fire to crackle and pop merrily.

Aria shrank deeper, trying to vanish into the armchair. She wasn't eager to discuss her failures with anyone. Talking about it out loud would make it worse.

But Carolina was already settling opposite her with an easy confidence, the glass beads hanging from the brooches on her robe settling with a soft clink.

'You know, the first weeks are rough,' she said casually as she began plaiting her chestnut hair, 'even the first *year*.'

Aria looked up, her own tangled hair falling across her face. 'How did you know?'

Carolina's smile held a hint of old pain, her fingers never faltering in their rhythm.

'People talk. But let's just say I understand what it's like to feel different, to worry you're doing everything wrong.' She faced the window. 'My mother sent me reminders every month of my first year, reminding me about expectations to excel. To make the family proud.'

'And you... got better?'

'No.' Carolina smoothed her finished braid over her shoulder, fingertips testing each twist. 'But my father – well, he understood. He travelled the world, studying archaeological sites. He always told me there was more to magic than just power or technique. It's about understanding its heart.' Her voice softened. 'I found solace in that.'

'What if I can't find the magic?' Aria whispered. 'I just feel empty.'

'Empty?' Carolina's fingers stilled on her braid. 'No, the magic is there. But sometimes... Sometimes, I think it's getting harder for all of us to reach. My father told me magic flows like rivers through the earth, but just like rivers, it can run dry if we don't protect them.'

'I think...' Aria stared at her hands. 'Maybe it was a mistake... choosing me, I mean.'

Carolina leant forward, waiting until Aria met her brown eyes. 'Nature doesn't make mistakes. If there's one thing I've learned from studying alongside mages, it's that your power is innate. You have to learn to tap into it. Occasionally that means being willing to try different approaches. You know, think outside the box.'

'I don't know how.' Aria's voice caught in her throat.

'Neither did I, at first.' Carolina's smile turned thoughtful. 'But you know what helped me? Not stewing on it by myself.' She rose, adjusting her blue robes and leather belt, showing off her long green-blue plaid skirt and her white blouse underneath. 'I have to get going, but hey, I think you might surprise yourself this weekend. I reckon you might even have some fun.' She gave her a wink and walked towards the door, her braid swinging like a pendulum against her back.

Aria turned back to the window. The fog had lifted now, the sky painted gold by the rising sun. Her hand reached the pendant, the emptiness in her heart lingering like a fungus. Could Carolina be right? Did Aria just need to learn to tap into magic, try different things? Maybe the professors were completely incapable of teaching her how to use magic.

The morning chill followed her down to the Mead Hall. She

found Finn at their usual spot, under one of many lamps illuminating the Hall, highlighting the golden curls of his hair. He pushed a teapot her way.

'Sitting with the first-years again, Frida?' a passing Lundgard student called to a tall Lundgard girl reading nearby, her locs woven with strands of bright red.

She looked up from her book, her russet eyes warm with curiosity.

'I need distance from you, Roger,' she laughed. 'How else am I to focus on my runes before the exam?' She gave a quick chin-nod to Finn. 'Besides, someone has to keep an eye on these guys. My brother Taye is a bit of a troublemaker.'

'We're perfectly fine,' Finn said with a side smile.

As if summoned, Taye burst in.

'Did you hear? Winddrift game on Saturday! Oh, it's going to be amazing!' He sat and bounced on the bench, incapable of being still.

'Winddrift?' Aria said as she curled her fingers around the mug. She'd never been good at games. This was a problem.

'You've never heard of Winddrift?' Taye nearly stumbled from the bench beside Finn, adding porridge into his wooden bowl. 'It's only the most exciting game in the world.'

Aria raised her eyebrows at Finn. 'Is it a Swedish thing?'

'We have it in Ireland, too,' he said. 'Most magical communities have their own version.'

'Because it started with the Vikings,' Taye said, 'and Vikings were literally everywhere! They used to play this game where they'd throw things back and forth on their ships—'

'That's not exactly—' Frida began, but Taye was already standing on the bench, waving his spoon.

'You have these platforms, right? Way up there.' He pointed at the ceiling with the spoon, sending porridge flying. 'And a glowing rune marker, like a magical flag, except it floats. The wind currents helps carry it, see?'

'The wind carries it?' Aria frowned.

'That's where the windweavers come in,' Finn explained, rescuing a nearby student from Taye's enthusiastic gesturing. 'Their staves are carved with runes to help you feel the air flow. You don't need to make magic, just work with what's there.'

'Like a conversation with the wind!' Taye grinned. 'Which I am excellent at, by the way. Last summer, my cousin and I—'

'Got tangled in a flag post,' Frida said dryly. Unlike her brother's constant motion, she remained perfectly still, though they shared the same warm eyes. 'My brother's talent for disasters is legendary.'

'Creatively tangled, might I add,' Taye said. 'Anyway, you pass the marker between teammates using the wind currents. The more times you get the marker on the opposite platform, you win! Super simple!'

'Unless you're afraid of heights,' Finn added.

'Oh, the platforms aren't that high anymore.' Taye waved his spoon dismissively. 'Not since the great windstorms of the 1860s, when apparently half the players ended up somewhere in the forest. Now they're just high enough to make it interesting. Plus, there are safety charms everywhere. The worst that can happen is you float down looking absolutely ridiculous.'

'The thing is,' Finn added after noting Aria's apprehension, 'it's one of the few magical games that doesn't need formal spells. And different magical communities adapted it, which is pretty neat.'

'Yeah!' Taye said. 'In Japan, they play it with paper lanterns, and in Egypt, they use sand markers. Listen,' he concluded, finally sitting down, 'it's not about being the best at magic. It's about feeling the wind, trusting your team, and occasionally making a spectacular fool of yourself. Which, coincidentally, I also excel at.' Taye passed his fingers over his perfectly formed eyebrows.

'Anyway,' he continued. 'October's match is on Saturday – a sort of initiation game for first-years. Just wait until you see it, Aria. It's like... like dancing with the wind itself.'

'Sure, right,' Aria said, crossing her arms. 'Sounds like yet another way to prove myself the laughingstock of the whole Academy.'

'Don't be too harsh on yourself,' Finn said. 'You might actually have fun. You're not the only one that has never played Winddrift. I mean, Fraser hasn't played it before, for sure.'

They looked at Fraser, who tripped over his own feet walking towards them, sending his stack of books cascading across the floor.

'Point taken,' Aria said, trying to hold a smile.

The next few days whirled past like the leaves caught in the autumn wind. The whole Academy had Winddrift fever, looking forward to Saturday's match. Yet, for Aria, the idea of participating in a game was a nightmare, particularly now when whispers of her incompetence followed her through the halls.

By Saturday afternoon, the whole Academy headed to the Arena, banners of the three Krets hanging in mid-air.

'Welcome, first-years,' said a voice amplified across the field, 'to what's gonna be an amazing afternoon!'

The audience cheered. Aria's stomach turned into a knot.

On a tower was Jonathan Thomson, Head of Stenvald, dressed in a shimmering ember red robe with a chain of light red and white glass beads attached to two brooches on either side of his chest. Around his waist hung a tool belt, and tucked behind his ear, a pen. The sun highlighted the warm, earthen tone of his skin and the sun-touched ends of his thick locs. A bobcat padded along the berm of the tower, its movements fluid and deliberate, shoulders rolling with every silent step.

Aria scanned the crowd, trying to settle her nerves. Astrid was finding a seat at the centre of the stand, wearing a large straw hat with a wide brim. Professor Halvard sat calmly in the stands, a relaxed smile on his face as he soaked up the atmosphere. Carolina gave her two thumbs up and a broad smile. But it was Professor Kiran who made her apprehensive. She was looking directly at Aria, steady and unwavering. A smile curved on Professor Kiran's lips, though from a distance, Aria couldn't tell if it was genuine or not.

As the crowd's buzz quieted down, Jonathan raised his hand and grinned.

'Alright, listen up! As most of you know, this little initiation game is a yearly tradition for all our new students here at Oakspire Academy. And since every one of us survived it,' he paused for dramatic effect. 'Let's make sure they know exactly how high the stakes are. No pressure, first-years!'

The crowd cheered loudly, mixed with laughter and a few playful jeers. Shouts of encouragement filled the air: 'No pressure at all!' and 'Show 'em what you've got!' Some clapped in exaggerated support, while others called out names of the first-years they knew, adding to the hype.

Jonathan raised his hand again, and the chatter died down. 'Alright, here's how it goes. Players will be forming teams of four – so pick your teammates carefully. This isn't about magic skills. It's about wits and collaboration.' He flashed a mischievous grin. 'Once the game starts, players can't hold the marker, and you'll need to pass it using wind currents – so keep it smooth. The rules are simple: no physical contact with other players, and no magic other than wind manipulation with the windweavers. If you try any magic, the field will mark you in red. And no blocking the platform access, so don't even think about it.'

He paused.

'You score by landing the marker on the opposite platform. Each match lasts only twenty minutes; it's a test of raw spirit, not drawn-out endurance, or we'd be here forever. Each successful landing gets you one point. The team with the highest score after twenty minutes wins. Got it? Let's make it a good one, folks!'

The first-years began to shuffle around, nervously eyeing each other. The pressure of forming teams hung in the air. Aria glanced over at Taye and Finn, who both smiled reassuringly.

'Looks like we're together,' Taye said with a grin. 'We need one more, though.'

'I'm in,' a voice said behind them. Aria turned to see Inaiê with the kind of determination usually reserved for battle.

'Perfect!' Taye bounced on his heels, energy practically radiating off him. 'I'll take the centre. Aria, you're with me for the Drifter role – pass, move, control. Finn, you're our Windguard, don't let them near the platform. Inaiê, you're our Stormweaver. You'll keep the currents flowing in our favour.'

'Got it.' Finn gave him a tight nod.

'Let's make it happen!' Inaiê said, eyes narrowing.

'So, wait, do I just move it along?' Aria said, scratching the back of her neck.

'Trust me.' Taye's eyes sparkled. 'You'll get into it fast.'

The four of them huddled together to strategise. The buzz of excitement and nervousness filled the space around her.

On the far side of the field, Kaija's team positioned themselves, standing tall and confident. Kaija stood with her arms crossed. Beside her was Victoria, Inessa, and Jun, who appeared unfazed, like they had done this a hundred times before.

'Okay, bring it in!' Taye said, his hand outstretched. 'On three, Air Force Fun!'

'Air Force Fun?' Inaiê raised an eyebrow. 'Seriously? How about Wind Raiders?'

'Wind Raiders?' Taye's eyes widened. 'It's Winddrift, not a protest!'

'At least it has dignity,' Inaiê said dryly. 'Unlike whatever children's party name you just made up.'

'It's fun! It's catchy! It's—'

'Brilliant,' Finn said with a half-smile. 'Though we could just be Wind Wanderers.'

'Embarrassing.' Taye crossed his arms. 'I refuse to chant that.'

Jonathan's voice rang out over the field, a mix of authority and excitement. 'The two teams closest to the platforms go first. Please, take your spots! The game is about to begin!'

'That's us!' Taye said. He stepped forward and the rest of the team followed. A rush of adrenaline rushed through Aria.

'Oh, this is going to be so beautiful, baby!' Taye shouted as Kaija's team marched onto the platforms, all sharp angles and focused energy. The tension between them hung heavily in the air like the calm before a storm, each player waiting for the signal to explode into action.

'They will eat dirt,' Inaiê said with quiet intensity.

'Just try not to get tangled in any weathervanes, Taye,' Finn said, laughing.

'That was one time!' Taye protested.

Aria inhaled deeply. Her heart raced like a mouse darting over snow. She knew this game was more than just a test of skill. It could be her chance to prove herself, in front of the whole Academy and against the girls who think of themselves as superior beings.

Kaija flashed a small knowing smile. She adjusted her windweaver and stood ready at the front, in the Stormweaver position, facing Inaiê. The contrast between Kaija's polished confidence and Aria's own uncertainty felt stark. The knot in her stomach tightened.

'Here's a tip,' Kaija called over to Aria. 'Try not to look so terrified. It's embarrassing for all of us.'

Aria clenched her fists, holding her windweaver tightly, her knuckles white.

'Start!' Jonathan shouted.

The horn blared, and the platforms shot upward with such force that the weight pushed the players down. The glowing marker sprang from Taye's grip with desperation to escape, hovering above them, pulsing with a mischievous light.

Aria looked down. Her legs wobbled beneath her. The platforms were five metres high, but it could easily be fifty. She held her windweaver tighter for balance.

Ahead, Inaiê planted her feet wide and swept her windweaver in a wide arc, her black hair in a ponytail flowing with the wind. The runes flickered to life, causing fibres of silver winds to float through the air like ribbons of moonlight, turning the space between the platforms into a spider web of shimmering currents.

Taye was already in motion, bouncing effortlessly between platforms as if gravity was a mere suggestion. The gaps between the platforms were big enough to allow them to fall, yet small enough to jump with ease. Aria struggled, as she was not ready for such a physical sport.

Like Taye and Aria, Victoria and Jun were Drifters, but they moved with the synchronised grace of dancers. They snatched the marker with faultless coordination, twisting the wind currents together into a perfect spiral.

'Finn!' Taye's voice cracked with urgency. 'Any time now would be brilliant!'

As Victoria and Jun rushed forward, Finn raised his windweaver, sending a wall of churning air upwards. It scattered the opponent's careful pattern into wisps of confusion. The marker shot up, and Aria could have sworn she heard it giggle.

The marker floated high between the teams, dancing in place, enjoying the chaos it caused.

'Now!' Taye launched himself forward with recklessness. The crowd gasped. He caught Inaiȇ's wind current, guiding the marker in a tight arc that sent it whizzing past Victoria's ear. She yelped in surprise, but Jun was right behind her, moving to intercept it with the calm efficiency of a player who had seen this trick before.

Behind them, Kaija waved her windweaver in elegant circles, creating a perfect lattice of wind currents. Victoria twisted and turned her windweaver, creating a spiral that intertwined with Jun's. The marker ricocheted off like a pinball, shooting from the lattice towards the opposite platform.

Finn raised his wind barrier again, but it might as well have been tissue paper. The marker shot through it, leaving trails of scattered silver current in its wake. It struck their platform with a musical chime that made Aria wince.

One point.

'Perfection, Victoria!' Kaija called out, already weaving new currents into existence. She created two separate wind streams that spiralled around each other like a double helix. Victoria and Jun caught these streams instantly, adding their own force.

Inaiȇ stood unmoved at the centre, each stream she created locked into place like the foundation of a building, creating a stable network of silver lines.

'Stay in the pattern,' Inaiȇ called. 'And Aria, don't just stand there – listen to the flow!'

Listen? Aria wanted to laugh. But before she could do anything, Victoria and Jun had shot the marker, this time darting forward through the air.

Taye and Aria moved together, their windweavers raised in desperate defence. Inaiê's methodical currents intersected around them in a perfect grid, each stream reinforcing the others. When Kaija's wind currents met hers, they didn't clash. Instead, Kaija's elaborate spirals scattered against Inaiê's unyielding structure.

But Kaija adjusted instantly, her currents flowing around their defences like water finding a new path. Victoria and Jun followed her lead, and the marker slipped through a gap in Inaiê's mesh.

Another chime.

Two points.

Kaija began to orchestrate the next attack, and that's when Aria heard it. A sort of whistling harmony as the wind currents crossed.

Her fingers loosened on her windweaver. In the next attack, Aria didn't try to block the currents, she let it move like a conductor's baton, following the currents' song. A new stream formed, gentle but true, redirecting the marker into Taye's waiting winds.

'That's it!' Taye whooped as he sent the marker sailing forward. Inessa threw up a barrier, but it wasn't soon enough. A resounding chime.

One point.

They found their rhythm after that. Inaiê's wind flows grew stronger, Finn's barriers became more precise. Aria stopped overthinking altogether, and Taye spun back and forth like a ballerina.

Two points.

The crowd's cheers had reached a new high.

'Did you see that? Did you SEE that?' Taye yelled, running on the platforms towards Aria.

When Aria was about to give Taye a high five, the air shifted. A discordant note in the wind's symphony rang in her ears, like a string that snapped from an instrument. The tunes of the currents became sluggish, heavy.

Jun Park leapt between two platforms to get control of the marker, but the currents tangled, twisted, and—

'Jun!' Victoria screamed.

Jun tipped over the platforms, headed towards the ground, headfirst. The safety charms caught him like a net, allowing for a gentle descent. A collective sigh could be heard from the crowd.

Jun smiled and gave two thumbs up, enjoying his slow, controlled fall.

The blue shimmer of the safety charms flickered once, twice, and vanished completely.

Jun dropped like a stone.

'NO!' Victoria's high-pitched scream pierced through the sudden silence.

Professor Halvard stood up, and as he hurried to Jun, his hands moved in a swift, fluid gesture. Time itself rippled around Jun, slowing enough for Professor Halvard to weave a net of air that caught him just before impact, cradling him safely to the ground.

The platforms descended as the crowd gathered around Jun and Professor Halvard. Victoria jumped off once closer to the ground and ran to them, her composure returning almost instantly when she reached them.

'Well,' she said, brushing imaginary dust from her robes, her hands trembling. 'That was an unwarranted display of excitement, was it not?'

'Gently now, everyone,' Professor Halvard said as everyone gathered around Jun. 'Let's give him space to breathe.'

The Raven glided onto Professor Halvard's shoulder,

impossible light spilling from its feathers, amber eyes fixated on Jun.

'Find Sigrid,' Professor Halvard commanded in a low voice. 'Tell her to prepare the Healing Hall. Precautionary only.' The Raven vanished in a blur of motion.

Professor Nkeiru Okezie – the Magical Ecology professor – stepped forward, her movements calm and graceful. She knelt beside Jun. Her intricate, vibrant blue braids were pulled back into a bun, decorated with cowry shells hanging like precious jewels. Her hands moved above Jun as she cast diagnostic charms, the bright yellow robe accentuating the warm hues of her dark skin.

'Just winded,' she announced, a hint of relief in her voice. 'Though we should have him checked thoroughly.'

The remaining players caught up. The marker's cheerful glow was strangely at odds with the tension below, while Jun's snowy owl familiar circled overhead, its harsh screeches gradually softening to quieter calls of concern.

'Let me help carry him,' Carolina offered, pushing through the crowd with her wand ready in her hand. 'I'm good with levitation spells.'

Jun groaned, sitting up despite Professor Okezie's protests. He glanced at Carolina. 'Thanks, but I can manage.' He looked over at the platforms. 'Did anyone see where my windweaver landed? The theoretical alignment was perfect on that one...'

'Honestly, Park?' Victoria snapped. 'You nearly plummeted to your death and yet you fret over your windweaver?'

'The alignment hardly matters if your technique is flawed,' Kaija said, standing confidently, but her eyes showed hints of worry.

'Here,' Inessa said brutely, stepping forward with Jun's windweaver in her hands. 'The charm matrix appears undamaged. Perhaps you should verify it against the Seventh

Principle of—'

'If you're all finished theorising,' Professor Kiran interrupted, 'Mr Park needs to visit the Healing Hall now.'

Jun headed through the crowd to the Healing Hall with Professor Okezie by his side. Victoria, Kaija, and Inessa followed them. Jun's owl swooped low over their heads with one final mournful cry before joining its master.

'Okay, okay, everything's fine,' Taye said as the crowd dispersed. 'We're all fine. That was just... That was...' He trailed off, looking defeated.

'A draw,' Aria said with forced lightness. 'I guess it's a diplomatic way to end the game.' But her attempt at humour fell flat, even to her own ears.

'The safety net shouldn't just fail,' Finn said, frowning at the platforms. 'The nets are anchored to stop it from falling apart.'

As they walked back to the castle, Aria couldn't shake the memory of that discordant note in the wind's song, just before Jun fell. Like the magic itself had twisted out of tune.

CHAPTER ELEVEN

Birch

'I'm telling you, Halloween has its roots in Celtic traditions!' Finn declared, his Irish accent emphasised by his passion. 'It's all about honouring the dead and celebrating the harvest.'

Aria lay on an enchanted blanket that kept them dry and warm from the wet mossy grass beneath an old oak by the lake. Leaves had turned into dull shades of gold and brown, many hanging on the branches, while others had fallen. A shiver ran down her spine as a particularly cold gust swept by, prompting her to pull her dark blue cloak closer around her.

Taye crossed his arms, a grin spreading across his face. 'Sure, but there are plenty of cultures with similar traditions. You can't just claim it for yourself. We have our own customs where we honour our ancestors and the spirits of Nature, with roots going back to the old Norse mages.'

'You didn't just make that up?'

Taye gasped dramatically.

'Finn! I'm insulted! Do I look like someone who would fabricate stories for my own amusement?' He chuckled before his face changed in a microsecond into a sterner expression. 'No, but seriously, it's top secret. We can't talk about it. Foreigners aren't allowed to come, as it would insult the elves.'

He lowered his voice and looked Finn straight in the eyes. 'And you don't want to anger the elves.'

Finn shrugged. 'Right. Sure thing. Aria, do you believe this guy?'

Before she could reply, a sound caught her attention – or the sudden absence of it. The usual chatter of jackdaws that filled the Ancient Forest's edge had gone quiet. She turned to the silence. Hundreds of black shapes erupted from the trees like smoke, their wings beating in desperate unison as they fled North.

'Do jackdaws migrate?' she asked, the same discordant feeling she'd felt during the Winddrift game creeping up her skin.

Taye followed her gaze, his expression shifting to seriousness. 'No... That's bizarre.' His voice dropped lower. 'They're territorial. They don't just abandon their grounds unless...'

'Unless what?'

'Unless something's driven them out.'

'Should we tell someone about it?' Finn asked.

'Maybe...' Taye replied, his brown eyes unfocused for a moment. 'Though wouldn't it already be known? I mean, Halvard and Grünwald are often in these woods.'

'I suppose,' Finn said, patting his fingers on his leg. He looked down at his watch. 'Oh, crap. Magical Ecology – we're going to be late.'

Taye straightened up, all business. 'Right! If we miss it, we'll never hear the end of it.' He dusted off his cloak and glanced at the castle, the flock of birds disappearing behind it. 'But Finn's right. First the Winddrift charms fail, now this... Something's not right.'

Aria couldn't shake the feeling it was connected to something bigger. With a final glance towards the clattering of jackdaws, she picked up the blanket, rolled it under her armpit, and joined Finn and Taye. They hurried down to the edge of the Ancient Forest.

The forest stretched ahead like a painter's fever dream: birches and ash stood bare, elms fading to yellow-brown, and oaks crowned in reddish-brown and gold, their stubborn leaves flickering against the blue sky.

They sneaked into the back of the class, where Professor Okezie stood in a long bright blue robe. Her presence was as much a part of the forest as the oaks and rugged birches that surrounded them. The sun reflected the warm amber and copper hues from the autumn leaves, echoing the deep bronze complexion of her skin.

'Today we're not just talking about the ecosystem, we're becoming part of it,' Professor Okezie announced, her voice soft but full of authority. 'We'll explore how magic flows through the interconnected web of life in this forest.'

Aria exchanged a look with Finn, who gave her a bemused shrug, while Taye grinned widely, showing off his dimples. 'I think we're about to have a spiritual moment,' he whispered, earning a light nudge from Aria.

The class followed Professor Okezie down a winding path of the forest, their feet crunching over fallen leaves and twigs. The towering trees cast a shifting patchwork of shadow and light, their branches creaking gently, murmuring to one another. The deeper they walked, the taller the trees, their bark holding scars of history.

The students gathered around a particularly striking tree – a colossal oak, its thick trunk twisted with age, yet radiating with vitality. Its branches spread wide, with its brown leaves flickering like fire.

'This oak,' Professor Okezie said, placing her delicate hand gently on the bark covered with moss, 'has stood here for over a thousand years. It has witnessed the rise and fall of civilisations, the changing of seasons, and the passage of time. Each tree has a story – one that stretches far beyond your own lifetime, connected to every living thing around it and beyond, today and tomorrow.'

Aria leant slightly and listened, ready for another of Professor Okezie deep rooted lectures on the interconnectedness of the magical system in our natural world.

'Every specimen in this forest plays a role in its survival. This oak provides shelter for birds and insects, while its fallen leaves nourish the soil, supporting the cycle of life. The roots intertwine with others, forming a network that allows them to share nutrients and communicate. Magic is not separate from this process; it flows through every interaction, binding us all together.'

Professor Okezie crunched down to a shrub, placing her hand on its leaves. She closed her eyes, nodding seriously. 'Hmhm… I see, yes.'

'Is she… having a conversation with a bush?' Taye whispered, raising an eyebrow.

'The shrubs are particularly chatty today,' Professor Okezie said, without opening her eyes. 'This one is concerned about Fraser giving too much water to his spider plant on his bedside table.'

Several students giggled. Fraser turned red as a tomato.

'The wych elm, however,' she continued, moving to place her hand on the tree's bark, 'is more interested in discussing the philosophical implications of photosynthesis.'

'Honestly, same,' Taye stage-whispered. 'I also contemplate my life choices every time I'm in the sun.'

Professor Okezie's lips hinted at a smile. 'Mr Lundvik, these trees deserve respect.' She paused. 'Though the wych elm agrees with your assessment.'

A wych elm leaf chose that moment to land squarely on Taye's nose.

When the laughter settled, Professor Okezie's expression turned serious. She extended her hands, palms facing the canopy above, and her eyes closed in concentration. The forest grew still, sensing the magic she was about to weave. A soft, shimmering glow began to gather around her fingertips, like sunlight filtering through morning mist.

'Let's try to see how energy flows here,' she said, her voice low and meditative. 'Energy moves between every organism, from the tiniest insect to the tallest tree, each connected to the next in a delicate balance. Magic flows through this ecosystem as naturally as air and water.'

With a slow, fluid motion, she moved her hands, and the glow spread outward, tracing a golden web of energy. It started at the canopy, where leaves transformed the last of their sunlight into sustenance, flowing down through branches and trunks into an intricate web of roots below.

The entire forest came alive with shimmering pathways: fungi that carried nutrients between trees; fallen leaves decomposing into the soil; a black bird swooping above, spreading seeds.

Students watched in awe as tiny drops of light danced along these connections like fireflies, showing the pulse of life flowing through the forest. Each movement told a story: nutrients being shared, matter being broken down, energy being transformed in an endless cycle that sustained them all.

Aria's mouth fell open. She'd read about the interconnection of ecosystems in her textbooks, but this was simply incredible.

Then, the air changed.

At first, she thought she'd imagined it: just a trick of the light, perhaps. But no, there it was again. An aura of deep, ugly purple bleeding through the web of light, like poison seeping into veins. For one terrible moment, the entire web of energy convulsed. The forest itself was gasping for air.

Professor Okezie's hands froze mid-gesture. For the briefest moment, concern flickered behind her dark brown eyes. 'Most irregular,' she said softly, studying the forest with newfound intensity. She straightened her shoulders and lowered her hands. 'The forest's magic can be temperamental in autumn. Best we leave it be for now.'

The web of light faded at her command, but Professor Okezie's gaze lingered on the trees, searching for answers in the spaces between the branches.

Aria exchanged glances with Taye and Finn, both equally captivated and curious, even a little unnerved. But Professor Okezie's voice broke the silence once more, drawing their focus back to her.

'Let's try something else,' she continued cheerfully, her tone steady again. 'To truly understand how magic flows, you must learn to feel that connection. So, choose a tree, any tree. Place your hand on its trunk and close your eyes. Let its energy flow through you.'

Aria hesitated before stepping forward. She was drawn to an old birch nearby, its bark rugged with hints of its youthful silver bark, red golden streaks threading through it.

Tentatively, she reached out, pressing her palm against the tree. The surface was rough beneath her fingers, but that was all. For a moment, nothing happened, just the distant calls of birds and the rustling of leaves in the breeze.

Finally – a thrum. Faint, like a far-off drum, yet undeniably there. She could feel it beneath her palm, a steady rhythm that echoed deeper than any sound, resonating in her bones. It felt like the forest's heartbeat, steady and slow.

Just as she began to follow its rhythm, a sharp jolt

interrupted it, like a heart that skipped a beat. The rhythm stuttered, becoming erratic. Her fingers tingled, a strange sensation going up her arm.

Aria's chest tightened. *What is this?*

Determined to understand, she steadied herself, closing her eyes and pressing her palm firmly against the rough bark. Slowly, the erratic thumping softened, and the rhythm began to stabilise. Her muscles unwound as relief took hold.

Beneath her fingertips, the energy ran deeper than bark, deeper than roots. It connected her to a vast and hidden world. The roots of the birch stretched far below, interwoven with the roots of other trees, forming a network she could sense now. A network of life. Sensations of the sharp bite of winter frost, the heavy warmth of summer's sun, the gentle brush of countless animals – the memories of the forest were playing in her mind.

'Young guardian, at last, you hear,' a voice reached her, whispering in the wind.

She whipped her head around, certain she'd catch Taye whispering behind her. But there he was, hugging an oak tree with the enthusiasm of a long-lost friend. Finn stood beside him, his brow furrowed in deep meditation with an elm. The rest of the class was equally absorbed in their own connections to the forest, oblivious to what Aria had heard.

Her heart pounded. Did she imagine that?

She closed her eyes again. The hum returned, stronger this time. The wind rustled the leaves, carrying with it the subtle crunch of decaying branches, the soft crinkle of creatures tunnelling beneath the soil.

'Roots deep, branches high. The old song sings in you,' the voice spoke again, this time clearer.

Aria rolled her neck, trying to ease the tightness on her shoulders. Her throat was dry, but she managed to whisper aloud, 'Who's there?'

'Green life. Wild growth. Cycle unending. You are of us, yet not,' the voice answered, wise and ancient.

Mind racing, Aria tried to make sense of it. 'Are you... the forest?'

'All breathes as one. Feel the spirit where earth touches the sky.'

'I-I think I do. There's a rhythm... something.' Aria's voice was barely a whisper, caught between wonder and uncertainty. As she spoke, her own heartbeat fell into step with the muted thump of ancient life.

'The forest remembers. The forest—'

'Alright, class!' Professor Okezie's voice cut through the moment like a knife. 'Remember that magic and nature are connected. Please read Chapter Twelve before next class. There might be an exam on that next week.'

Aria's eyes fluttered open, the connection abruptly severed. She stared at the birch, its aged bark silent and still. The moment had been nothing more than a dream, her mind swirling with fragments of the strange, primordial conversation.

'That was WILD!' Taye practically danced down the forest path to the castle. A tiny forest mouse paused its foraging to stamp its paw indignantly at the disturbance, scolding him for interrupting its winter preparations.

'Apart from the mishap with that web of light,' he continued, 'Professor Okezie was all like "commune with nature" and I swear me and the oak had a moment. Though, now the tree's probably like "this kid needs therapy."' He spun around to face Finn and Aria, walking backwards. 'Did anyone else feel like they were in a spiritual yoga retreat? Cause, baby, I am all for it!'

Aria hugged the blanket roll closer, trying to hide her trembling hands. 'Did either of you... hear anything?'

'What do you mean?' Finn asked. 'Did you feel something through the magic currents, or was it more... direct?'

'I totally felt that!' Taye jumped in before Aria had a chance to reply. 'It was like...' He pressed his hands to his chest and adopted a mock-serious expression. 'The tree's energy spoke to my soul. It said, "Taye, my child, you need to let go of the pressures societies have placed on you" and I said "Absolutely!"'

Aria managed a weak laugh, but her mind was still spinning from the experience. 'No, but seriously—'

'Oh, my word, Aria actually heard something, didn't she?' Taye stopped walking, causing Finn to bump into him. 'Look at her face! She's got that "I just experienced something life changing, but I'm trying to play it cool" look!'

Finn studied Aria with quiet consideration. 'You know, the old mages believed trees were keepers of ancient knowledge. Or, even that trees have spirits themselves. If you did hear something, it's not that far-fetched, given how deeply they're connected to the earth's magic.'

'I don't know what I heard,' Aria said quickly. 'Maybe I'm just going crazy. On top of being magically challenged, now I'm hearing voices...' *Again,* she added to herself.

'Hey' – Taye's voice softened, dropping the theatrics for a moment – 'if anyone's going crazy here, it's definitely me. I mean, I just spent fifteen minutes hugging a tree and telling it my life story. Pretty sure it'll ghost me after that.'

Aria looked down at her boots.

'Look,' Taye continued, 'I don't know what's going on, but hearing voices? It's not exactly *crazy*. Nature led you here for a reason, and now they are trying to get your attention. I think that makes sense!'

'Maybe you're just... attuned to it differently than the rest of us,' Finn said.

Aria stood frozen, like the ground had been pulled from under her feet. Different is not what she wanted. She was different all her life, and Oakspire had the promise to be a place she could call home. Instead, she was to continue being a stranger.

That night, lying in her bed, Aria stared at the ceiling of her box bed, the tree's words echoing in her mind. *Green life. Wild growth. Cycle unending.* What did it all mean?

The castle's usual nighttime creaks were different now. The stones whispered to her as she fell asleep.

CHAPTER TWELVE

Wolf

Aria stood on the edge of a wasteland, the red sky above oppressing, and the silence deafening. A poisonous smog clung to the bare land like a suffocating veil. She tried to take a breath, but the air was thick, filled with the scent of ash and rotten eggs.

A low rumble made the ground tremble beneath her feet. Her heart jolted.

Through the fog, a massive wolf with fur as dark as midnight moved with terrifying grace. Each step sent cracks rippling through the earth as though the ground itself recoiled in fear.

The wolf's eyes glowed yellow, locking onto hers as it walked slowly, methodically. The coldness that swept through her was paralysing. Her blood turned to ice. Every step it took spread a wave of ache into the air, a pulse of pain that made the sky seem redder – the smog thicker, the silence heavier.

She wanted to run, but her legs were as heavy as lead. The wolf towered above her, its breath hot and repulsive like decay. It opened its mouth, saliva dripping from its teeth, creating puddles on the ground. Instead of a growl, there was only silence, an emptiness so profound, it could have swallowed the world whole.

The wolf flickered, and for a moment, a person emerged behind it. Ragged and tired, yet powerful and relentless. They blurred together, indistinguishable from one another.

As the fog swirled around them, she noticed a body by her feet, frozen in its final moments, covered in ash. A hand stretched towards her, desperate, pleading. Someone she was meant to save but couldn't. Her heartache was unbearable, even though she did not know who they were.

Aria woke up startled, her forehead slick with sweat. For a moment, she just lay there, looking at the ceiling of her box bed, catching her breath. From the corner of her eye, green and violet light painted the walls like an aquarium.

What in the world...?

She peeked out from her box bed to the window. The lights embraced her soul.

Across the night sky, Northern Lights swirled with life. A tapestry of colours rippled across the stars. For the briefest of moments, she was at peace, even though she could not shake the weight on her chest. The dream lingered still, vivid and raw as she took in this breathtaking view.

She never had a dream this intense. It felt so real. *Too* real, even.

A snore brought her back to reality. Suraya, fast asleep on her bed, was all curled up. Louis dozed peacefully on the windowsill.

They must be dreaming something nice, she thought. Not of death or wolves with the breath of decay. Definitely nothing that leaves the taste of ash in their mouths.

'Right,' she muttered under her breath as she sat up, folding up her knees. 'First, I hear voices, and now I'm having apocalyptic dreams. Couldn't I just dream about failing an exam like a normal person?'

Grunting, Aria leant her head against the box bed's wooden wall. She wanted to scream, or hit something, but at the same time, she was lost.

No. There was no time for self-pity.

Standing up, she walked to her wardrobe, got dressed, and headed down to Fossheim's common room, hoping a change in scenery would help deal with the dread. The wolf. The devastation. The hand. Images warped in her mind like a hurricane, leaving her in a haze. Who was the person she didn't save? Or could it be a person she was meant to *be* saving?

But I am in no capacity to save anyone. The thought unnerving.

She slumped on the sofa in front of a fireplace in Fossheim's common room. The emptiness made it a lot larger. The space made her feel isolated, exposed. And even though the Northern lights lit the folk drawings on the cupboards – giving the impression of dancing in tune of silence – Aria felt danger.

A mist materialised into view. A ghostly fox lay by her feet, curled up with its head on its front paws, taking in the comforts of the fire.

What is this? Aria thought, for *this* was not an ordinary Oakspire's resident animal ghost. Its fur had a shimmering hue, and it was a lot less translucent.

The ghostly fox turned its face and looked at her with recognition. Its large amber eyes smiled so subtly, Aria could have missed it if she wasn't staring at it in horror. Without warning, it dissipated into thin air.

'Don't panic,' Aria muttered, but her pulse disagreed. She hugged herself and looked around the empty room, the Northern lights giving way to the dim light of pre-dawn twilight.

She curled her fingers into fists and shook them out,

flinging away the adrenaline clinging to her skin. The dream had left her on edge, anxiety threading through her body, and the ghostly encounter only deepened it.

Hands shaking, she reached for her pendant. Should she tell Taye and Finn about the dream? Aria hesitated. Taye would probably try to lighten the mood with some jokes, which might not be at all bad. Finn would listen – and possibly understand. He often helped her understand this magical world, so maybe he could even explain what this dream could mean?

But she wasn't sure she had the heart to burden them with this. She didn't even have the courage to say it out loud. It would make it more real.

Gradually, the common room began to stir with life.

Tenzin walked down the stairs, their green fringe bouncing with each step. A full smile spread across their face, eyes squinting against their sun-kissed cheeks. So carefree, so content, Aria almost wished some of it could rub off on her.

They mustn't have seen Aria near the fire, otherwise she knew they would have joined her. Instead, Tenzin pulled a necklace over their head, made of golden beads. They sat in the far corner of the room, where it was semi-enclosed, with pillows on the floor – a spot many used for reading – closed their eyes, crossed their legs, straightened up, and took a deep breath. As they moved the golden beads with their fingers, a golden aura formed around them, a light flowing within like water. Their smile softened.

Aria could tell it was in this position, inside that aura, they were fully and entirely anchored to the present.

Moments later, Carolina strutted down the stairs, frowning slightly, deep in thought. Her hair was up in a ponytail. She wore a sweatshirt and black leggings, so Aria knew she was going out for her morning run. Suraya ran down the stairs, hugging her notebooks, her hair in a messy bun, glasses slightly crooked; Louis hung onto her shoulder for dear life. Aria attempted a wave, but Suraya was out the door, probably hurrying to the library to study.

'You look like you've been possessed by a Mare.'

Aria jumped. Taye stood there, one brow raised, his brown skin glowing with the warmth from the fireplace.

'A what?'

'A Mare. A nightmare spirit, old folklore.' He flopped into the chair opposite, pulling out a crumpled brown wrapping parchment from the pouch hanging from his belt over his ocean blue robe. 'They say they sit on your chest while you sleep, causing you nightmares.'

He unfolded the parchment and revealed a slightly squashed sandwich. 'Want some? It's lingonberry jam. I added a refrigerating charm on the parchment, so it's still fresh.'

'Not going down for breakfast?'

'Not today. I'm more curious to see the shadow lynxes.' He grinned, already breaking it in half. 'They are most active during dawn, and I heard some are passing this way. Migrating.'

Aria took half of the lingonberry sandwich, which, to her surprise, was remarkably fresh and tasty. They spent the rest of the morning on the lookout for the shadow lynxes that never came. Disappointment set in from not having gotten to see such fascinating creatures but, at the same time, relief for having something else occupying her mind, especially with Taye's incredible ability to talk.

As the morning progressed, Fossheim's common room was filled with movement; many hurried down to breakfast, some did their homework in a hurry, while others practised a dance holding water bowls.

'Is that for the Harvest Feast?' Aria asked. The Harvest

Feast was just around the corner, and each Krets was to prepare an act for entertainment for the ancestors.

'Sweet merciful Odin,' Taye exclaimed, clutching his chest dramatically. 'If they don't flood this place with that horrid dancing, I will be incredibly shocked.'

Aria laughed. It was cringeworthy to watch, like second-hand embarrassment.

A tremor hit.

It was subtle, just a slight shiver through the wooden floor, not big enough to make the dancers trip.

'Did you feel that?' Aria asked Taye, her eyes widened.

'Your brain exploding from this tragic performance?' Taye grinned from ear to ear. 'Nope, missed it!' he said with a wink.

'No...' she mumbled, but Taye didn't hear her. Was Aria the only one who felt it? Everyone was too caught up in their own chatters. Yet, judging from the sudden stillness of the plants next to her, maybe she wasn't the only one who knew something wasn't right.

In the afternoon, they headed to the Training Hall for Vitality and Combat Arts. The tremor nagged at her thoughts throughout the morning, intertwining with visions of the wolf from her dream. Could the tremor be the wolf? The thought alone was terrifying to even consider.

The Training Hall stood on the west side of Oakspire grounds. It was a large wooden building; its ceiling arched like a cathedral. Light streamed through the windows of the tower, casting beams of light onto the stone floor below. Along the wall, torches aligned, adding light to the open space.

Exhausted after being up since before dawn, Aria knew Master Torben Stormgaard's class would not end well for her.

'If I have to balance another chicken on my gorgeous head, I will literally die,' Taye said, moving his fingers through his curls as they entered the Hall. 'My hair cannot take that kind of trauma again.'

'Say what you want, but this crazy training actually helps.' Finn shrugged. 'Even if I'm still finding feathers in my robes.'

'I'm sorry, but I still think using chickens like that is animal abuse,' Aria said, frowning.

Before they could continue the conversation, Master Stormgaard's voice rang through the Hall.

'Today,' Master Stormgaard announced while the first-years gathered around, 'we'll test your coordination and balance.'

A wave of disappointment echoed from the walls.

Master Stormgaard walked around the Hall, a worrying twinkle in his grey eyes, as fire reflected on his bald head. His full beard had a blend of dark and lighter tones, giving him a weathered, rugged appearance. Though what was more remarkable was the scar he had running down his left eye, from his pronounced brow to his high cheekbone.

Aria had heard rumours the scar came from a draugr, which is essentially a zombie, according to Finn. Master Stormgaard went to a barrow in the northern mountains, chasing whispers of a lost relic. The draugr rose with eyes like burning coals, its voice cold enough to freeze blood. Stormgaard didn't flinch. He fought it through three nights and two blizzards, armed with only a double-edged axe and runes inked in his arms, which gives one superpowers, according to Finn.

The draugr's sword kissed his face just once, leaving him that mark. Stormgaard, filled with rage, split its skull with a single blow. He walked away with the relic wrapped in a blood-soaked pelt.

Of course, it might not be true, but from the way he moved and the intensity in his eyes – of a man who had stared at death and told it to sit down – Aria knew there was more truth to the tale than not.

'Partner up: mage and wizard!' Master Stormgaard said with a deep voice. With a wave of his hands, stationary logs flew across the Training Hall into neat rows, hovering slightly above ground. 'Two duelists per log. Your goal is simple: stay up there while defending against your partner's attacks. And please, stick only to the spells we have practised for the past weeks.'

'Great, just another creative way to get our arses handed to us,' Taye muttered, rolling his eyes. 'Honestly, I think he enjoys seeing us suffer.'

'Exactly! And "simple" is not the word I would have chosen,' Aria said as she bit her lip, staring at the logs. With her mind scattered, keeping balance while dodging spells, or even blocking them, was a recipe for disaster.

'Just go with the flow!' Finn shouted as he stepped on an empty log.

'Well, well, well, if it isn't our resident chosen one,' Kaija stepped onto the log opposite Aria. 'I know you are struggling with magic so badly. But don't worry, I will not take that into account. No special treatment from me.'

'Oh, come on. Couldn't you go bother literally anyone else?' Aria groaned, knowing Kaija would love to knock her off the log just to prove a point.

'I like how the light hits me in this particular spot.' Kaija tossed her deep brown hair back, the sun accentuating her porcelain complexion.

Before anyone could begin, a high-pitched voice echoed in the Hall.

'This has to be illegal somewhere! I'm pretty sure this violates at least three human rights conventions, and my policy against facing death before dinner!'

Taye pointed dramatically at Inessa, whose large brown eyes stared him down like a predator. Even though slightly shorter than him, and with that soft pink hair of hers, she looked intimidating from afar.

'Mr Lundvik, I am sure you have the skills necessary to handle this exercise with flying colours,' said Master Stormgaard. 'Please get into position.'

Taye grunted and reluctantly did as he was told. On the other side of the Hall, Finn was facing Victoria. It was clear this was an orchestrated attack. *Very well,* Aria thought. She was determined to wipe those smug looks off their faces. She might end up flat on her face, but she wasn't going to let Kaija see her fear.

'Begin!' Master Stormgaard called out cheerfully, while the class desperately wiggled on their logs, trying not to fall.

A flash of blue light zoomed past Aria's ear as she stumbled backwards, waving her arms for equilibrium. She barely regained her balance when another spell flashed towards her. Aria turned her body just in time, the spell hitting a string of hair, which coiled from impact.

Kaija threw spell after spell. Aria tried and failed to avoid them. She fell off the log many times, threw her hands up but nothing happened. Her body ached from being hit by Kaija's aggression.

'Remember!' Master Stormgaard's voice rang out over the mayhem. 'In real combat, you rarely fight on perfect ground. Adapt!' He paused to observe the Jensen twins, one of which was a mage and the other a wizard. 'Excellent defence work – though perhaps save the synchronised backflips for the talent show? Mr Lundvik, excellent shield charms, I knew you had it in you.'

A yelp and thud announced Fraser's inevitable fall, who had the balance of a newborn giraffe. 'Hurry, Mr Murphy-Mussa, get up! In battle, there is never time to linger. And Miss Renwood, find your centre!' Master Stormgaard called out.

'Work with your magic, not against it!'

Work with it? She barely understood what "it" was.

Kaija's eyes narrowed as she muttered the next spell. White light shot from her wand like an angry wasp. Aria threw up her hands instinctively, and that's when it happened. The magic surged through her like a tidal wave, tingling on every nerve ending. The floor cracked as roots burst through the stone, twisting upwards, alive like wooden serpents rushing to strike.

'Oh please,' Kaija scoffed. She pointed the wand at Aria, and as she opened her mouth to cast another spell, roots coiled around her ankles. She tilted dangerously backwards, her eyes alarmed and her arms looking for a place to hold herself steady.

It wasn't just Kaija. Several screamed as roots snaked past them, some thick as tree trunks, others delicate as threads. They writhed and twisted through the air, creating a forest of living wood throughout the whole Training Hall. The stone floor became a maze of broken stones and emerging roots.

Aria's heart sank as she took in the scene before her. She had no idea she was capable of this. Her surprise soon turned into embarrassment, her cheeks burning as everyone stared at the chaos she'd created. Of course, after a month of nothing, her first magical act would have to destroy the Training Hall instead of something simple, like making a lamp glow and water ripple.

'Master Stormgaard, this is *not* part of the curriculum!' Kaija shouted, pointing at Aria as she held on tightly to a thick root, her legs bound by thin threads.

Master Stormgaard laughed above the gasps and shrieks. 'Well, Miss Renwood, that's certainly one way to approach the exercise. Perhaps next time, you'll want to tone it down a little. Mr Murphy-Mussa, please stop fighting the roots. They are your best chance of not falling flat on your face from there.'

To Aria's relief, the class was dismissed. At least Master Stormgaard had the common decency to recognise a floor riddled with holes might pose a safety risk.

The energy prickled through her palms like an unexpected storm. What had just happened? How? She didn't mean to do it; she didn't even know she had it in her.

'I am LIVING for Kaija's face!' Taye bounced beside her as they made their way to the Mead Hall through the corridor of the main castle, their footsteps squeaking the old wooden floor. 'She looked like she just sat on a pinecone when that root knocked her perfect posture sideways.'

'Uncontrolled magic is dangerous,' Kaija spat as she stormed past, hair unkempt. 'Someone could have gotten seriously hurt.' Inessa and Victoria flanked her, their usual poise undermined by wrinkled ember red robes.

Aria stared down at her trembling hands. 'I didn't mean to,' she whispered. 'How did I even...?'

'I think,' Finn said quietly, making them both turn, 'you might be fighting it. Blocking your magic somehow. Which is why it exploded like this.'

Heat rose to Aria's face.

'Blocking my magic?' Her voice rose. 'Are you saying it's *my* fault now? You think I did it on purpose?'

Being told every mistake, every humiliation, every failure at the Academy was somehow her doing was not what she needed to hear. It'd been hard enough as it was. She'd been doing *everything* she could.

The corridor windows gave a faint rattle. Finn and Taye exchanged a glance.

'It's just...' Finn said, choosing his words carefully. 'Like when you're playing a game and overthink the rules instead of just playing? Maybe it's like that. You're trying to do magic with all the rules, but that's not how it works for you.'

'Oh, so now I'm just trying *too* hard?' Aria snapped. 'What's next? Are you going to suggest meditation and manifesting inner peace?'

'Actually—'

'Don't even finish that sentence,' Aria interrupted.

'What our socially awkward friend means' – Taye threw his arms around them both – 'is that maybe you need to go with the flow and forget the recipe books.'

Aria looked up at the drawings carved into the corridor's wooden ceiling panels, their faded blues and greys telling old stories.

The words hit harder than she wanted to admit. Her throat went dry.

Was Finn right? Had she been fighting herself all along?

They walked through the long echoing corridor in silence as the descending sun faded behind the windows.

CHAPTER THIRTEEN

The Harvest Feast

Fog lingered on Oakspire's grounds, thick enough to hide a dragon. From the Mead Hall, the tall windows looked frosted as the sun set. Torches on the dark wooden-panelled walls warmed the space, while decorations of autumn leaves on the tables brought the outside in.

It was the evening of the Harvest Feast.

The Mead Hall was reorganised into three long tables at the centre, one for each Krets. A fire burned on an iron ceremonial basin at the front, its flames reaching tall, creating shadows along the high table ahead, where the Academy staff sat.

Professor Halvard sat in the centre of the high table, his hair immaculately combed, and his beard gathered by a golden tube at its tip. In contrast, Professor Grünwald left his hair wild and wore his signature vest, nodding excessively as Professor Thistlecroft leant in with a smirk, as though the feast were merely an excuse to share the latest gossip.

Aria winced as another burst of laughter echoed off the walls, a migraine thumping with a heart of its own. She wanted to escape outside but knew she would probably walk straight into the lake by mistake. Or worse, into the deadly embrace of a bear. Instead, she sneaked into the Mead Hall early to avoid having everyone turn to see her come in and sat by herself on the empty Fossheim table.

Her magic went from non-existent to out of control overnight. The day before, her sneeze had made all the snapping orchids sing opera in the Greenhouse. Herbology Professor Rosemary Salvia still hadn't managed to stop their dramatic soprano solos. On any other day, Aria would have found it a little funny, but after weeks of being the Academy's laughingstock, she found herself avoiding people altogether. Might as well, because everyone kept their distance from her these days. Well, nearly everyone.

'Are you seriously still brooding about the snapping orchids?' Taye said, fist-bumping softly at her arm as he sat on the bench beside her. 'You should be swelling with pride! They weren't half bad! And, this way, they won't bite anyone either.'

'I'm fine. Just enjoying the luxury of having my own blast radius.' Aria gestured at the empty benches around her with mock grandeur. 'Highly exclusive club. Membership requires at least one accidental explosion per week.'

She caught the blond Jensen twins whispering to each other, shooting glances her way before quickly finding seats at the far end of the Hall at the Lundgard table. Sure, they weren't necessarily friends, but it still stung.

The Harvest Feast would, at least, offer a distraction to whisper about, giving Aria a break from the unwanted attention. If she could just keep her magic under control for one evening. One perfectly normal, hopefully not catastrophic, evening.

'Oh, that's because not everyone has come yet. And will you look at that.' Taye waved eagerly at Tenzin and Suraya, who entered the Hall.

He leant closer to Aria and dropped his voice. 'You know, I waited in the common room for ages, but Tenzin was late –

again. Suraya, the loyal queen she is, stayed and waited for them, because someone had to come keep you company, knowing you would be overthinking about everything!'

'I wasn't overthinking. I just didn't want to talk to anyone.'

Taye's eyes softened. 'I know.'

More people entered the Mead Hall, among them Professor Okezie, who changed her braids to orange for the season, plaited in neat rows across her scalp and gathered into a large, elegant bun. With her white and dark-orange robe, she radiated a warm, dignified confidence. Beside her was Professor Haruki, his pinkish robes wrapped and tightened at his waist, with wide sleeves. The fabric swayed around him as he walked, his long black ponytail brushing against his back.

Aria's head throbbed, and the noise in the Hall scraped against her skull.

As Tenzin and Suraya reached the table, Taye placed his hands on his hips. 'Seriously, Tenzin, you *desperately* need to work on your timing.'

Tenzin dropped into the seat in front of them, grinning like nothing was wrong. 'I thought I said five minutes?'

'That was a lot more than five minutes,' Suraya said, laughing.

'Oh...' Tenzin said. 'Well, I'm here now!' They gave two thumbs up, unbothered.

Their expression changed in a split second and frowned. 'Hm, do you think we will lose the competition?'

'What competition?' Taye said. 'There's no competition tonight. It's more like entertainment for the ancestors to celebrate the harvest.'

'Then why will everyone be so sombre?' Tenzin asked, their dark eyes looking between them, concerned.

They all stared at Tenzin.

Aria tensed. The hope of a normal evening became a lost

dream floating away.

Tenzin shrugged. 'I don't know. Temporal energy has been unstable lately. Maybe it's nothing.'

Kaija passed by, her posture straight, walking with a confident stride. She ignored Aria, for once, as she talked with an older Fossheim girl Aria didn't recognise.

When the Mead Hall was finally filled with every student and staff alike, at the high table, Professor Halvard rose. Conversations faded in waves with his commanding presence.

'Look around you,' he said, surveying the Hall, his mouth curved slightly, pride gleaming in his eyes. 'Over nine hundred years of tradition gathered in this Hall.'

A weight shifted. The Hall became fuller. Shadows moved along the wooden-panelled walls. A presence Aria could only guess belonged to those who came before.

'As wild animals inherit migration routes stretching back through generations,' Professor Halvald continued. 'Magifolk celebrate the harvest, year after year, honouring the ancestors who passed down the old ways, preserving Nature in her infinite wisdom.

'Tonight isn't just about filling our bellies with this year's yields. It's about filling our hearts with gratitude to the remarkable system that provides not only water, food, and shelter, but magic, too – perhaps her most extraordinary gift of all.'

He raised his drinking horn high. The rest of the Hall followed suit, raising their wooden cups. 'Let us share this drink, as our ancestors did. To those who came before us, to those who sit here now, and to those yet to come. Enjoy the Harvest Feast!'

The Hall cheered, cups clunking in a lively symphony. Rapidly, the noise escalated with laughter, chatter, and plates clattering. Aria pressed her palms against her ears, eyes closed as the migraine flared, sharp and relentless. The banquet in front of her, with elk stew, root vegetables, and mushrooms, made her stomach turn.

'Here,' Finn said, standing behind Tenzin, holding a plate with a piece of bread drizzled with honey and fresh scent of mint crushed over it. 'This should help.'

'How did you—'

Finn shrugged with a slight smile. 'You've looked like you've been in pain for a while, so I made you something that could help. My dad taught me some easy remedies when I helped him out at the healing centre.'

She hesitated and took the plate. 'Thanks,' she said, taking a bite. The warmth of the honey and mint spread through her like a balm.

Satisfied, Finn turned to Taye. 'Is this the feast you're not supposed to share because of the elves?'

'No,' Taye replied with a slightly exaggerated sigh, his Swedish accent thickening. 'And honey, we don't speak of Álfablót in public like this. It's disrespectful.'

'Oh, elves!' Suraya interrupted, sitting up straighter, adjusting her glasses. 'I read about Norse private ceremonies. My mum says the energy patterns during private rituals are completely different—'

'Suraya,' Taye intervened, rolling his eyes. 'Cultural boundaries please, this is not science.'

'But scientifically—' Suraya began.

Taye cut her off with a dramatic wave of his fork. 'Some things,' he said, raising his voice for effect, 'are not meant for your mother's research papers.'

Before Suraya could reply, a ripple of movement and anticipation passed through the Fossheim table. At the far end, one of the older boys struck his wooden cup against the table's surface in a steady beat. Within seconds, the whole table joined, banging their own cups on the table, following the same rhythm.

'Here we go,' Taye whispered, grinning wide, his frustration forgotten.

Finn waved them goodbye and walked back to his seat at the Lundgard table to watch the first entertainment act.

Ten Fossheim students stood on their benches, facing their table, each with a bronze water bowl hovering above one of their palms. They circled the berms of the bowl with the other hand, creating a soft, melodic harmony that washed over the Mead Hall. A magical display of light reflected on the wooden walls, giving the illusion of being underwater.

The performers burst to song, with various others joining in.

'We gather now as seasons turn,
We all sing loud as fires burn,
The water dances beneath the moon,
Washing hope through every tune.'

'Oh, I don't know the words,' Aria whispered to Taye in panic.

Behind her, Carolina tapped her shoulder and handed her a piece of parchment, then continued down the table, passing them out to the rest.

'The song book!' Taye grinned as he picked up his.

They sang in unison, the water illusion rippling with the music. By the time the chorus returned, the whole Hall joined in. Astrid clapped and sang along on the high table, her black-painted nails glittering with the movement, while Professor Salvia's ivy crown swayed to the beat, the flames casting a warm glow over her platinum hair and her cheeks flushed with a rosy hue. Professor Grünwald thumped the table in delight, his deep laugh ringing.

'Flow, flow, flow, O waters flow,
Through the fog, the rain, the snow.
Tra-la-la-la, O Fossheim child,
We are born to roam the wild.'

As the music flowed, the performers danced on the spot to the sound, robe tunics moving gracefully.

Aria couldn't stop smiling. The singing, the stomping, the watery magic – it was all beautiful. For a moment, she forgot about everything else.

The final note was held in a long, trembling harmony, joined by the entire Fossheim table with lifted voices. As silence fell, laughter and applause soared from the other Krets.

'Loved it!' Taye said, flushed. 'Not half as bad as I thought it would be. And the performers did not drop any water!'

When Stenvald's turn came, a mist moved in from the outside. The mist bundled into various small balls of smoke, held by every Stenvald. They whispered into them, and let them go, allowing the balls of smoke to move around the Hall, descending to other Krets' tables.

What has hands, but cannot clap?

Each ball of smoke turned to riddles, dancing and twisting. The words hang in the air, whispered by unseen voices for all to hear, puzzles waiting to be solved.

'A clock!' Tenzin shouted, pointing at the first riddle. The ball of smoke exploded into a dazzling burst of light. The crowd nearby clapped.

What has one head, one foot, and four legs?

'A bed!' a girl shouted from the Lundgard table, succeeded by another explosion of light.

One by one, riddles exploded in a display of fireworks,

ending with a large applause and laughter.

'That was incredible!' Aria said, joining the applause at the end of the entertainment act.

During dessert, which to Aria's delight was apple crumble with whipped cream – something she was used to, for a change – the Mead Hall darkened. From the centre of the Lundgard table, an illusion of a forest grew within the Hall, a starry night above. Fireflies flew around, creating a magical atmosphere. Suraya's jaw dropped in awe.

A short boy stepped onto the bench, his shadow cast tall by the firelight. The rest of the Lundgard table sat still, eyes closed, humming softly.

The boy held an apple and spoke with a voice deeper than expected.

'As the wind moans through the hollow night and creatures of fire rise with burning might. How canst thou be bewitched by love, when the stars themselves adore it from above?'

He paused and bit his apple with a crunch. 'But if love's a spell, then curse me twice, so long as it comes with mead and spice!'

The humming continued through the whole soliloquy, and at the last word, silence fell and the fire at the front of the Mead Hall flared. From the ashes, butterflies rose. Hundreds of them fluttered out across the forest illusion. Tenzin let out a breathless laugh and goosebumps went up on Aria's arms as the butterflies slowly faded away above them.

Aria was overjoyed by the evening. Even her migraine had improved, thanks to Finn's remedy. The music, dancing, and magic all created a timeless night, making her forget about root explosions, opera singing orchids, and people treating her like a ticking bomb.

But the joy didn't last long.

The ground shook beneath her feet.

'Woah, woah, WOAH!' Taye's voice rose dramatically as the iron chandeliers swayed above. 'Is anyone else feeling this? Please tell me I'm not the only one feeling this earthquake right now!'

It was the sound that made Aria squeal. It was twisted, wrong. The magic in the Hall had been disturbed. It wasn't like the first tremor she'd felt. This was stronger, darker. The weight pressed on her chest.

Down the table, Carolina's usual confidence had faltered, her cup frozen halfway to her lips. Pale as though she had seen – or felt – a horrific truth. Whatever was happening was not ordinary. It was dangerous.

'I don't want to be dramatic—' Taye said.

'That would be a first,' Suraya muttered.

'—but from the professors' concerned expressions, this must be the end of times!'

At the high table, Professor Kiran straightened in her seat, a lock of short chocolate-brown hair falling across her forehead as she leant towards Professor Haruki to whisper something quick. Squinting his dark eyes, he leant in to answer, but Professor Kiran was already striding to the back door.

Professor Haruki rose slowly, pulling out his ever-present notebook from his pocket. He scribbled, his thin lips moving as though doing calculations out loud.

Professor Salvia's ivy crown was standing on its end, like a cat arching itself in the face of danger. Her hand reached for Astrid's, who nodded, her face pale. Professor Okezie wrapped her arms around herself, looking around warily.

Master Stormgaard was the only one unfazed by the tremor. His weathered face frowned as he took a slow sip from his drinking horn. He scanned the Hall, his eyes narrowing and lingering on every corner to find the culprit.

Finally, Professor Halvard stood, his presence calm. He lifted his hands.

'Students,' he said, 'please continue your meal. Professors Kiran and Haruki are investigating what appears to be a minor disturbance. Nothing to concern yourselves with.'

The words were meant to be reassuring, but as his blue eyes flickered towards the high windows, a hint of unease crossed them. Aria followed his gaze, and her heart skipped a beat. What were the tall dark shadows moving outside through the white mist?

'Right...' Taye said dryly under his breath. 'Sure, nothing to worry about. Just an actual earthquake where earthquakes never happen.'

Professor Haruki moved between tables heading to the main entrance to the Mead Hall.

'Fascinating resonance pattern,' he murmured. Every student near him followed him with their eyes as he passed. 'No need to worry, this is an absolutely normal and completely documented occurrence,' he added in a cheerful tone, but his face twisted in a microsecond, suggesting the contrary.

'Normal?' Suraya said to the group as she set her fork down. 'This doesn't feel normal to me.'

A hand grabbed Aria's arm. She turned to Tenzin, who stared at her with distant eyes.

'The earth bleeds North,' they said, their eyes burning with intensity. 'The fox wanders as the great ones roar. Again and again, the cycle holds. It's not the end, merely the beginning.'

'Erm... Tenzin?' she asked, one eyebrow arched. 'Are you okay?'

They blinked and a grin spread across their face.

'Hah! What?' Tenzin said as they snatched away their hand. 'I keep getting out of body experiences around here. It's weird.'

'Do you, erm... get training for this particular skill?'

'Not yet! But that's why I came here. Professor Halvard is a well-known timeweaver, so he's going to train me in the coming years.'

The ground shook again, this time strong enough to make a couple of students fall off their bench. A sound cut through the Hall – a bell struck underwater, wrong and deep, pressing on her eardrums. It came from everywhere and nowhere at once. Aria put her hands on her ears, but it made no difference. Was it in her mind? No one else reacted to the sound.

Across the Mead Hall, flames shivered, their golden warmth turning to a diseased purple, stretching long shadows across the terrified faces in the Hall.

'This is so wrong,' Aria whispered, more to herself than anyone.

Beside her, Taye had lost his usual grin, his face pale as he stared at the pulsing purple light. The sticky purple colour made Aria want to crawl out of her skin.

Every hushed conversation stumbled to a halt as every single flame went out, leaving only the memory of the otherworldly purple glow in their mind.

In the darkness, the silence was eerie while the outside fog crept in. The ancestors that once filled the Hall with their presence had left, for the Hall felt emptier now.

In a split second, the warmth of the fire and the candles came back. An audible sigh could be heard, relief it had passed, but tension was palpable with nervous chatter.

'Given the escalation of these events,' Professor Halvard began, 'I must ask all students to return to their dorms immediately. Head of Krets, please guide your pupils back safely. I will ask the kitchen to bring an array of warm beverages and buns to the common rooms.'

Footsteps echoed in the long corridors; murmurs filled the

silence as they headed to their dorms.

'So,' Taye said, 'it all got way too real for my taste.'

'Yeah...' Aria's mouth went dry. The wolf's yellow eyes flashed in her mind, the hand outstretched, the body covered in ash. Her hand instinctively went to the pendant, the warm metal grounding her. Was this the beginning of the end?

Finn caught up with them. 'Did you notice the smell of rotten eggs? It was subtle.' He shot a quick look at Aria. 'Are you okay? You don't look so good.'

Taye looked at Aria. 'He's right, your face is all twisty, like you've eaten something sour.'

'Yeah, no, I was just thinking about... a dream,' Aria said.

'Wait,' Taye asked, his tone light but with a hint of concern. 'Was it the Mare? The other night? You should put linseeds around your bed. The Mare will be compelled to count them and that way you will avoid getting more nightmares.'

Aria hesitated. She couldn't tell them about the dream, especially not now. They wouldn't understand. It was too much to explain, and part of her still wasn't sure what it meant, or if it even meant anything at all.

'It's just a weird dream,' she said, giving them a small unconvincing smile. 'Nothing important.'

'Are you sure about that? You've got that look, the one where something's bothering you, but you're not saying it out loud.'

'I'm fine,' Aria insisted, a little too quickly. 'Let's just get to the dorms, okay?'

Finn exchanged a look with Taye and nodded slowly. They fell into step beside her, quietly, as they headed to the dorms.

The warmth from Aria's room was a welcome change from the chill of the Hall. Suraya joined her a second later without exchanging words. They sat quietly on their beds, staring out of the window, Louis white as a ghost.

Aria couldn't shake the unsettling weight on her chest, just beyond the edges of her awareness. She tried to brush it off, but still, a shift was unfolding. Subtle, elusive, and she couldn't grasp what it meant.

CHAPTER FOURTEEN

Cinnamon

The Mead Hall was unrecognisable the following morning. No trace remained of the previous disturbing evening. The tables stood in their usual places while orbs of light floated above, casting the warmth of a summer sun and flooding the Hall with golden light, though dawn had yet to break. The usual chatter had been replaced by clusters of uneasy whispered conversations.

'According to *Historical Magical Disturbances of the North*,' Fraser said, surrounded by his usual wall of books, with only his ginger crown of tight coils visible. 'Similar tremors were recorded in 1786 in Sweden, just before a major shift in the ley lines.'

Inaiê shook her head, her golden septum piercing giving a small sway. 'No, it's in the forest. It doesn't look quite right. Something has been off in the natural processes. I just can't put my finger on what it could be.'

'You feel it, too?' Aria paused buttering her toast, her chest aching for validation of what she'd been feeling. 'It's like the forest is hurting.'

Inaiê nodded with a half-smile in agreement, but her eyes flickered with a question.

Maybe Inaiê didn't know what Aria meant after all.

'It's not magic or the forest,' Tenzin said, fixing their green fringe with their fingers. 'Not exactly. I think it's time. It's fracturing and bending. The tremors are a sign of time itself shifting.' Tenzin gave a nonchalant shrug. 'But I might be wrong.'

Aria swallowed dry.

Finn leant back. 'If time were fracturing, wouldn't we notice? People ageing strangely, days skipping, the sun rising at the wrong hour? Tremors alone don't prove that.'

'I heard they've called in experts from the Magic Regulation Board,' Suraya whispered, Louis turned a gossipy yellow on her shoulder. 'Based on my own observations, magical disruptions like this should indicate—'

'If you say "fascinating energy patterns" one more time,' Taye groaned, 'I will personally feed your research notes to a mountain troll.'

'Actually,' Fraser perked up, his coal-dark eyes peeking from behind the book, 'there's an interesting book about mountain troll dietary habits—'

'*Cara.*' Inaiê placed her hand on Fraser's shoulder. 'Trolls are the least of our concerns right now, especially what they eat for breakfast.'

'Right, right, sorry,' Fraser said, nervously pushing his clear-framed glasses up his nose.

'It's just recalibration,' Carolina said as she walked past their table, balancing books in one arm, dark circles shadowing her eyes. 'Old magical wards need tweaking every few decades – standard procedure for a place this old. Honestly,' she added with half a laugh, 'all this talk about ley lines and time falling apart? You guys are being dramatic. We'd be the first to know if there was anything extremely serious happening.' She walked on, leaving a trail of quiet behind her.

'I don't believe that,' Inaiê said under her breath. 'It's simply not true. We would be the last to know if it was serious. And this feels deadly serious.'

'It's becoming embarrassingly obvious,' Victoria sighed from the table behind them. 'Renwood's magic is about as refined as a toddler let loose with a wand. Utterly atrocious. She's obviously responsible for the tremors, not to mention that dreadfully uninspired light display yesterday. *Purple?* Oh, darling, do have dignity.'

'Wait, wait—' Kaija straightened up, eyes gleaming with malice. 'Picture the headline: "Oakspire in Ruins! Prestigious Magic Academy Learns the Hard Way Why You Don't Lower Standards." Iconic, right?'

Inessa snorted her orange juice, joining Kaija and Victoria in laughter.

Aria had it with these three. If only she could explode their heads.

'Hey, Renwood,' Inessa called out, her voice laced with amusement. 'Now *that* would be a legacy!'

Aria opened her mouth, but before she could say anything, Tenzin muttered, almost to themselves. 'That's not how it happens...'

Silence.

Kaija turned to them, nose wrinkling, looking paler to the point of transparency. 'Sorry – *what?*'

A flicker of regret crossed Tenzin's face. 'I-I don't know,' they said quickly. 'I just... I've seen the ruins before. It wasn't because of her.'

Kaija took a slow sip of her tea, hiding her shock with an unimpressed expression. 'Oh, how *intriguing*. Do enlighten us, Oracle One.'

'Yes, please.' Victoria smirked, pushing her golden-brown hair away from her face with a graceful gesture. 'Do tell – how *will* our dear Academy crumble into oblivion?'

Tenzin shifted uncomfortably but stayed silent.

'Oh, come on, don't be shy now,' Inessa cooed. 'Or are your visions just as useless as Renwood's magic?'

They laughed again.

'Enough!' Aria's voice cut through the laughter, sharp and stinging. She was on her feet, fists clenched at her sides. 'Mock me all you want. I couldn't care less about the opinions of petty, self-important nobodies. But don't drag Tenzin into it.'

The Hall quieted as voices died down.

A flicker of surprise crossed Kaija's face.

'You sit there,' Aria continued, 'tearing people down and you think it makes you interesting. The sad reality is that it just makes you predictable. Small. And I refuse to waste another second listening to it.'

She exhaled sharply, willing herself to stay in control. 'So, go ahead. Laugh. Whisper. But if you think for a second, I'll stand by while you treat other people like this, you're even more pathetic than I thought.'

Kaija, Inessa, and Victoria stared at her, stone-faced. They turned to each other and burst out laughing even louder.

'Oh, look at that.' Kaija clapped slowly, a smug grin stretching across her face. 'Renwood found her spine. How adorable.'

'You're taking this far too seriously, darling,' Victoria said. 'It's not our fault you're so easy to rile up.'

'It's not worth it,' Finn said to Aria, gently placing his palm on her shoulder.

Taye stood up and sighed. 'Okay, well, as much as I'd love to sit here and relish in the sheer narcissism, we actually have important things to do.'

He linked his arm with Aria's and nudged Finn towards the door. Suraya, Fraser, and Tenzin followed them quietly. Suraya threw one last venomous glare over her shoulder, Fraser hugged his books tighter to his chest, and Tenzin dragged their feet. Inaiê remained motionless on her seat, eyes narrowing at Kaija.

'You think this is funny?' Aria yelled, her voice cracking with rage as she wrenched herself free from Taye's grip. 'You act untouchable, but the second stakes get real, you'll be the first ones crying for help!'

'Oh, I do hope you're threatening me, Renwood,' Kaija said with amusement. 'It would make this so much more interesting.'

Aria's hands tingled at her sides as her magic clawed at her, begging to be let out. Plants in the Mead Hall started to move, turning their leaves facing the girls, ready to strike.

Inaiê stepped between them, forcing Kaija to meet her eyes. 'If you think she's easy to rile up, you should try me.'

A slow smirk crept over Kaija's face while meeting Inaiê's gaze, but she said nothing.

Finn grabbed Aria's wrist as the plants vibrated around them. 'Aria, we better go.'

Aria grunted and stormed out, her magic seething under her skin. Inaiê snorted at the girls before following Aria out.

The moment they were out of sight in the corridor, Aria punched the nearest wooden-panelled wall.

'Argh!' she shouted in agony, shaking her hand. 'One day,' she said through her teeth. 'One day, I swear—'

'Yeah, yeah,' Taye cut in. 'You'll make resin fall onto their heads, forcing them to shave their hair off. But not today.'

Aria couldn't help but smile at the image. *One day,* she thought, rubbing her sore hand.

Finn held her hand. 'It's not broken, but if you keep clenching like that, you'll make it worse. Aria, loosen it up.' He pressed his palm against hers until her fingers uncurled.

'Those girls are not worth it,' Suraya said, rubbing her arm. 'They're the lowest of the low, the dirt of humanity. They'll sabotage anything just to look better. I've seen it in every class we have together. You wouldn't believe the way Kaija manipulates others to do her bidding. Urgh, it makes me want to throw humiliating spells at her everyday just so she'd feel the pain she inflicts on others.'

Inaiê leant against the wall, arms crossed, eyes narrowing. 'Watching them squirm around like they own the place... it's despicable. Classic power trip.'

Fraser shuffled nervously behind them as the group went quiet. The muffled sounds of the Mead Hall filled the corridor. A ghostly owl zoomed silently above. Tenzin tilted their head, observing it intently.

'Right,' Taye said, pushing Aria down the corridor to the Front Hall. 'Let's go before those sorry souls decide to come this way and bore us with their lack of personality.'

Aria walked, rubbing her knuckles, now red. Her thoughts spun faster than her feet could carry her. Kaija, Victoria, and Inessa were insufferable, calculating, predictable. And why her? Mockery and assumptions followed her like a shadow, all her life. Aria clenched her fists, trying to quiet the storm in her mind.

By the time her thoughts slowed enough, the library doors loomed ahead. Only Finn and Taye walked beside her.

'Where's...' Aria started, looking between them. 'Did the others leave?'

'They're off doing their own thing,' Taye said. 'We figured you needed a little peace and quiet.'

Finn gave a small smile, concern in his eyes. 'Best to focus on something else for a while.'

'It's fine,' Aria said, wanting to desperately think of something else. 'Let's do that.'

The library was massive, with an atrium surrounded by three floors of shelves that rose all the way up to the ceiling. Autumn light from the rising sun streamed through the windows highlighting the dust particles in the air. A fluttering noise made them look up, and a ghostly bat flew above them into a bookshelf where it had made its home.

Aria welcomed the quiet, though her ears still buzzed with adrenaline.

They sat at their usual table near the Mímir's Vault deep in the library – a closed-up room which protected the most valuable and rarest books. The massive wooden doors were carved with intricate interwoven patterns that subtly shifted and flowed like water. At its centre was an iron lock, circular in shape, with delicate runic channels carved on the metal. On each door were ravens, carved from the wood itself. They were both part of it and rising from it, breathing and moving like living creatures. One turned its head and stared at Aria with its black stone eyes. Aria looked away in an instant.

Taye sprawled across one of the worn leather chairs, picking up his books from his bag.

'So,' he said, trying to urgently change the conversation, 'does anyone understand what Professor Okezie meant about magical frequencies? Because I've read this paragraph five times, and it might as well be in Old Norse.'

'It's like...' Finn closed his eyes for a moment. 'Think of musical notes vibrating. Everything in nature has a frequency, a sort of natural hum. Magic flows through these frequencies, and if something disrupts them, it throws everything off balance.' He grabbed a piece of parchment, drawing a ripple-like pattern. 'See? If the natural frequencies are out of sync, magic won't flow right.'

Aria watched her two friends discussing magical theory, when *she* was so out of tune. Her own struggles of magic were now a distant problem when destruction was stirring in Oakspire. How could she focus on homework when every tremor was a step closer to the wasteland she'd seen in her dream? Surely, it was not because of her.

Was it?

'Oi.' Taye waved his hand in front of her face. 'Don't let them take up your energy. They're not worth it.'

'Sorry,' she mumbled and perked up. 'You know what, we shouldn't be doing homework at all. I suggest a protest! We should have more information about last night.'

'Protest? Yes please! With banners and all?' Taye said excitedly.

Finn gave her a long, quiet look. Aria shrugged in response. Could he see right through her? See she was drowning in everything she couldn't say?

A slight tremor ran through the floor, rattling some books behind them. A soft thud of a book falling from its shelf echoed in the library, making the ghost bat fly above, finding safety on the other side of the atrium.

Aria's fingertips tingled. The plants around the library stretched and reached for her. Automatically, her hand clutched her pendant, and she closed her eyes, trying to calm herself.

'Wait, what's this supposed to say?' Taye flipped back and forth between pages in the textbook from the library, frowning. 'There's a whole chunk missing about resonance patterns in... something. The page has been ripped out.'

Finn leant over. 'Which chapter?'

'The one about energy flow in magical networks. Look – it jumps from talking about resonance patterns to advanced channelling, but there's clearly something in between that's missing.' Taye looked up at the ceiling with a sigh. 'Great. Just great. Watch Professor Okezie test us on exactly whatever's missing.'

Aria stared at the torn edges in the textbook, but all she could see were the walls inching closer with every heartbeat. She swallowed hard, but the lump in her throat wouldn't budge. She could hear her pulse in her ears, drowning out their voices.

A light touch on her shoulder made her jump. Finn slid a piece of chocolate across the table, one of those with runes that added a buzz on the tongue. He offered a smile, but she couldn't smile back, knowing what she knew. She couldn't shake the thought that Oakspire would turn to ash, the sky would burn, and people would—

No, they can't.

Take a deep breath, Aria, she thought.

She turned quickly to the window, watching the first snowflakes of the season. The kind of weather that made her want to curl up by the fireplace with a hot cocoa and a book. But here she was, feeling suffocated. Even more now, knowing this peaceful winter landscape would inevitably burn to ash.

She couldn't breathe. She could no longer pretend everything was normal when she knew what would happen.

'I just remembered,' she said, her voice faltering as she fumbled to gather her books with trembling hands. 'I promised to help with the...' Her hand fluttered vaguely at the windows, her mind scrambling for an excuse. '...the Greenhouse.' The words tumbled out, rushed and unconvincing, as she blurted the first thing that came to mind.

Taye barely looked up from his frustrated page-flipping. 'Since when are you into gardening?'

'I... um... it's a new thing,' she muttered, already taking a step back, her movements awkward and unsure. Her eyes flickered to the entrance, searching for an anchor. Maybe the Greenhouse wasn't such a bad idea – to be near something growing and alive. The opposite of that terrible wasteland imprinted in her mind. 'I'll catch up later?' Her voice wavered, an unspoken plea for understanding hanging in the air before she turned and hurried out of the library, leaving them confused behind her.

The Greenhouse glowed bright like a lantern on such a cloudy, moody, snowy day. Its glass dome of a thousand windows created a green haven amid the fresh snow that fell from above. Once inside, the rich scent of earth and the sweetness of flowers filled her senses with glee.

All around her, exotic tropical plants from faraway lands perked with her presence. One had bioluminescent flowers that created dancing patterns of light and shadows. Large trees stretched high, reaching the glass ceiling of the Greenhouse. Insects flew throughout, making it buzz with life, ignoring the arrival of winter.

Beside a large tree, with large thorns on its bark, was Astrid, attending a patch of delicate blue flowers. Her hair was styled in an intricate braid resting on her head like a crown, her hands gentle as she handled the plants.

'I could use a little help here, if you are willing,' she said as Aria stepped closer. 'Between you and me, I think they are just being dramatic. A little water and attention should perk them up.'

'I wouldn't know...' Aria shifted on the spot. 'I'm not good with plants.' *Or anything else right now for that matter,* she added silently.

'Everyone is good with plants,' Astrid said, waving her to kneel next to her. 'Here, help me with these seedlings. They're ready for bigger homes.'

Astrid placed a collection of small clay pots with tiny green shoots before her. She handed Aria a larger pot and a bag with rich, dark soil. 'See how the leaves are reaching the edges of their pots? That's them telling us they need more room to grow.'

Aria picked up a seedling, surprised by how delicate and alive it was in her hands. The cool, damp soil crumbled between her fingers, grounding her in the moment. Yet, even as she helped nurture this new life, her mind wandered back to the wasteland where nothing grew, a moment where death had touched everything. The stark contrast between the vibrant green shoot and her memories was painful.

Astrid's hand appeared in her ray of sight, gently steadying Aria's trembling one where the seedling rested on her palm. Aria looked up in surprise, aware of the warmth of Astrid's hand. The simple touch sent an unexpected ache through her chest. When was the last time someone had reached for her with such casual tenderness? Such moments belonged to other people's childhoods, to mothers and grandmothers she'd only observed from a distance.

'I think,' Astrid said with kind firmness, rising to her feet and dusting off her green apron, 'this is the perfect moment for tea and one of my cinnamon buns. They're still warm from the oven, and there's nothing like the smell of cinnamon to calm the mind.'

Aria nodded, not trusting her voice. She slowly planted the seedling in its new pot before she stood, wiping her hands on her robe and following Astrid through the lush sanctuary into the winter air outside. Gone was the soft rustling of leaves and bustle of lively insects, replaced with a subtle tapping sound of snow falling on dead leaves. Aria shivered, drawing her cloak tighter as they made their way towards the warmth of the small red cottage beside the Greenhouse.

'Make yourself at home,' Astrid said, opening the door.

Aria stepped in, and the home embraced her: herbs drying by windows, mysterious potions bubbled on wooden shelves beside numerous books on botany, and the scent of cinnamon enveloped her. The crackling fire and soft glow of candles made the cottage feel cosy, and when she sank into the plush sofa, she felt held and protected.

'How do you like your tea?' Astrid asked, moving a small kettle on the stove in the kitchen. 'I have chamomile, mint, and even nettles. All of which I grew myself.'

'Chamomile sounds lovely, thank you.'

'Perfect choice,' she said as she poured hot water over the fragrant tea leaves and offered Aria a steaming mug, along with a freshly baked cinnamon bun.

Sitting across from her, Astrid leant forward, her expression softening. 'Now, tell me what's on your mind. Clearly, you're having a difficult time.'

Aria wrapped her hands around the warm mug, breathing in the herb's soft, wild scent. The question hovered in the air. She took a sip before the words tumbled out on their own. 'Have you ever known something was going to happen before it did?'

Astrid turned to the window, distant thoughts crossing her face. 'What you're describing could be heightened awareness. Sometimes, the world tells us everything we need to know through our subconscious.'

Aria looked down at her tea. 'Everything feels wrong,' she whispered. 'Like I'm caught in a story where pages are tearing themselves out and rewriting as I go, and my hands—' She clenched her fingers, making the herbs hanging from the ceiling sway slightly. 'They won't stay quiet anymore.'

Astrid studied Aria for a moment, setting her tea down. 'It reminds me of a saga my grandmother used to tell,' she said. 'The Saga of Vavtrudner.'

Aria looked up. 'That's a mouthful.'

Astrid smiled. 'It's the name of an old tale, one about a

giant known for his immense wisdom and knowledge of the past, present, and future.' She paused and watched herbs swinging on the window. 'You know, giants aren't big brutish beings. They were the first. Before gods, before men, before the world had even taken shape. They were the chaos before the order, the storms before the sky knew how to hold them. And some of them, like Vavtrudner, understood the chaos.'

Astrid smiled knowingly, watching a leaf detach itself from the vine above.

'Odin, the Allfather, wanted to test him. So, he travelled to Vavtrudner's Hall, far beyond the places where the gods dared to go. He challenged the giant to a contest of knowledge. They sat across from one other, and Odin asked the hardest questions he could think of.'

'What kind of questions?'

'The shape of the cosmos. The first dawn, the first breath of wind, the first death. And Vavtrudner answered every single one. He spoke of Ymir, the first giant, whose body became the land we walk on. He spoke of the rivers and stars, of how the earth was carved from chaos itself. And he spoke of the future, the unravelling. Ragnarök.'

'The what?'

'The end of this world. The great wolf breaking free, the earth trembling, the sky splitting apart. The giants knew of its coming, not because they wanted destruction, but because destruction is part of the cycle. And Vavtrudner saw it all. Can you imagine knowing something like that? Feeling the world shift beneath you and knowing what it means?'

Yes, Aria knew that feeling intimately. She swallowed dry and forced her voice to redirect the conversation. 'Did Odin win?'

'He did. But not because he was wiser. He asked a question no one could answer: what did Odin whisper in the ear of his dying son, Balder?'

Aria frowned. 'That's not fair.'

'No, it wasn't. But that's the thing about knowledge. Sometimes, you don't actually know it all.'

Aria stared down into her tea, ripples forming within.

'This is to show that even the wisest must listen,' Astrid continued. 'Even Odin doesn't rely only on his own wisdom; he sought out the giant's knowledge. So, true wisdom isn't just knowing but also listening.'

'And how do I listen when everything is falling apart?' she asked quietly, biting her lip, her voice trembling.

Astrid smiled, her eyes softening as she reached out to hold Aria's hand.

'One step at a time, Aria. You've already started listening. The world doesn't rush, and neither should you.'

The leaf drifted towards Aria's hand and settled at her fingertips. She picked it up, turning it over in her palm, its edges delicate and curled with the memory of the life it lived.

Astrid leant back, watching her with quiet understanding, and smiled, holding her mug on her lap.

'You're not alone in this,' she said. 'The world speaks to you, and around are those who will listen.'

CHAPTER FIFTEEN

Yule Market

'No one will steal them,' Finn said, adjusting the brooch pin on the shoulder of his green winter cloak. Aria stood in front of a row of bicycles propped against the stonewall, their metal frames dusted with fresh snow.

'I half-expected a horse-drawn carriage or some kind of magical transportation to Eldviken,' Aria said.

'What, you thought we'd waste magic or use animals on something we can do ourselves?' Taye patted his bike's seat affectionately. 'Are you mad?'

'You thought it was nice to cycle in the snow? I felt my face being torn to pieces by microscopic razor blades! And I can't feel my ears anymore.' Aria pushed down her blue woollen beanie to better cover her ears.

'Come on, that's part of the charm! Besides, it's excellent for your complexion and – oh my goodness!' Taye grabbed Aria's chin and inspected her face. 'You desperately need it.'

Aria shook him off. 'Excuse you! Have you seen yourself in the mirror lately?'

Taye gasped theatrically.

Finn chuckled. 'What if instead of exploring each other's pores, we can give the Yule Market a chance before the rest of

Oakspire arrives?'

'You don't need to ask me twice!' Taye hooked his arms with Finn and Aria's and walked to the Eldviken village centre, where the annual Yule Market was taking place.

The village near Oakspire held echoes of the past. The houses were made of massive timber logs locked together at the corners in intricate puzzle-work. Runes carved in the wood glowed faintly between them, which Taye pointed out was for protection against malevolent spirits, bad luck or even thieves. The sweet scent of pine bark and spices lingered in the air, carried by the smoke rising from dragon-headed chimneys.

Aria welcomed it all. It was a comforting distraction from the tremors at Oakspire, now happening daily for the past month and a half since the Harvest Feast. It had become the new normal, with professors barely pausing their lectures as the ground shook, while students joked about Oakspire having growing pains. Aria joined them, laughing it off, jealous they dismissed it when she knew, with a terrifying certainty, they weren't random.

The Yule Market stretched across the snowy square. Stalls built from dark wood stood in neat rows, their rooftops heavy with snow. Pine garlands and red woollen ribbons hung between them, with small orbs of light in glass bulbs along it. Smoke rose from iron braziers throughout the market, adding warmth to this otherwise cold, snowy day.

Music drifted from a corner where fiddlers and lute players played festive melodies, while children ran through the market, chasing a dog with a thick coat with white and black markings. The stalls were packed with people, looking into all sorts of curious artefacts and edibles. Aria was itching and eager to explore what the market had to offer.

'Well, well, well,' a cold voice cut through their wonder. 'Has the walking disaster decided to spread the chaos to neighbouring villages now, too?'

Kaija stood in their path, Victoria and Inessa beside her, their black cloaks clear from snow, shielded from it by some unseen charm.

'Brave of you to show your face in such a public setting, Renwood,' Victoria added. 'I am sure rumours about you spread with speed in these parts.'

Heat surged in her cheeks, a mix of anger and frustration bubbling under the surface. She forced a smirk, leaning into her response. 'Jealous, are you? That people talk more about me than you?'

A flicker of irritation passed across Kaija's frosty blue eyes, enhanced by the black fur hat, her cheeks and nose rosy-red from the cold.

'Darlings, those cloaks are absolutely *stunning*,' Taye gushed, not giving her a chance to respond, his voice light and exaggerated with mischief in his eyes. 'What's the material? Angora wool, surely, enchanted by the finest tailor in the land? You *must* give me the name. But not today, we have crafts to see, people to meet. Bye!'

Kaija's lip curled in spite as Taye waved his hand at her face. She rolled her eyes and turned away, facing Inessa and Victoria. 'Come on, I want to see the crystals by the light elves before Renwood destroys them, too.'

'Absolutely vile, those three,' Taye said as they watched them go.

'Their problem, not ours,' Finn replied.

'Hm,' Taye agreed. He turned back to Finn and Aria, his grin widening as he bounced on his feet. 'To start off your first Yule Market, let me have you both try something.'

Finn and Aria shared a glance and followed Taye through the crowd of locals, travellers, and various students from Oakspire.

They walked up to a stall where an old woman arranged golden spice buns on a wooden tray, their sweet scent swirling with cardamom and saffron.

'Three, please!'

Taye handed them a warm bun, its hue glowing faintly in the soft light of the Yule Market. The bread was shaped into a circular braid, its twists and turns evoking the endless cycle of the seasons. Dotted with dried berries and glazed with a thin sheen, the smell of saffron rich and inviting.

'Solkattring, fresh from the hearth,' Taye said with a grin.

Aria and Finn shrugged. As they took a bite, Taye nodded in anticipation. 'Well? It's basically sunshine in bread form, isn't it?'

'Oh! It's sweet,' Aria said as the flavours exploded on her tongue.

'The saffron,' Finn said, studying the bun. 'It's subtle, but it changes everything.'

'Yes! It's a Yule tradition!'

'Wait, are those... *dwarves*?' Aria said loudly, pointing at the far end of the market, where sparks flew.

Two figures huddled over an anvil, their forge burning with blue flames as they shaped metal with intricate hammers. They could have stepped from the old tales – not much shorter than grown men but broader, with soot-dark skin and eyes that glinted with molten ore.

'Oh my gods, *yes*! We absolutely have to go there!' Taye declared, weaving through the crowd. He stopped and turned. 'Dark elves. They're dark elves. Not dwarves.' He pirouetted and vanished in the crowd.

'Will we ever get through this market at a normal pace?' Finn asked dryly, biting into his solkattring, trailing Taye towards the dark elves' stall.

Aria chuckled. 'We'll be lucky if we leave before the sun

sets.'

'Hurry up, you two!' Taye shouted from afar, his colourful beanie sprinkling with light.

The stall was surrounded by a crowd watching the dark elves crafting elaborate detailed metal work on blue fire.

'Excuse me! I want one of those,' Taye said, pointing at a compass on the table, its needle pointed to a perfect North. 'This will be excellent for the summer hikes in the fells.'

One of the dark elves looked up from her work, her thick grey braids clinking with metal beads. 'Of course,' she said simply, her voice rough. She wrapped the compass in soft leather, her movements precise despite her broad fingers.

'Is this similar to the original ones? The ones from the legends?' Taye said, holding his wrapped package beaming with pride.

'This one is good enough for finding North, yes. But the old ones...' She paused, running a calloused thumb over another replica. 'Those were forged to guard earth magic itself. Found more than just North, they did. Found trouble brewing in the depths.'

Taye's eyes sparkled. 'Oh, I love this! So, you're saying the legends are true! What kind of trouble are we talking about? Like, "run-for-your-life" trouble or "best bring snacks, this is gonna be interesting" kind of trouble?'

'The kind that makes smart folk turn back, kid.'

Taye grinned widely, rubbing his hands together, his compass now safely guarded in his yellow backpack. 'The bigger the trouble, the more fun, right?' He winked. 'Thank you very much. Wishing you a wonderful day!'

An ethereal glow from a stand on the far end of the market caught Aria's attention. Two figures stood tall, graceful, arranging crystals that shimmered with inner light. Their silver-blond hair was partly hidden behind their long sage-green hooded cloaks, with complex golden details along it. In discussion with one of the figures was Kaija, negotiating prices over a large violet crystal.

'Light elves,' Taye said, following Aria's gaze. 'They come here from Alfheim. They try to spread good in our world. Real beings of light and beauty.' He lowered his voice slightly. 'But don't let it fool you. Light doesn't mean harmless.'

Finn raised an eyebrow. 'Are those the elves you warned me not to offend?'

'Exactly. Though, also the dark elves we just met. Same roots, but they're connected to earth instead of light. Álfablót honours both, in its own way. Balance, you know? You give the ground what it's owed – and the sky, too.' He paused. 'Still think I made it all up?'

Finn didn't answer right away. He watched the light elves with furrowed brows, lips pressed into a line. 'Let's just say, I'm re-evaluating.'

Taye grinned. 'Progress.'

Aria listened to their interaction, half smiling while watching a grumpy garden gnome, barely as tall as a child. His red pointy cap was crooked as he demonstrated his enchanted garden tools that worked while house owners slept. Astrid was there, observing the stall with interest, a woollen brown beanie on her head, her red hair filled with snowflakes. She examined a belt with various pockets. Aria could only assume it was to hold knives, scissors, and other small gardening tools.

Beyond them, in a narrow space between two stalls, partially hidden by hanging dried herbs, stood Professor Kiran. She spoke with a hooded figure, their face hidden in the shadow. What struck Aria wasn't so much their secluded location or even the hood covering the stranger's face, but Professor Kiran's demeanour: shoulders tense, gestures sharp and contained as she spoke in hushed tones.

Aria pushed herself through the crowd to get closer, to catch what they were talking about.

'The balance is shifting,' she caught Professor Kiran saying. 'We need to act now—' The rest was lost in the noise.

The hooded figure handed her a small globe-shaped object made of crystal, perhaps? Professor Kiran picked it up with one hand and quickly placed it inside her worn leather satchel. Yet Aria managed to glimpse an unusual green-blue sheen, moving erratically inside the sphere.

'Time grows short,' the hooded figure said. 'The signs are clear.'

Professor Kiran nodded, her expression grim.

The exchange had the weight of importance wrapped in secrecy.

To challenge Aria's suspicion, Carolina stumbled on a patch of ice near Professor Kiran, who shot her hands out immediately, steadying her before she could hit the ground.

'Careful there, Miss Valencia,' she said, her earlier tension completely replaced by warmth. Her hand lingered on Carolina's shoulder, a maternal gesture. 'These cobblestones can be treacherous in winter.'

'Thank you, Professor,' Carolina mumbled. There was something vulnerable in her expression Aria had never seen before, a flicker of uncertainty, quickly hidden by her smile.

'Come see me after class next week,' Professor Kiran said with a calmer demeanour. 'We should discuss your progress on the Quest for Knowledge, make sure you are reaching your milestones.'

'I was about to suggest the same,' Carolina said. 'It is a lot more complex than I anticipated.'

'That's why it's called a Quest,' Professor Kiran said.

Carolina laughed. 'Right! See you next week, then,' she said, blending back into the crowd.

Professor Kiran straightened and adjusted her red scarf. It was tied into a knot and tucked into her long black cloak, buttoned up at the front with silver buttons. She put up her hood, protecting her hair from the snow, and stepped back into the flow of the market, once again the picture of composure.

The hooded figure she had the secret exchange with was now gone, melted into the crowd.

Professor Kiran smiled warmly at a group of second-years admiring wooden sculptures of ravens and other mystical animals on the nearby stall. As Aria's eyes followed her through the crowd, something warm was thrusted into her hands.

'Honeymead,' Taye said. 'Drink up, thank me later.'

She held the wooden cup of honeymead and took a sip. The warmth spread through her, making her realise how cold it actually was. She turned back to Professor Kiran, but she was no longer there. She shook her head and took another sip. *Tomorrow's problem*, she told herself.

They wandered through the market, Taye leading them from stall to stall. By the time darkness fell, during the afternoon, Finn bought himself a handmade flute and wool mittens, and Taye an assortment of candy for all three of them. Aria had no money to spend, but she didn't mind; she was too mesmerised by the magic of her first Yule Market.

The majestic Yule Ash stood tall in the centre of the market. Its twisted, naked branches reached up into the night sky, adorned with iron runes and other symbols that shimmered in the firelight.

The tree looked magical, even without its leaves.

'That one's for protection,' Taye said, pointing to one of the iron symbols in the shape of a hammer. 'Thor's hammer, Mjölnir.'

Aria touched the juniper bushes at the tree's base, warm to the touch.

'To ward off malevolent spirits,' Finn said, also taking it all in with curiosity. 'A protection for the coming year. We have similar traditions back home.'

Taye handed Aria a small iron boar charm, which he took from a basket at the bottom of the tree.

'For Freyr,' he said. 'Maybe, just maybe, we get a better Harvest Feast next year.'

As Aria lifted the charm to place it on the tree, a cold hand gripped her arm. She turned to find an old woman studying her with eyes pale as winter ice. Animal bones clinked at the woman's waist, and her grey braids hung, thick and knotted, woven with raven feathers. Her cloak, blood red and twilight blue, bore runes that shifted in the shadows.

'The wolf stalks your dreams,' the woman's voice rasped, like dry leaves in the winter wind. 'I taste ash in the air when you draw near, child.' Her thin fingers tightened, cold as the grave. 'The old magic runs thick in your blood. Seidr-magic. Wild magic.'

The woman's eyes went wide with recognition – or fear. She snatched her hand back as if burned, the bones at her belt rattling with warning. Without another word, she stepped back into the crowd, leaving only the heaviness of her words and the lingering scent of wood smoke.

'Sweet merciful Odin,' Taye whispered, watching the woman disappear into the crowd. 'She was a völva.' He stopped, reading Aria's face. 'Are you okay?'

Aria rubbed her arm where the woman had gripped her, heart racing. 'She knew about... about my dream.'

'What dream?' Finn asked, staring at her with curiosity.

'I...' Aria rubbed her face. 'I've had this dream. About a wolf, and ashes, and—' She stopped, the words sticking in her throat.

As she described the nightmare, Taye grew uncharacteristically still, his usual animation replaced by focused attention. Finn leant forward slightly, his presence steadying her. Now she understood. *This* was why she should have told them sooner. They weren't looking at her with judgement. They saw Aria still – just Aria carrying something too heavy to bear alone.

'Well,' Taye said finally, his voice unusually serious, 'that explains why a völva just grabbed you in the middle of a market. But also? This is clearly about you. Your magic, this dream, Nature choosing you. Maybe it's time to stop pretending you're not special.'

'We'll figure it out. But carefully,' Finn said while he gave Taye a pointed look. 'No rushing into things.'

'Of course! You seem to have lost faith in me.' Taye's usual grin returned. He turned to Aria, his eyes softening. 'First, let's have time to process and, you know, make sure we're not all having creepy wolf dreams.'

Aria took a shaky breath, grateful for how Taye could give a sense of adventure to mysterious seers and nightmares, and how Finn's calm attitude kept her grounded.

The snow fell heavier, muffling the market's happy chatter and music. Aria took a deep breath of the cold, fresh air and looked up, seeking guidance from the stars hidden behind clouds. Snowflakes fell softly on her face, each one a gentle reminder she wasn't alone. The dream's burden felt different now, shared between friends.

At last, Aria breathed out, feeling lighter.

CHAPTER SIXTEEN

Yule

The melodramatic moonflower on Aria's desk let out a mournful sigh as another tremor rippled through Oakspire. Its purple petals drooped dramatically, while Aria looked straight out to the moon reflecting on the lake below, trying to ignore the ground shaking.

Not much had been discussed about the dream since the encounter with the völva. All their professors realised winter break was upon them and collectively decided to torture their students with the biggest assignments yet.

Professor Salvia gave each student a plant to nurture over the holidays, making sure they kept a mood journal. It made no sense until Aria got back to her room with her assigned melodramatic moonflower, a purple flowering plant known for its ability to turn every minor inconvenience into an operatic tragedy.

Between that and Professor Kiran's assignment to track elemental fluctuations during the winter solstice, Master Stormgaard's combat stance practices in the high snow, and Professor Vinke's challenge to enchant winter hats to remark on one's body temperature, there was little time to actually contemplate anything else.

Aria wandered the corridors, mostly empty now that winter break had begun. The animal ghosts drifted along as usual, but everyone else was away: Taye up north for Yule, Finn back in Ireland with his father, Suraya off in France for a huge family gathering she was fretting about, Fraser visiting relatives in Mozambique, and Inaiê enjoying the summer sun in Brazil. Even Kaija and her pair of ice princesses had gone home at last, much to Aria's relief, leaving her with a rare moment of peace.

She entered the Gathering Room beside the Front Hall, now completely transformed for Yule. The ancient iron hooks that once displayed Viking shields now held pine branches, bringing in the wild scent of the forest. Candles cast moving shadows, reflecting through the windows where snowflakes drifted outside. The fire hissed and popped, radiating warmth.

Carolina waved at her to join her by the fire. She wore a rich red boat-neck top with long sleeves, its smooth fabric tucked neatly into high-waisted black wide-legged trousers. Her hair fell in soft, natural waves, pinned neatly behind her ears to reveal her face and accentuate her features.

Aria sank into the leather armchair next to her and pulled up a wool blanket across her lap. She was clearly underdressed, wearing a simple burnt orange turtleneck sweater, an oversized grey knitted cardigan, and charcoal trousers she found in her wardrobe.

'It's almost like Christmas,' Aria said.

'Kind of,' Carolina said. 'It's more about the winter solstice here. The longest night, the end of a cycle, the start of another. It's poetic, really.'

'How come you didn't go home for Christmas?' Aria asked. Why would someone not spend time with their family if they had one? She herself didn't have one to go to, at least.

Carolina twirled her chestnut wand between her fingers,

watching the fire dance to the tune of a violin Aria didn't recognise, its neck lined with wooden keys, its bow gliding by unseen hands in the corner.

'Mother's new partner, António, is... traditional. Exceptionally traditional for my own taste. He thinks we should stick to the old ways. As if the old ways never hurt anyone.' She clicked her tongue and stopped twirling her wand, her voice hardening. 'Papa understood. He was working on something revolutionary when he passed away...' She sighed and faced Aria with a tight and practised smile. 'Anyway, better here than listening to another lecture about proper magical conduct.'

Aria shifted in her armchair, her throat tight. 'I... I didn't know.'

Carolina smiled but shook her head. 'It's fine. It was a long time ago. Let's enjoy the moment. Yule in Oakspire is special. The founders chose this spot for a reason. The magic is so much stronger this time of year. During solstice, the veils between realms are thinnest. No wonder the old Norse folk chose it for the offerings.'

Aria nodded in silence. Her friend sank back into the armchair and took a slow sip from her mug as the firelight caught the weariness in Carolina's face.

Laughter made Aria turn her head to the seats by the tall windows where Jonathan Thomson, Head of Stenvald, and fifth-year Lundgard Tove Bjørnstad sat. Jonathan told stories that made Tove's blue eyes light up through the stray strands of her short platinum hair. Another group of kids sat awkwardly, in silence, gathered together by circumstance, not friendship. In the far corner, Tenzin sat crossed legged on a sofa, a book in one hand and a fork in the other, eating from a plate filled with different foods from the Yule Smorgasbord. Aria made a mental note to greet them in a minute.

Across the room, Professor Haruki sat with a cup of mulled wine, immersed in a conversation with Professor Okezie, whose winter-white braids cascaded down her back for the season. Nearby, Professor Kiran leant casually against the wall, arms crossed with her oversized tweed jacket, her eyes scanning the room. Their eyes met, and Professor Kiran offered a small nod and a soft smile.

Aria hesitated. She forced a faint smile in return. The memory of Professor Kiran at the Yule Market was fresh in her mind and Aria was convinced it was malice. Why else would the figure be hidden in the shadows? Why have a meeting between stalls, in the shadows? Aria stood up and carefully placed the wool blanket on the armchair, to avoid any interaction with Professor Kiran, even from a distance.

'I'm going to get something from the Smorgasbord,' Aria said to Carolina, who nodded absently, staring at the fire.

Aria sympathised. If there was anything they had in common, it was losing a parent, the emptiness during festive seasons. But Aria was used to it, for she had no memory of her parents whatsoever.

At the Smorgasbord, she picked up a plate. The scent of spiced mead mingled with the rich aroma of pickled herring, cured salmon, and the roasted boar. Among the lavish dishes, only gingerbread was familiar. It made her heart ache – not so much for the children's home, but for the foods, people, and culture she was accustomed to. She even missed Mrs Mabbott, who baked them gingerbread cake for Christmas, which always tasted divine. Mrs Mabbott tried to bring joy to a home of unhappy children who just wanted to be with their families. Last year, she wore an ugly Christmas sweater with a reindeer, whose nose blinked brightly. Aria's chest lightened to this fun memory.

Did they still think of her now? Astrid told her on the very first day in Oakspire that the home considered her adopted the moment she passed through the stone. Maybe it was true. Maybe she'd already been forgotten, and they'd moved on, as if she had never belonged there at all.

'Everything here tells a story,' Professor Halvard said, droplets sparkling on his white beard. 'This boar isn't just any boar. It's Freyr's sacred animal. In the old days, they would sacrifice the boar in honour of Freyr for the Yule feast. But nowadays' – he leant in conspiratorially – 'most put intention into the meal instead. I think Freyr would appreciate that just as well.'

Aria smiled, unsure what to say. She knew nothing of Norse gods but trusted that whatever needed to be done to please the gods was being done.

'Now, the pickled herring is a delicacy,' Professor Halvard continued. 'Caught locally. Pickled in different ways. It reminds us of the season's rhythm – when the seas give plenty, we preserve with care.'

Aria shifted her plate from one hand to the other. 'I've never actually had herring before,' she admitted. Her stomach twisted at the sight of the pale, shiny raw fish.

Professor Halvard tilted his head and smiled. Without a word, he reached for the plate with the gingerbread cookies and brought it closer to her. 'A gentler start,' he said. 'You can decide when – or if – you want the herring.'

Aria took a piece and carefully placed it on her plate. Her shoulders, tense since arriving at the Gathering Room, lowered slightly.

Once satisfied with her plate of new and familiar tastes, Aria made her way to Carolina, who was now in the company of Jonathan, Tove, and Tenzin. Aria slid onto her armchair and nibbled gingerbread, then sampled a bite of roasted vegetables, listening to Jonathan telling stories of magical mishaps that left the professors fuming. Each story made her grin, her tension loosening like the first thaw of spring.

Throughout the evening, the Smorgasbord grew emptier, the trays gradually cleared as students made trip after trip, filling their plates and their bellies. Aria let her laughter ripple freely, which mingled with the quiet chatter in the Gathering Room. Every refill, every shared smile, made the day feel less daunting, less foreign.

Professor Halvard's voice rang out, cutting through the music and chatter. 'I believe it's time for a beloved Oakspire tradition: the singing toast! If this is your first Yule, go with the flow, and speak the words that come into your mind.' His eyes sparkled with enthusiasm, and excitement rippled through the room.

Aria frowned, shifting in her seat. *Singing? Toast?* Her stomach fluttered with a mix of nerves and uncertainty. No one told her about this singing toast.

In contrast, Carolina looked positively giddy.

'I'll start.' Professor Halvard cleared his throat dramatically and raised his cup. 'To the trees that tower high, and the stars that light the sky, may our magic flow like streams and our hearts be filled with dreams!'

Students and staff alike raised their cups in response. Aria joined them, though she couldn't help but feel a drop of awkwardness as, one by one, others stood and continued to sing cheerfully.

'To friendships, bright and true, with laughter by me and you!' Carolina sang, her voice strong and clear.

'To the elements, so bold, let the connection unfold,' Professor Kiran sang with a playful smirk.

'To the bonds that tie us tight, through the dark and through the light!' Professor Okezie sang cheerfully, her voice soft.

'To the time we have to share, spreading light through gentle air!' Tenzin sang, gesturing at the snow falling outside.

As the toast circled around the room, each person added their own unique flair. Aria's mind raced, scrambling for something to sing, and in that second, Taye's perfect smile and Finn's kind eyes took foreground.

With a spark of courage, Aria raised her cup, and with a nervous lump in her throat, she sang, 'To the family we found, who help keep us strong and sound.'

Applause and laughter filled the room. Warmth spread in her chest as everyone enjoyed this intimate gathering.

Professor Halvard clapped his hands together, beaming at them. 'What a lovely performance! Thank you for this pleasure. Please, enjoy the rest of the evening.'

As the chatter died down, Astrid stepped in through the door, patting her thick winter cloak to remove the snow. She exchanged a few words with the headmaster, and they both left in a hurry.

Odd, Aria thought. Instinctively, she hurried after them, out of the Gathering Room, down the corridor, and into the Front Hall. She found them just ahead, two shadows, their voices low but sharp in the otherwise quiet Hall.

Aria slipped behind the towering statue of Eiríkr the Stormbringer, one of the legendary founders, whose likeness stood tall and imposing. She pressed her back to the warm wooden panel, heart racing, but she couldn't just walk away now. She needed to know what they were talking about.

'The Great Ash is sick,' Astrid said, her voice trembling with concern. 'I've been monitoring its vital signs for weeks now.'

'Are the runes not working?' Professor Halvard asked, his voice low and encouraging.

'Barely. Something is draining its life force in a way I've

never seen before.'

'This seems more than just a single tree's decline. This could be a systemic collapse.'

'My thoughts exactly. But there's something else.' Astrid took a step closer, lowering her voice to a whisper. 'There are signs the vaesen are waking.'

Silence.

'We need to deal with this at once,' Professor Halvard said. 'I regret that you must forgo the Yule festivities.'

'This is more important.'

They turned sharply towards the doors and stepped outside. A sudden cold gust swept in the Hall. Aria shivered.

Panic crawled up her skin. She had to follow, to understand what was going on. Without her winter cloak, she'd be nothing more than a frozen statue – Aria the Reckless, she would be forever known.

Pacing up and down the Front Hall, Aria's mind raced. *Systemic collapse. Vaesen awakening.* She didn't know what vaesen was, but something awakening did not sound good. The words echoed in her head, sending a rush of adrenaline down her spine.

She paused, slapping her palm against her forehead. 'The changing room!' she said out loud.

With a quick turn, she headed to the door underneath the Grand Staircase, where fieldwork attire was stored and available for all.

'Gotcha!' She picked a thick woollen green cloak with a hood. 'And you're coming with me, too,' she added to the worn wooden snowshoes hanging by the door.

Aria threw the cloak over her shoulders, pinning the ring needle on the left shoulder. She hurried out of the Front Hall, facing the cold head on, and placed her snowshoes.

Large snowflakes made the visibility low. Aria looked

around for footsteps but found none – they had been covered already. Suspecting they had gone directly to the Great Ash, she went that direction.

The Great Ash looked naked without its leaves, thick layers of white blankets heavy on the branches. Astrid and Professor Halvard weren't there. Aria grunted, disappointed she didn't follow them directly, to uncover what was causing the tremors. Surely, it had to be related.

As she took a step closer to the Great Ash to investigate, the runes on its bark pulsated with a warm colour. It didn't look sick, it just looked dormant, as any tree would in winter.

Snow muffled the world into a calm hush. Aria couldn't imagine any systemic collapse. She looked up, flakes falling on her face, taking in the silence. It was eerie and calming to be in the presence of this tree on the shortest day of the year.

A movement was caught in the corner of her eye, a shadow slowly climbing down from the highest branches. Aria took a step back as the creature observed her with curiosity, a creature with the form of a small woman. Its face looked human, yet not; its eyes were large and black, its nose thin and narrow, and its cream-white skin had the rough texture of bark.

The creature reached the ground and crouched, looking up at Aria with unwavering focus. Quietly, it stepped closer without leaving footprints, its long black hair covering its naked body, intertwined with ash leaves and twigs.

Horrified, Aria took another step back, her chest filled with panic.

Without warning, the creature moved with incongruous speed and wrapped its hand around Aria's neck. She gasped. She tried to move but couldn't, tried to scream, but no noise came out. All the hairs on her body stood up.

Aria was in danger.

A sickening energy swirled through her from the creature's fingertips, a disease taking over her body – first heat, followed by chills with a deep muscle ache she couldn't shake.

The creature did not move, did not blink. Its eyes locked onto Aria's, its face disturbingly expressionless.

Aria's adrenaline peaked, and exhaustion took hold. She knew now this could be the end. Her eyes were heavy, her body limp, and her mind empty.

She dropped to her knees on the cold snow, disoriented. The creature had let go, and jumped back, closer to the tree.

A mage came out of nowhere and stood between them, feet wide and commanding as they manipulated the air, creating a barrier of air between the creature and them.

The creature hissed, pacing from side to side, trying to find a way through the barrier.

With precise, deliberate movements, the mage traced a pattern in the air before lifting their palm. In response, iron flakes emerged from the ground. As they floated between them, the mage snapped their fingers, causing them to spark with a bright white glow.

The creature watched as the mage put down the barrier with one hand and pushed the iron flakes towards it with the other. The creature screeched in pain, a scream of death. It turned to the Great Ash and dove into its roots, vanishing from sight.

The mage turned to Aria, lowered to her level and helped her up from the ground.

'Askafroa,' she said. 'Dreadful creatures.'

Aria held on to the mage's hand, not trusting her legs would hold her. She looked up at the stranger. Professor Kiran stood before her, eyebrows drawn together.

Why was she here?

Professor Kiran took a knife from her pocket and held out

her hand.

'I need a locket of your hair to do an offering. It will help you recover faster.'

Aria obliged. She took her hair from under the hood and Professor Kiran cut it. She carefully placed it at the base of the Great Ash and said a few words, which Aria struggled to understand. Professor Kiran picked something from the floor and placed it in her pocket, then wrapped one arm around Aria to hold her steady.

'Let's get you back to your dormitory. You need to rest.'

'I am going to be okay?'

'I believe so. Askafroa is a tree spirit tied to the oldest ash trees; by showing respect, they tend to lift the curse.'

'Curse?'

'They attack when the ash is under threat, and you being near it, it saw you as the attacker.'

Aria didn't have much energy to reply. She let herself be guided to the empty Fossheim dormitory, welcomed by the warmth of the fireplace.

She sat on an armchair in Fossheim's common room, breathing fast and shallow, while Professor Kiran went through a door to the small kitchen. She came back with a mug with hot water, took a piece of wood from her pocket, conjured fire and burned it into ash. She put the ashes inside the mug.

'Here,' she said, hand stretched. 'Drink it like tea. This will heal you by tomorrow.'

'Thank you,' Aria managed to say.

'And please, don't start wandering into the forests alone. It's reckless behaviour, and you clearly cannot handle the danger.'

'I... Sorry, Professor.'

'Drink that and go to bed. I'll have to report this to the

Headmaster.'

Professor Kiran left without another word, leaving Aria alone with a conscience that prickled uncomfortably. What would Professor Halvard say when he found out? Imagining it made her temples ache.

Exhausted, Aria walked into her room on autopilot, put on her pyjamas, and stood before her bed, guided there by an unseen hand. The room was warm, a soft cocoon in contrast to the cold, snowy night outside. She slid beneath the covers, weak and sick, picked up the mug from the side table and drank the ash tea.

Aria gagged. 'Absolutely disgusting,' she mumbled.

The laughter from earlier belonged to another world now, replaced by the haunting image of the Askafroa staring at her with dead eyes. Astrid's and Professor Halvard's words looped in her mind, pulling her thoughts back to the tremors and the wolf's yellow gaze.

CHAPTER SEVENTEEN

The Fox

Sleep was fragmented and restless, with dreams of shifting shadows and forests riddled with strange creatures. Angry giants loomed in the distance, their footsteps shaking the ground. Aria twisted and turned all night, trying to escape them.

She jolted awake, gasping for air, cold sweat soaking her bed. The faint light of the full moon peeked through the curtains, its serenity amplifying the turmoil inside her. She sat up, hugging her blanket as she looked out the window.

With the pain and fever gone, Aria felt stronger now. The realisation she could have died yesterday if not for Professor Kiran sent a shudder through her. But why was she there? Did Professor Kiran follow her? If so, why? Did she suspect Aria had seen her in the Yule Market? In which case, why save her from death, instead of letting her be silenced forever?

Aria slid out of bed and put on her slippers and a woollen sweater.

'Oh sure, pretend I'm not even here! I'm just a MERE PLANT after all! Not like I've been photosynthesising my heart out ALL NIGHT!'

Exhausted from having to deal with this loose-lipped

homework, Aria glanced at the plant, its mouth somewhere inside the trumpet flower, which amplified its voice even louder. 'It's three in the morning. You're not photosynthesising anything.' She made a mental note for her journal: *drama queen thinks photosynthesis works at night.*

'The AUDACITY! The SLANDER! I'll have you know moonlight is PERFECTLY adequate for my needs!'

'Sure, it is,' Aria mumbled as she walked towards the door. She needed tea, or hot chocolate, or literally anything that would get rid of the dry mouth. 'Just... try not to wake up the entire Academy with your theatrical crisis while I'm gone?'

'ABANDONED in my hour of need! And after I noticed you tossing and turning all night! The TRAGEDY of it all!'

Aria paused at the door. 'Tell you what,' she said, 'I'll bring back some water with a drop of honey in it. You can tell me all about your dramatic suffering then.'

The Moonflower's leaves perked up immediately. 'Well... I *suppose* that would be acceptable. Though I prefer lavender honey. The regular kind makes my leaves itch. NOT that anyone ever asks about my preferences...'

'Noted.'

Aria opened her door, only to see Carolina hurrying past in the corridor, still dressed in her elegant red top. Odd for three in the morning.

'Oh, Aria.' Carolina paused, startled. 'Couldn't sleep?'

'No,' Aria said. 'I just need some water.'

Carolina nodded. 'Same here. I've been restless all night.' She hesitated, and added quietly, 'Papa used to make hot chocolate with cinnamon when I couldn't sleep. This time of year... I miss him more.'

'I'm sorry,' Aria said softly, not sure what else to say.

'Just memories, you know?' Carolina's fingers tapped lightly against her leg. 'Anyway, I should get some sleep. See you tomorrow.' She gave a quick smile and walked off down the corridor.

Aria frowned. Restless from the feast? Maybe. But an uneasiness pressed on her shoulders. Was there more to her words? Did she know about the Great Ash?

The days following the winter solstice blended into a tapestry of calmness and peacefulness, punctuated by the melodramatic moonflower's daily theatrics. The plant would wail, its dramatic soliloquies a constant backdrop to Aria's winter break. Each day, the plant found new ways to lament its existence, fainting dramatically at temperature shifts and composing tragic odes to the cloudy winter days. The latest was the sun. 'The sun ABANDONS us!'

Christmas morning arrived with a peculiar assortment of presents on her bedside table. An unexpected surprise to wake up to, one that she didn't even know was possible, for she would have heard if someone had come into the room.

At its centre was a miniature Christmas tree, clearly Taye's creation. Traditional ornaments were replaced by an eclectic mix of protective runes carved on wood hanging from the pine branches – much like the ones from the Yule Ash in Eldviken. At its base, tiny goats made of straw, no bigger than chess pieces, pirouetted around the trunk with an un-goatlike grace.

One of them paused in its dance to head-butt her finger affectionately, while another posed dramatically, clearly waiting for applause.

Aria clapped and the entire herd launched into what had to be their grand finale, complete with miniature lighting effects.

She laughed. It was a perfect Norse twist to a Christmas tradition.

The colour-changing package beside the tree revealed a wooden case with five glass cylinders of colourful dust floating inside them, embodying the delicacy of exotic specimens. Aria recognised them immediately – Echodusts of Professor Halvard's expeditions, which Taye mentioned not once but ten times. She still didn't know how they worked but was looking forward to getting a demonstration.

The first glowed with gentle waves of green and blue, which was about the great northern dragons in their natural habitat. Another shimmered with gold and shadow, documenting the lives of the hidden folk. The largest cylinder contained a dust of deep ocean colours, recording Halvard's legendary expedition to the underwater cities of the merfolk. Each cylinder was labelled in Taye's careful calligraphy: "Halvard's Dragon Sanctuaries", "Secrets of the Hidden Folk", "Depths of the Merfolk Realm". Aria was delighted to get a glimpse of a world she had never experienced, yet she belonged to.

Finn's package was wrapped with brown paper and a sprig of dried rowan berries tucked into a fold. It was a leather satchel, protective runes woven in its surface, which contained its own patch of night sky inside. A note explained it was bottomless, enchanted to clean itself and adapt to whatever she needed to carry. She could place anything inside, and with a single thought, it would appear in her hand. Just the sort of practical magic she'd expect from Finn.

The new satchel made her glance at her battered beige backpack in the corner; a second-hand thing from the children's home. Once, letting it go would have felt like severing her last tie to England. Now, watching the starlight shimmer in her new bag's depths, she found she was ready to pack away that part of her past.

She sat cross-legged on her bed, taking it in, when a mist gathered on Suraya's empty bed. It coalesced into a familiar shape: a fox, made of a silver substance, thicker than a ghost but less solid than anything living. Amber eyes watched her, deep wisdom emanating from it.

It spoke.

'You must come,' the Fox said, voice like frost forming on glass.

'I'm sorry, what?' Aria asked, acutely aware she was having a conversation with a creature that shouldn't exist.

'The forest is unbalanced,' it said simply.

'I know, but what has that got to do with me?'

'You've been summoned. I've been asked to bring you to them.'

'To whom? If this is a trick to take me back to the Askafroa, you are barking at the wrong tree, my friend,' she said, wary of the fact she was arguing with a misty being. It should have felt impossible, but after everything she'd seen, part of her wasn't even surprised. Of course this would be happening.

'The Ash spirit has made its peace with you. She understands now you are not the cause for the sickness of the Great Ash.'

'Well, thank you for that. She should have asked instead of trying to murder me.'

'Askafroa are not known for being the communicative types,' the Fox said. It jumped off the bed, its form shimmering like moonlight on snow. 'For now, Aria Renwood, you must follow me. The ancient ones wait.' Without a noise, it walked out from the room through the closed door.

Aria pursed her lips. Should she follow the Fox?

Her brain screamed at her to stay put, while her heart recognised an odd kinship with the creature. She shrugged and put on her cloak, boots, thick blue woollen beanie, and her new satchel, in case there was anything interesting to bring back.

She followed the Fox down the stairs, through the corridors, and into the winter grounds outside, all the while watching its fur move in impossible ways – rippling, liquid silver, shifting between solid and spectral.

What *was* this creature?

The first rays of sun illuminated the horizon, a white blanket glittering in the light. Aria pulled up her cloak closer, feeling the burn on her cheeks from the crisp air. The silence was deafening, broken only by the soft crunch of her boots on the fresh snow.

The Fox ran with ease without leaving footprints, heading towards the North Forest. Aria struggled to keep up, walking through the knee-high snow, her cloak brushing over it. Not the exercise she was expecting to do on Christmas morning.

They walked deeper into the North Forest, the cold air numbing her face. She had not been this deep in the North Forest. It was dense, the pine trees large, and the underbrush covered in a white rug. The little light that pierced through the canopy of an otherwise dark forest.

A growl. It came from up ahead, vibrating every cell in her body.

A disembodied growl, for Aria could not find its source.

The Fox looked up at her. 'We're close.'

Aria regretted this already.

The growl rumbled through the air again, and Aria hugged herself tight. What on earth was she doing? Walking into the forest, alone, following a silver translucent being she just encountered, in the dead of winter. Was this the vaesen awaking?

She should be petrified, yet somehow the forest felt... right?

The Fox stopped, causing Aria to nearly step on it. It hovered more than it sat, neither fully solid nor completely transparent.

Three enormous figures she'd mistaken for boulders slowly turned and faced her. Sunlight caught their moss-covered shoulders, dusted with snowflakes, while their skin bore the roughness of bark and the coldness of stone.

Her mouth fell open.

Giants. Real giants.

Adrenaline rushed through her body, ready to fight or flee. Though something about these beings pulled at her heart, the same way she felt when she encountered the barkfox and raven. It was a connection older than her.

'Hearken,' the smallest giant said, its voice like stones grinding beneath glacial ice. 'The balance frays.'

Silence. A breath.

'Magic wanes,' the middle giant said, with the edge of thunder. 'Torn. Extracted. Roots are forgetting their song.'

The largest giant leant down, moving with the slow grace of a continental drift. Its frost-blue eyes held winters of wisdom, locking on Aria with curiosity. 'Not power,' it spoke, each word weighted, 'but memory awakens.'

'I don't—' Aria began, but the giants' collective gaze silenced her – a look of unspoken wounds and unhealed violations.

'Child of whispers,' the smallest said, 'your strength lies where you cannot see. Listening is the first song. Listening breaks no bones. It is the oldest weaving, the magic that knits what has been broken. In silence, worlds are born.'

The middle giant's voice rolled with the power of distant storm, tinted with sorrow slicing through like a sharpened stone. 'The earth remembers what humanity's heart has turned away from. And, in that turning, magic withered, and the river strangled from its source.'

'Attend the breath of being,' the largest added. 'Hearken the tree's lament. Your magic flows not from command but from deep knowing. Guard against the ravaging that would leach the world's sacred breath.'

Their forms began to shimmer, becoming more landscape

than being.

'Wait!' Aria reached out, desperate to understand more. 'What am I supposed to do?'

The smallest giant produced a smile that was ancient, beyond time, sharp with purpose. 'Listen,' it said. 'Only listen.'

'The forest unfolds its secrets,' the middle giant added, 'should your spirit remain open to its whispers.'

Aria watched as the giants dissolved into the forest's texture, their forms blending into bark and shadow, no longer creatures, but a living breath of the landscape itself. She could not say if they had vanished or simply become invisible, only that the air itself was transformed.

Aria stood still, her mind spinning. *What just happened?* she thought. Her breath caught in her throat as she pressed her hand on her chest, where her pendant was hidden under layers of clothing. A wave of panic mixed with a strange, unexpected excitement bubbled up inside her.

The Fox brushed against her leg, now solid enough to touch.

'They speak in a language older than words,' the Fox said. 'A language of water and fire.'

'What do they want from me?'

The Fox's amber eyes flickered with an unearthly light. 'Not want. Recognise. You are a bridge where others only see a boundary. They are the memory-keepers of the world's deepest rhythms. When magic fractures, when the sacred connections between earth and spirit grow thin, they awaken in this realm.'

'Will I see them again?'

'If need be. For now, remember what they told you. Remember when you listened with more than your ears.'

Aria followed the Fox back to the edge of the forest, the sun now fully exposing the winter landscape. She welcomed the warmth on her face.

'Thank you,' Aria said. 'For bringing me to them.'

'The giants do not choose their witnesses lightly,' the Fox said. 'This was as much your beginning as their examination.'

'Examination? What are they testing me for?'

'Some truths must reveal themselves at the right moment.'

Aria shifted on the spot.

The Fox stepped closer. 'You're not alone. We sylvandir walk with mages by ancient promise,' the Fox continued. 'Our spirits are bound; it's how we link mages to nature's deepest power.'

The Fox's presence became less an outside force and more an extension of herself. A companion. A guide. Deep inside her, a window she didn't know existed opened, letting in a draft of ancient, wild air.

And for the first time, Aria understood listening wasn't just about hearing. It was about becoming.

The Fox dissolved into a mist, threads of silver light whispering softly.

The winter silence hummed around her with new awareness, and deep underneath her feet, vibrations announced the giants moving within the forest.

CHAPTER EIGHTEEN

Mímir's Vault

'A sylvandir?' Taye practically bounced in his seat, his curls bobbing lively. 'Incredible! I can't wait to meet mine! I bet it's a Bear! No! A Wolf! My aunt's sylvandir is a Wolverine. She named it Linda! The Wolverine is not too happy with its name, though.'

'What exactly is a sylvandir?' Aria asked, scratching her head.

She had told Taye and Finn about everything that had happened over the winter break. They sat by the fireplace in the Gathering Room downstairs, unusually quiet for this time of day. The flames shifted colours with each turn of her tale, while snowflakes gently tapped on the window.

'They're primordial beings,' Finn said, leaning in, his green eyes softening. 'They're nature spirits that guide us through the deeper currents of magic. Every mage has one, but they only appear when needed the most – during a magic-heavy ritual or a life-threatening situation. Though, in your case, it was connected to a message from mystical beings. Once you connect with your sylvandir, you're connected for life.'

'I think I've seen them before, though. Misty clouds in the forest?'

'They are intensely curious and attracted by the magic in our blood. I've seen them, too, never as many as during the Wild Claiming. Now that was fascinating!'

'Yes, yes, yes, but GIANTS?' Taye interrupted, sitting on the edge of his seat, waving his arms on each syllable. 'Real, actual giants! Why does all the good stuff happen when I'm away?' He slumped on the sofa with an exaggerated sigh.

Finn sat back, his fingers tracing runes carved into his chair's armrest. He tilted his head thoughtfully, causing his blond soft curls to fall over his fair skin. 'With the Great Ash dying, the Askafroa, and surely other vaesens, and now giants, are literally waking up... Your magic is part of a larger pattern we're only beginning to understand.'

'Right. No pressure or anything,' Aria said, her voice dripping with sarcasm. 'Just another Tuesday. Wake up, have breakfast, meet ancient giants to save a collapsing ecomagisystem, maybe grab a cup of tea afterwards.'

'Hm, he's got a point, though,' Taye said, sitting up. He tapped his fingers on his lips, his golden rings clinking against each other. 'It's too much of a coincidence. But we'll figure it all out!' he added with a glint in his eyes. 'I can promise you that.'

The words had barely left his mouth when a sharp commotion erupted in the Front Hall. Voices rose and fell in urgent tones, cutting through the usual holiday quiet.

'It's been broken into, Headmaster!' a voice shouted, raw with alarm. 'During the winter break. The lock to Mímir's Vault has been tampered with!'

'Dear, dear,' Professor Halvard said, his voice measured. 'This is most concerning. Would you show me, Magnus?'

Aria turned to Taye and Finn, who read her mind. Along with the others in the Gathering Room, they hurried out the door into the Front Hall, where they were faced with a crowd.

Professor Halvard walked up the Grand Staircase beside librarian Magnus Nordfell, whose hoverchair rose with ease up the stairs, lifted by invisible hands.

The crowd followed, and so did they.

A ring of students surrounded the outside the entrance of the Mímir's Vault when they arrived, whispering to one another. The circular lock on the Vault's open doors had its delicate runic channels scorched black in places, their usual silver sheen disrupted by magical burns. Small shards of glass glittered on the floor in front of it.

The librarian positioned himself beside the massive doors, cleaning his red-framed glasses, his mouth tightened into a thin line of disapproval. He had long, flowing hair past his shoulders, brown with subtle ash-blond highlights. Even though his hair looked sun-kissed, his skin was pale from hours inside organising books. His strong jawline emphasised the severity of his frown.

'As you can see, Headmaster, someone tried to force a counterfeit key,' he said, turning his hair to the other side. 'But the door rejected it' – he guided his hoverchair closer to the lock and traced the scorched runes around the lock with his finger, nail painted black – 'spectacularly, judging by broken pieces of glass. The magical backlash should have been enough to knock any thief unconscious. Yet, they still managed to resort to...' – he gestured to a burn mark that cut through the ancient runes – '...more direct methods.'

When he reached out to touch one of the carved ravens flanking the open door, his hand trembled slightly. The birds carved in the door, normally alert and watchful, remained motionless under his touch, their eyes dull as ordinary stone. 'They've bound the guardians into dormancy. This was no amateur break-in, Headmaster. Whoever did this understood our protections intimately.'

'Most worrying, Magnus... Most worrying, indeed,' Professor Halvard said, stroking his white beard. The quietness of his voice made several students step back instinctively. 'Do you know what book has been taken?'

'I'll determine it now.'

Magnus placed his newly cleaned glasses back on with practised precision. He took out his wand, black and shiny, and traced an intricate pattern in the air, muttering under his breath. Golden threads weaved through bookshelves beyond the door.

'The perpetrator left magical residue all over my classification system – muddy footprints on freshly polished floors, if you will.' He clicked his tongue in disapproval, though his hazel eyes sparked with the thrill of the puzzle. 'Section 14-B, Primordial Currents. Specifically...' He made his way towards the empty shelf space inside the vault, his wand lingering over the shelf, reading invisible braille with his fingers.

His confident expression faltered. 'That's strange,' he said as the threads dissolved into smoke. 'The tracking charm. It's been...' He paused. 'It's as if someone erased it.'

'Remarkable,' Professor Halvard said. 'In all my years here, I've never seen anyone counter your security measures. Most concerning.'

'This will require a more thorough investigation than I anticipated.'

'A situation of this magnitude requires our utmost attention. Please proceed.'

A glimmer of satisfaction broke through the librarian's concern.

Professor Halvard turned to the gathered students, acknowledging their presence at last. His blue eyes scanned the group. When he spoke, his voice carried that rare note of disappointment that would make even the most hardcore troublemakers feel ashamed.

'Stealing is punishable by expulsion. It is something we simply cannot tolerate at this Academy,' he said, his eyes hardening. 'However, if the book is returned by the end of the day – anonymously – we shall let the matter rest.'

He glanced at Magnus, who was now meticulously reorganising already-perfect rows of books. 'Otherwise, I have complete confidence Mr Nordfell will uncover the truth.'

The subtle emphasis on "truth" made the librarian's hand pause mid-motion. His posture straightened with the reverence of a scholar receiving rare praise. He brushed the strand of hair that fell on his forehead, tucking it behind his ear.

Professor Halvard gave the librarian a nod and made his way through the group of students, who instantly moved to make way. A heavy silence followed Professor Halvard's footsteps, and once he was out of sight, the chatter filled the library.

Magnus shushed them away and retired to his desk by the entrance of the library, rifling through his catalogue with utmost urgency, the pages rustling loudly.

'Wow,' Taye whispered once the library was deserted. 'I've literally seen Halvard coo at angry dragons, but this? Disappointment? Terrifying.'

'These burn patterns. It had to be a wizard,' Finn said, crunching by the lock with keen curiosity.

'How do you know?' Aria asked, joining him at the door.

'Look at the lock,' Finn said. 'See those little scorch marks with a tiny lightning bolt pattern? That only happens when a wand's magic hits ward-runes. I read it in a book once, about the differences between spell impact patterns.' He traced the edge of one particularly dark burn. 'A mage would manipulate the metal itself, which leaves warping marks. But these are classic wand signatures.'

Aria squinted. Indeed, there were faint marks around the keyhole, barely visible unless you knew what to look for.

'But Professor Kiran is a mage,' Aria said.

Taye and Finn stared at her with total surprise written on their faces.

'I saw her in the Yule Market, talking to someone,' she continued flustered, realising she forgot to mention it to them. 'They exchanged something round. They said something along the lines of hurrying up, but I couldn't hear much. Maybe it was the counterfeit key?'

Taye's eyes lit up. 'Oh! What if she's part of a secret protection society? Underground resistance fighters!' His enthusiasm was infectious, but Aria clenched her fists in rising frustration. Why did everyone always assume the best?

'Professor Kiran has been working on figuring out what's causing the tremors,' Finn said. 'It could be related to that?'

Aria crossed her arms, her eyebrows coming together with anger. The evidence was there, if they'd just look at it objectively.

'Though, the secrecy is weird, I'll give you that,' Finn added rapidly.

'Of course!' Taye leant in, speaking faster. 'She's probably trying to protect the Academy!'

'I'm keeping her on my list,' Aria said firmly. 'Even if I'm the only one who does.'

Taye studied her for a moment. 'You know what? That's perfect. We're a real detective squad now – everyone bringing their own theories to the table.'

'Good, thanks,' she said, feeling some of the tension leave her shoulders.

'We have History in five minutes,' Finn said, eyeing the

wall's clock, which wagged its minute hand disapprovingly at them.

'I will not have Professor Thistlecroft shame me in front of the class again!' Taye said, striding towards the door.

Through the corridor, Finn walked beside Aria, opening and closing his mouth several times with the energy of a nervous fish.

'Oh, just tell me,' Aria said.

'There's this meditation group in Lundgard,' Finn said, quickly passing his hand through his curls. 'We meet in the East Garden. It's helped me with focus, especially now with the daily tremors. I thought it might help you connect with your magic more easily, maybe?'

'Finn...'

'I just thought, with everything happening, your magic bursting through you, the Askafroa and giants...' He trailed off, looking so genuinely concerned Aria's annoyance eased a little.

'Meditation, though?' Aria stopped walking, the sunlight from the window creating a spotlight on her. 'Seriously? I don't need to sit around humming. I need to figure out how to control it.'

'It's not about humming,' Finn said. 'It's about learning to be still, be with yourself. You did with the tree before, but this time, it's intentional.'

'That was different. It just... happened. I can't just make myself connect that way.'

'Maybe that's why it would help. You already have this natural ability to sense things others miss. The meditation group works with that kind of sensitivity. Not forcing it, just... understanding it better.'

'You're not letting this go, are you?' Aria asked with a mix of resignation and grudging curiosity. As much as she hated to admit it, learning to control whatever had happened with the tree during the Magical Ecology lesson might be useful. Especially now, when her magic was chaotic and everything hinted at danger unfolding.

'Tomorrow morning, before breakfast,' Finn said.

'*Before* breakfast?' Aria groaned. 'You're really not selling this, you know.'

'Trust me.'

'Famous last words.'

'What's tomorrow morning?' Taye turned back, realising they had stopped walking.

'Meditation,' Finn said.

'Oh! Can I come? I've been dying to try it out!' His face lit up with sudden inspiration. 'We could make it a whole thing—'

'We're going to be late,' Aria cut him off, half smiling under her breath. Having friends who cared this much was both wonderful and exhausting.

CHAPTER NINETEEN

Snowdrops

Aria suppressed another yawn as she walked down to the East Garden. Her brain was fuzzy and she regretted agreeing to meditation. Taye was instead wide alert, walking with rhythm beside her.

'Come on, it's not even that early!' he said. 'I've woken up much earlier to watch the arrival of the red-breasted swifts in spring.' He paused and closed his eyes, as if devouring a tasty memory. 'You should have seen it. Their song is visible through red vibrations in the air that can only be seen in the dark. It's the most mesmerising thing you will ever witness!'

'Bet it is, but I refuse to wake up this early again.'

The garden was enclosed by an invisible dome, a strange sight of greenery surrounded by the frozen landscape beyond. The sun had not risen yet, but Aria was used to that by now, for the night stretched into morning during the winter. Instead, there was a ball of light floating above, emanating the warmth of a summer's day. Her mood improved slightly.

In its centre was a semicircle of cushions, some occupied by students sitting with their legs crossed, eyes closed. They weren't only Lundgard students, but she didn't know any of them.

'Let's go over there,' Finn whispered behind them.

They sat on some cushions beside a young birch tree, their backs to the Ancient Forest, trying to copy the others.

Tove, the fifth-year student with short platinum hair Aria had met at the Yule Feast, settled on a cushion facing them. A Norwegian Forest cat curled up beside her on the folds of her deep green robes, its thick fur coat gleaming and its bushy tail flicking lazily up and down. Her familiar, Aria assumed.

'Welcome, everyone,' she said, her voice soft as the morning mist. 'I'm Tove Bjørnstad and I will be guiding your meditation today. I see we have some new faces. Have you meditated before?'

'No, but I am eager to learn!' Taye said a little too loudly.

Aria just shook her head in silence, fighting another yawn, her hand covering her mouth.

'Perfect.' Tove smiled wide, her blue eyes looking around the room. 'Sometimes it's better to come with a fresh mind, no expectations. Though, perhaps a little more awake,' she added with amusement, causing others to giggle. Aria shifted uncomfortably.

Tove closed her eyes. 'Let's begin with relaxing our bodies.' Tove's gentle voice guided them. 'Close your eyes. Feel the weight of your body sinking into the cushion.'

Aria closed her eyes. The soft cushion grounded her body, but her mind wandered: the memory of giants emerging from mist; Kaija's smirk in class; the purple light from the Harvest Feast.

She shook her head and adjusted her position.

'Now, focus on your feet... your legs... letting all tension wash away...'

The silver flowing body of the Fox. The golden streaks of the birch tree that spoke to her. Esmeralda, Carolina's golden eagle, watching her with judging eyes.

'Release the tension on your shoulders...'

Aria's shoulders hunched up to her ears. She released them.

'Soften your jaw...'

Her teeth were clenched so tight, her face hurt. She tried to relax, but her mind flashed to the wolf in her dream, its massive jaws, the outstretched hand.

'Now, imagine you're holding a seed of light in your hands. Feel its warmth. Watch it grow as you inhale. Hold...' She paused for a couple of seconds. 'And release.'

Aria peeked one eye open. Tove was the essence of peace, smiling softly, as did everyone else in the garden. How? Aria closed her eyes shut, shifting on her cushion to find a better position, but her legs were sore.

'The light grows branches,' Tove continued. 'Spreading down through your arms, into your chest. Feel the light spread through your body, connecting you to the earth below, roots deepening into the Earth...'

Aria was stiff, awkward, and increasingly frustrated. Her mind raced, refusing to settle. She tried to force herself to focus but only made it worse. Time stretched, honey-slow, each minute an eternity of failing to do what seemed to come so easily to everyone else. When would this ever end?

'Let the light fade naturally.' Tove's voice sounded distant. 'Slowly return to your body... Whenever you're ready, open your eyes.'

Shoulders slumping, Aria opened her eyes. Others stretched, their faces peaceful. Taye sat there for a little longer, eyes closed.

'What did you think?' Finn whispered next to her.

'It didn't work,' Aria said. 'I couldn't reach that calm state. My mind just wouldn't—' She stopped. In her frustration, she clenched her fist and hit the grass.

Where her fist touched, tiny white flowers sprouted.

Did I do that? Aria thought, staring at the snowdrops.

'Maybe you weren't distracted after all,' Finn said, following her gaze. 'Maybe your mind needed to reorganise your thoughts.'

The snowdrops swayed lightly. Tiny flowers she created without trying, yet another reminder of how her magic refused to behave, how it burst out in ways she couldn't control.

'I need to go,' she said, gathering her things. 'Elementals.' She didn't want to hear any more about centres or light or relaxation. Her mind was loud enough.

'Aria—' Finn started, but she was already walking away.

Students flowed into the packed corridors, and Aria was grateful for the noise and bustle that drowned her thoughts. Each student at Oakspire was so normal, hurrying to class with their books and wands, complaining about homework, planning weekend trips to Eldviken. None of them felt magic erupting from them in ways they couldn't control. None of them felt the tremors in their bones. None of them had apocalyptic dreams.

Professor Kiran lounged against her desk in the empty Elementals classroom with her usual casual grace, reading a book open in her hand. Aria hesitated at the door. *Bet it's something evil,* she thought wryly.

Aria took a deep breath and stepped inside. Moving as quiet as a mouse, she slipped into her seat by the window, hoping to avoid notice. Whether Professor Kiran saw her or not, she gave no indication, her gaze never lifting from the book. Aria was content with that. No words exchanged meant no unwanted attention.

She turned to the window, where sunlight gleamed over the frozen landscape. The blue sky stretched endlessly, and the low winter sun bathed the horizon with light.

As the classroom filled, the chatter of Kaija, Victoria, and

Inessa floated through the air. Taye and Finn followed them in.

'Look at her, trying meditation now,' Victoria's crisp voice carried a touch of mockery. 'Is nothing sacred in the East Garden? To have certain individuals of such ilk partake in an ancient custom.' She gave Aria a pointed look, side of her lip up with disgust.

Kaija sighed. 'Just once, I would want to see people focusing on the actual problem instead of jumping on trends. They wouldn't understand meditation's purpose, anyway. They'll probably say they "felt magic" and leave it at that.'

Inessa snorted as they sat on their seats.

Finn gave Aria a small, sympathetic shrug, as he settled on his seat, while Taye rolled his eyes at Kaija and Victoria.

Professor Kiran pushed off her desk, snapping the book shut. 'Today we're working with earth,' she announced, her voice cutting through the chatter. 'Raw earth magic – the kind that built mountains and carved valleys,' she continued, her gaze sweeping the room before lingering on Aria, which made her chest tighten as though she'd been singled out.

'Some of you might find it resistant,' Professor Kiran added. 'Others will discover it's been waiting for them all along.'

Professor Kiran picked up a smooth river stone, rolling it between her fingers with practised ease. 'Watch,' she said, her voice dropping to that compelling tone that always made the room lean forward.

The stone rippled in her palm, reshaping itself fluidly before settling back into its original form. 'Earth doesn't resist change and it remembers every shape it's ever been.'

Taye immediately grabbed his stone. 'Oh, this is going to be epic! I mean, how hard can it be to – oh!' His stone remained a stone, earning a few giggles from nearby classmates.

'Less drama, more focus, Mr Lundvik,' Professor Kiran

called out.

Professor Kiran pointed at the words on the blackboard behind her. 'Wizards, use your wands and say *umskapa*.'

Kaija raised her silver wand, tracing a pattern above her stone. '*Umskapa*,' she whispered. The stone responded instantly, reshaping itself with mathematical precision.

Aria picked up her stone, her brow furrowed in concentration. She tried to sense the earth's energy, to coax it into movement. But her thoughts rebelled. *Rich, coming from Kiran,* she mused bitterly. *Talking about earth magic when the earth is literally dying.*

'Remember.' Professor Kiran's voice carried across the room. 'Earth energy is about foundation and stability.'

Sure, it is, you would know. Aria's frustration bubbled over, and in response, the plant on the windowsill came to life. Its vines shot upward, spiralling around the window frame as new leaves unfurled in rapid succession. Delicate red flowers bloomed and scattered their petals across her desk, while the main stem curved near her, ready to strike.

Finn's eyes widened as he witnessed the plant's explosive growth, a flicker of both wonder and unease crossed his face. The plant was reacting to her emotions – not just growing, but almost... guarding her.

'Focus, Miss Renwood.' Professor Kiran's voice was closer now. She stood over their desk, her presence electric. 'The stone. Not the...' – she gestured vaguely at the increasingly agitated plant – 'everything else.'

Aria didn't look up. She ground her teeth and squeezed the stone harder. Why couldn't she just do this one thing normally? The pressure continued building inside her, and her stone sprouted moss, tiny green tendrils weaving across its surface in living lace.

'Well,' Professor Kiran said, examining Aria's moss-covered

stone. 'Life from stone. Remarkable as it is, you need to learn the formal techniques. Otherwise...' She paused, studying Aria with intensity. 'Stay after class, Miss Renwood. I think it's time we discussed your unique talents.'

Excuse me? Something in Professor Kiran's voice made Aria's stomach clench. Even the moss on her stone shrank away a little from Professor Kiran's touch, surely sensing what Aria already knew.

After the class ended, the first-years packed their books and left. Taye hesitated by the door, but Aria gave him a small nod. 'Don't worry. I'll catch up.'

The classroom was colder with just the two of them. Professor Kiran leant on the desk in front of her.

'Your connection to nature is raw,' Professor Kiran said, examining the moss-covered stone. 'Untamed, even.' She set the stone down carefully. 'I could help you understand it better. Train you properly, outside of class constraints.'

Aria's heart pounded. The plants along the windowsill straightened themselves up. 'Thank you, Professor, but I'm fine with regular classes.'

'Are you?' Professor Kiran's smile didn't reach her eyes. 'Your magical mishaps do not go unnoticed. Someone with your abilities should learn to control them properly.'

Aria thought of the dying Great Ash, the purple glow, everything wrong with magic. 'I appreciate the offer, but no thank you.'

For a split second, a microexpression flickered across Professor Kiran's face. Was it frustration? Anger? 'Think about it. Power flowing through you needs guidance. The wrong path could be devastating.'

'I'll keep that in mind, thank you.' Aria stood up and backed towards the door. The plants reached for her as she passed, trying to pull her away from the professor. 'But I have to go. I'm already late to Magical Ecology.'

She didn't run from the classroom, but it was close.

In the corridor, she pressed her back against the wooden wall, trying to steady her breathing. She found comfort from her pendant, warm in her palm.

Why would Kiran want to help me? What's in it for her?

Various possibilities crossed her mind to answer her question, but none made sense. Squaring her shoulders, she resumed heading to Magical Ecology class, determined to continue investigating Professor Kiran.

CHAPTER TWENTY

Nightwing

As winter turned to spring, Aria strolled through the Oakspire grounds, soaking in the last rays of sun as it dipped behind the forest. The crisp air was filled with the scent of fresh earth. Crocuses and snowdrops pushed through the soil, adding a splash of colour to the otherwise barren landscape. The sound of birds chirping filled the air with promises of new beginnings.

A sense of hope blossomed within her after months of frustration clouded her mind, suppressed by the winter darkness. The world around her was now awakening after being dormant and she couldn't help but feel a part of it all.

As the sky turned into hues of orange and pink, she ran to keep up with the group of first-year mages who made their way towards the North Forest for their night of fieldwork. Ahead of them, Professor Grünwald's lantern bobbed with the mystery of a ghostly light hovering above them. Excited whispers rippled through the group about what creatures they might encounter.

Within the forest, misty creatures moved between the trees. Was the Fox, the sylvandir bonded with her, among them? She hoped to see it again.

‘I can’t believe we’re finally doing this!’ Taye said, his eyes sparkling with anticipation, twirling with his blue cloak, showing off his outdoor cargo trousers and Nordic jumper underneath. ‘What if we see an echo owl? They’re supposed to be able to sing across time – imagine hearing the same hoot as your ancestor in this same place! Or maybe even an ice vole! My cousin swears she saw one making ice flowers in Jokkmokk last winter! Some sort of mating ritual.’

‘According to Magifauna Monthly,’ Finn said, adjusting his green beanie, ‘ice voles only reveal themselves to people who can stay still for more than thirty seconds. Maybe work on that first.’

‘Oi! Rude! Did you not see me excel in meditation next to you? I am more than capable of being still, thank you very much.’

Aria smiled, her fingers tracing the soft edges of her pendant as the shadows deepened between the rugged pines, their branches casting intricate patterns on the ground from the moonlight above. The magic in the air thickened. Could the giants be around? Watching them?

As they approached their destination, the old pine trees let out creaks to acknowledge their presence. They gathered in the clearing, where snow was still melting on moss. Professor Grünwald gestured for them to settle, the tools in his vest jingled as he did. His grey cloak was pinned on the side, by a golden circular pin.

‘Tonight, we will be observing the luminous salamander,’ Professor Grünwald said. ‘They thrive in the shadows, hidden under dead wood. But remember, young friends, the forest comes alive at night! Keep your senses sharp!’

Taye’s and Finn’s expressions mirrored Aria’s excitement. This was more than just a lesson. It was an adventure, an opportunity to connect with the wild magic of the forest, perhaps even discover more about herself along the way.

The class spread out. Professor Grünwald's lantern multiplied and followed each one of them, casting warm pools of light against the engulfing darkness. The forest came alive with shuffling sounds all around them. In the distance, a great grey owl hooted. Overhead, a flash of vibrant green zipped by. Aria looked up sharply, her heart skipping a beat.

'Did you see that?' she whispered urgently to Taye, who was arching his neck beside her.

'A Nightwing!' he breathed, eyes wide with wonder. 'Some believe they are an omen, to warn us of what's coming.'

She shuddered as her dream of ash emerged in her mind. She pushed the thought away but couldn't shake the feeling there might be some truth in what Taye said.

'But hey,' Taye whispered, 'it's just folklore.'

Beside them, Tenzin stumbled, pressing their hand against the tree trunk to steady themselves. Tenzin hadn't been themselves since they arrived in the forest.

'Are you alright?' she asked them.

'Why? Yes!' Tenzin said, their expression changing rapidly. 'It's thrilling to do fieldwork at night! I just wish it was somewhere where the temporal energy was less wobbly.'

Aria gave them a smile and returned to exploring the forest floor. The luminous salamander was characterised by fluorescent polka dots, so finding it would not be a problem. However, considering how many hours they'd be looking, she wondered if they were here at all.

The forest shifted. The usual night sounds stopped to a halt and an unnatural quiet took over.

'Does anyone else feel...?' Tenzin's voice trailed off as they stumbled again. 'Something's not right.'

As they said it, the lanterns began to change. The warm glow shifted, taking on an unsettling purple tinge. The strange hue spread through the trees, ink in water, transforming the forest into something alien and wrong. The air grew thick, heavy with discordant vibrations she'd felt during the Harvest Feast. Dread took hold.

'Professor?' Fraser called out with uncertainty. His voice muffled, the forest itself absorbing the sound.

Tenzin swayed, their face pallid in the purple light. 'Could you...' they whispered, stretching their arms to Inaiê, who was nearest. But before she could reach them, Tenzin crumpled.

Everyone looked in shock to find Tenzin collapsed on the ground. Professor Grünwald walked to them, but his lanterns flickered once, twice – and died. Darkness rushed in, thick and immediate, swallowing them whole.

Gasps rippled through the forest as students collided against each other in the sudden blackness. The wrongness made Aria's skin crawl. Taye's cold and trembling hand reached for her own. She gripped it tightly, feeling his squeeze in return as shadows pressed in around them, thick and unyielding.

'No need to worry,' came Professor Grünwald's voice, unexpectedly close behind them. Aria flinched, barely holding back a gasp. The professor's hands glowed faintly, casting a warm, wavering light that crept across the trees. The first-years looked at each other, some nervous, others petrified.

The ground trembled, causing everyone to sway, gripping each other's arms for balance.

Professor Grünwald hurried to where Tenzin had fallen and knelt beside them. When his fingers touched their wrist, his face froze and lost colour. The light emanating from his hand flickered and in the next second, he slumped forward, barely catching himself on his hands. The group gasped as darkness closed in again, more suffocating than before.

A dull thump broke the silence, followed by a terrifying

scream echoing in the darkness.

'I think Fraser might have collapsed, too.' Finn's voice broke the silence.

'What in Odin's name is happening?' Taye shouted, more high-pitched than usual.

The energy in the air was erratic; a heartbeat struggling to find its rhythm. Aria pressed her hand to her abdomen to quiet the panic, but the pulsing magic grew louder, more desperate. The forest itself was losing control.

Fire illuminated the forest, conjured by Inaiê's hands. Her dark eyes were wide. 'Gather sticks! We need to keep the light going and help those who've fallen. Hurry!'

Everyone scrambled for anything dry enough to feed the flames. Along the ground, Aria's fingers found a branch. But as Inaiê tried to strengthen the fire she conjured, the flame wavered and died completely.

Another heavy thump followed.

'Inaiê!' Aria's voice cracked through the dark.

'Something's wrong with the magic itself,' Finn murmured beside her. A moment later, he raised his voice. 'Don't use any more magic. It's what's made them collapse!'

'But we need to see!' Aria shouted. 'How else can we help them? How can we even find our way out?'

Specks of silver light appeared around them, illuminating in the distance below the trees, like stars dropped from the sky above. The lights moved towards them without a sound – no crunch of leaves, no snap of twigs – just a glow cutting through the thick dark.

Aria stretched her fingers, tensing her muscles to strike at whatever approached them. But as they all held their breath, she sighed in relief when she recognised a familiar energy. The Fox stepped out of the shadows, its amber eyes meeting hers. In that moment, all her fear melted away.

As she was about to kneel to greet the Fox, other misty creatures emerged from the shadows. First an owl, its wings woven from autumn leaves, silent as it descended from the canopy and landed on a low branch. A stag, whose antlers had a living crown of moss and morning dew, head raised high. One by one, sylvandir stepped forward. Aria counted at least twenty, which rapidly filled the clearing with ethereal light, pushing back the oppressive darkness.

Aria glanced around at her classmates. Every single one of them stood frozen, open-mouthed, caught between awe and terror. The sylvandir moved around them with deliberate grace, forming a perfect circle.

The wild, erratic energy that had been making Aria's teeth ache smoothed. A wave of stillness settled, emanating from the spirits themselves.

A Wolf stepped forward from the circle, larger than any Aria had ever seen. Its fur was a deep blue-black of twilight, with hints of silver smoke. It padded towards Professor Grünwald, moving with the fluency of water. It touched its nose to the professor's chest with the gentleness of an old friend. With deliberate care, it positioned itself over his chest. A soft blue aura pulsed between them, a second heartbeat trying to keep the first one steady.

A Crane with its white feathers twinkling like glitter, its black neck like the night sky, walked with long, measured strides towards Tenzin. It positioned itself next to them, laying its head on their still form. A Jaguarundi emerged next, its coat moving like smoke. It padded slowly and curled itself around Inaiê. Finally, a Squirrel, small but radiant, its tail streaming with light, hopped from a tree down to Fraser. It wrapped around his neck like a living scarf.

Aria didn't dare to breathe as the sylvandir worked their magic. This was nothing she had learned in class. This was older, a lullaby hummed in her bones, familiar and strange all at once.

A cold air brushed against her leg, breaking through Aria's trance. She looked down to find the Fox looking up at her.

'They're keeping them alive,' Fox said.

'Good. Could you get help? We can't carry them out of here alone,' she said. The Fox's ears flicked in agreement and looked up.

A Snowy Owl materialised from the darkness, its glow pure as fresh snow under sunlight. With a single powerful beat of its wings, it shot through the canopy towards the castle, leaving a trail of starlight in its wake.

Aria paced the clearing, her hand fidgeting her pendant. Every few steps, she'd stop to check on each of those that had collapsed, though nothing had changed. The sylvandir remained steadfast in their healing vigil.

She paused by Professor Grünwald and couldn't help but admire the beautiful connection that seemed deep and true, between the mage and his sylvandir. The Wolf had its eyes closed, focused on keeping the professor alive. The magic flowing between them made her heart swell and skin prickle at the back of her neck. What an incredible gift, to be a mage and be bonded with these sylvandir.

Around them, clusters of first-years huddled together, watching over their fallen friends. Silently waiting, hoping.

'I should have noticed something was wrong sooner,' Aria muttered as she sat on a mossy rock.

Beside her, Taye held Tenzin's hand, checking their pulse. 'Why is this happening? I mean, look at them. They were so alive a minute ago and now seem close to dead. Tenzin's my roomie. I can't deal with this!' He rubbed his sleeves over his watery eyes.

'It's not random,' Finn said, sitting on another rock near

them, alert but posture relaxed. 'Look at the sequence. First, Professor Grünwald's light spell failed, then he fell trying to help Tenzin—'

'But Tenzin wasn't casting anything,' Aria interrupted. 'They just... collapsed.' She paused. 'Though they were acting strange since we arrived in the forest, did you notice? They kept stumbling, holding onto trees for dear life.'

'They're a timeweaver,' Taye said. 'They mentioned something about time energy being off here. Maybe that weakened them.'

'That makes sense,' Finn said. 'The corrupted magic would have overwhelmed them faster than the rest of us.' He knelt at Fraser's motionless body. 'Fraser passed out trying to help Professor Grünwald.'

'And Inaiê...' Taye added. 'She went down right after conjuring fire.'

'Exactly,' Finn said. 'There's a pattern here. Something about this particular area is affecting magic. But what?'

Aria didn't know. She closed her eyes for a moment, concentrating on the strange pulse beneath her feet; weaker now, but still there. What could be causing this?

A flash of light burst from the castle's highest tower, brightening the forest like a meteorite streaking towards Earth. Everyone looked up from their silent vigil.

Help was coming.

CHAPTER TWENTY-ONE

Moonhare

'Magical exhaustion, the whole lot,' Aria heard the healer say. 'Their core was completely depleted, as if they had used all their magic. If it wasn't for the sylvandir...' Her voice caught in her throat. 'I don't think they would have survived.'

'Thank you, Sigrid,' Professor Halvard said, his voice low with concern. 'I trust that you have everything you need to help them recover?'

'Yes, Professor,' Sigrid said. 'It will take time. I've called upon their sylvandir to continue anchoring their energy, and I've prepared a tonic of rowan and nettle to replenish what was lost. With rest and care, they'll regain full strength. For now, they mustn't attempt any magic.'

'Very well,' Professor Halvard replied, glancing at Professor Grünwald. The Wolf at his side shifted, stretching before settling back down, its eyes half-closed with his ears alert.

Professor Halvard left the Healing Hall, his heavy boots echoing against the stone floor. Aria sat with Taye beside Inaiê, Tenzin, and Fraser, fighting against the pull of sleep. Returning to the dorms felt wrong. None of those who had been there last night had left for their rooms, all of whom either fell asleep on the empty beds or sat uncomfortably on the available chairs.

Sigrid had reassured them earlier, her tone kind but firm. 'Your presence here is a healing circle. You're grounding them with your care and intention. Your friends are lucky to have you.'

Aria leant her head back, her thoughts drifting. 'Much like the sylvandir,' she mused, her eyelids growing heavy.

Sigrid walked up to Fraser, with serene focus. Her long brown hair went down over her blue robe. Her fingers weaved invisible threads over him, knitting the air itself. She hummed a melody, while a white Raven perched on her shoulder, its feathers glowing strongly in the dim light. It watched her work with an almost otherworldly calm. Fraser's Squirrel, curled near his chest, twitched its tail in time with Sigrid's movements. Its amber eyes, once filled with unease in the clearing, glowed faintly now, reflecting the comfort of her magic.

Dawn crept through the windows of the Healing Hall, the warmth of the sun painting stripes of morning light across rows of white-sheeted beds. The night's chaos was contrasted by the neat medicinal Hall: healing runes glowed along the walls, the sharp scent of juniper and yarrow hung in the air, and a colourful tapestry of Eir – the goddess of healing, according to Taye – covered part of one side of the room.'

Finn slipped quietly into the Hall, dark circles around his eyes. He handed Aria and Taye a cup of tea before slowly sitting on a chair next to them.

'Something's happening outside,' Finn said. 'I saw Astrid on the way here. She said magifauna are gathering. Species that usually avoid each other are huddling together. Like they're trying to keep warm.'

'That's ominous,' Taye said, frowning as he took a sip of tea.

Aria's throat went dry. Of course it wasn't over. Nothing

had been solved. They just managed to survive the night.

She stood, sudden determination replacing her exhaustion.

'I want to see,' she said, her voice steady for the first time since the forest. 'We need to figure this out before more people get hurt.'

As she said it, Aria could see scenes of her devastating dream, which she couldn't ignore any longer, not with her friends lying here because she'd failed to act sooner. It was time to face it head on.

Finn and Taye exchanged a look, then followed her outside without another word.

Aria's skin crawled as they walked down the steps from the Front Hall. The view before them was bewildering. Scattered around the grounds, weak animals were grouped together: shadow lynxes, their fur matted without their blue vibrancy, together with one of their prey, the white-horned deer, its head rested on the lynx's belly, eyes closed. Farther down, by the lake, ducks huddled together with snakes, which was even more disturbing.

'How in Thor's name...?' Taye said as they passed by a group of three echo owls semi-hidden under the shadows of a spruce tree, eyes half shut. 'This is so heartbreaking.'

'It is,' Finn agreed, his expression mournful.

Near the oak tree, a couple of moonhares lay together, their fur uncharacteristically brown and lifeless. Beside them was a brown bear, motionless. An otherwise fierce creature who channelled their spirit to warriors in battle.

Aria approached them carefully, each step calm and determined. Finn and Taye watched from a distance.

She knelt beside the moonhares. Her heart sank. *Are they dead?* The thought terrified her. She placed her hand against the bear's broad head as pure instinct took over. She closed her eyes, took a deep breath, and listened.

Her mind ravelled.

'Magic winter spreads,' a voice of autumn leaves in the wind said in her mind. The brown bear spoke to her. 'Hibernation, but deeper.'

Aria gulped as images flooded her mind: the embers of life dying; rivers of magic crystallising; the darkness of winter, engulfing all.

'Little ones still have fire,' the bear said, its voice weak. 'Keep them alive.' Its consciousness fragmented, like ice sheets breaking in spring.

Aria opened her eyes, stomach turning as she realised they were indeed dying. She couldn't let them die; she had to try something. A tingling sensation formed at her fingertips as she reached for the moonhares, their fur soft and warm to the touch.

She closed her eyes, searching. Nothing. Their minds were silent, but Aria could feel a flicker of hope deep within.

'I can help,' said a voice. Aria opened her eyes to find the Fox fixated on the moonhares beside her. The fine hairs of her skin perked up all over her body, as though the Fox's presence was making magic more accessible.

Grateful, Aria returned her focus, fingers gently brushing the moonhares' soft fur as she thought of healing.

First – nothing. Just hopeful thinking, pretending.

Aria pushed through, and a surge went through her, from the earth, from the Fox, from the brown bear. Her whole body vibrated, warmth spread and radiated from her palms onto the moonhares. Aria's heart accelerated as raw energy flowed through her, connected with every living being, every leaf, every water droplet, every insect.

While it started as warmth, it soon burned. The power was too much. She released her grip and fell backwards, onto the soft ground.

'Aria!' Taye shouted as he and Finn ran to either side of her.

'Are you alright?' Finn held her under the arm to pick her up.

'Did it work?' Aria asked.

'What worked?' Taye asked, looking at the hares.

A soft sigh.

Silver light rippled from nose to tail as the moonhares' colour flooded back into their fur. Their ear tips began to glow with translucent radiance, and slowly, their eyes opened. They rose on unsteady legs and turned to the bear, bowing deep in acknowledgement.

Heart clenched, Aria understood the creature had stopped breathing entirely.

The moonhares bounded and turned to the echo owls under the spruce who were nearby. They circled them, silver light emanating from their fur like a waterfall, before bounding towards the Ancient Forest.

They paused at the edge. One turned back, as if thanking Aria for the gift of life, before disappearing into the Ancient Forest, leaving trails of silver light in their wake.

A hoot made them turn to the three echo owls, who awakened. They stretched their legs, head and wings, shaking out their white feathers, each tipped with a faint, glowing hint of blue.

One of them hooted – a loud, resonant sound that rippled through the grounds. Its head turned in a slow, fluid movement until both eyes locked onto them.

Taye gasped. Aria shifted, uneasy under its gaze, and beside her, Finn stood calmly, watching the echo owls without blinking.

The owls took flight, wings silent, splitting off in different directions and vanished among the trees.

'Echo owls,' Taye finally said. 'I have never... that's just...

and moonhares...' He swallowed. 'Aria,' he said quietly, with a hint of contained excitement. 'Did you just heal them? Like, actually heal them? Those moonhares were practically gone, and now...' He gestured in their direction. 'They're jumping around spreading moon magic through the land.'

'I think I did,' Aria said, still looking at the Ancient Forest, flexing her fingers to relieve the tingling sensation, a residual reminder of what she was capable of. The Fox was gone.

Maybe that's why the brown bear wanted them alive, she thought. Moonhares were surely a keystone species, especially vital now, when magic was running out.

Finn knelt with deliberate care towards the brown bear and pressed a respectful hand on the creature's fur. 'The bear didn't make it,' he said.

'I know.' Aria swallowed hard. She struggled to breathe as the remnants of the bear's words still circled in her mind. 'It told me to save them. It wanted the moonhares to live.'

'An honourable death,' Finn said as he stood up, patting away the dirt from his knees. 'You honoured its choice.'

'The bear still died.' Aria's heart ached for the death of a creature with whom she had a connection on a whole other level. Without taking her eyes from the bear, she was acutely aware of how many others still needed to be saved, animals whose life force was depleted, slipping away just like this one.

'Wait, wait, wait.' Taye straightened. 'The bear communicated with you? Actually shared thoughts?' He ran a hand through his curls, pieces clicking together behind his eyes. 'Of course! It makes perfect sense now!' His voice lowered to a chilling whisper. 'You're a wildkeeper.'

'What do you mean?' Aria turned to him, her mind brought back to reality.

'You know, like Tenzin is a timeweaver. You, my sweet, sweet friend, are a wildkeeper. Connected to the natural world and all its species. My cousin is one, too. You guys are essentially the keepers of balance of the ecosystem. Though I have to say, I don't think my cousin could have healed an animal on the verge of death like that. You're definitely more than just a wildkeeper.'

'But—'

'Hey,' Finn said as he looked around the grounds. 'I think we can discuss mage genetics later and instead try to figure out what is going on. I think these gatherings are showing us a pattern.'

'Should we go back and map them?' Aria asked.

'Actually,' Taye said, 'I need to show you both something. I've been connecting some dots this term. Let's go to my room, I think you will appreciate it.'

'But wait, shouldn't I be healing the others too?' Aria asked, rubbing her palms against her robes.

'Look... magic has limits. It's not an infinite well,' Finn said. 'If you heal all of them... you could be done. My dad once told me about a wildkeeper – same as you – who tried to mend a small forest after a wildfire. He managed it. The village was overjoyed, but he got frail, and when my dad was called to help him...' Finn let out a sigh. 'His life force was depleted. He had nothing else in him.' He looked at her, seriously now. 'You have to leave something for yourself.'

Aria couldn't breathe, a lump taking hold in her throat. Her heart broke with the thought that the creatures scattered around the grounds might die, and there was nothing she could do about it.

She held her pendant and turned back to the castle. 'Let's go. Let's fix it. I cannot take the thought of seeing them all die.'

The walk to Fossheim Tower was tense with unspoken questions. Aria caught Finn looking around with keen eyes at where the clusters of magifauna were positioned, while Taye was sombre, staring down at the floor.

'Don't mind the mess,' Taye said as they entered his room, clothes scattered all over the floor, his bed unmade, and a desk with scattered papers. He took a moment to look at Tenzin's bed, perfectly made, notebooks neatly organised on their desk, and an open wooden box with golden beads necklace by their bedside table. With a sigh, Taye went to his wardrobe and took out a narrow board. With practised ease, he propped it against the wall, unfolding the panels like opening a door to a mystery.

'Welcome to my passion project,' Taye said, smiling wide with pride, though pain lingered in his eyes.

The entire investigation sprawled before them. Aria's dream was painted in the centre: a large wolf with yellow eyes, reddish smog, and a person stretching out their hand. Her shoulders tensed. Taye hadn't just sketched what she'd described. He had captured it exactly, as if he'd seen it himself.

From the dream, there were threads of light connected to sketches, notes and clippings, which floated in mid-air, like a three-dimensional detective's investigation board. Among the clippings was a picture of giants in the forest. Finn's disapproving snort told her exactly what he thought about Taye ripping a page from a library book for that one. The threads also linked to sketches of the Fox and notes about the library break-in.

'You've been tracking everything,' Aria whispered, in awe to see it all organised.

'Do you have parchment?' Finn asked, walking towards Taye's desk.

'Yeah, yeah,' Taye said. 'First drawer.'

Finn took a parchment and sat down. He drew the map of the grounds with utmost precision. He marked the animal gathering points in the park; the moonhares, the echo owls, the ducks. One by one, the map filled up with gatherings, from the lake and the edges of the Ancient Forest to the ones closest to the castle.

'How do I put this on the board?' He ran his hand through his blond hair and got up. 'It will be easier to spot patterns.'

'Frida taught me this trick,' Taye said, picking up the map. 'Hold it where you want it and focus on your intention...' He held the top of the parchment with one hand and made a knot in mid-air with the other, tying an invisible thread. 'You make a knot at the top and trace your finger to where it'll hang on the board.' A faint shimmering thread followed his fingertip as he drew a line through the air. When he reached the board, he pressed his finger to it for a few seconds and let go. The thread held and the map floated, gently bobbing in place.

'There! Done.' He grinned.

'That's pretty cool,' Aria said.

'Ah, wait a second! Let's accentuate the points.' Taye ran to his wardrobe and grabbed a cup filled with brushes of different shapes and sizes. He picked one and opened a tiny pot of red paint, dipping the tip carefully.

'The moonhares by the oak...' he murmured, dotting the map with a precise flick. 'The echo owls under the spruce...'

Another dot bloomed, the red deepening as it dried.

He painted each dot where Finn had indicated the gatherings, which shimmered faintly.

'Let's add the other strange events,' Aria said, taking Taye's brush from his hand. 'The North Forest, where everyone got sick last night; the Mead Hall during the biggest tremor at the Harvest Feast; the Winddrift Field, where Jun fell through the net; and... am I missing anything?'

'The crystalwing,' Finn said. 'Fraser mentioned—'

'Don't remind me of my near-death experience,' Taye groaned. 'The trauma!'

'You weren't going to die from a crystalwing,' Finn said,

rolling his green eyes. 'Fraser said it was mating behaviour, but these dragonflies only mate in spring. Should we count it?'

'Yes,' Aria said. 'Something must be affecting the magifauna's behaviour too. And remember that Magical Ecology lesson in the Ancient Forest? When Okezie's web of energy got all weird?'

'Yes!' Taye exclaimed. 'Let's add that, too.'

The three of them stared at the map. The dots formed a pattern that could be straight lines, but Aria couldn't grasp what it meant.

'Could the animals be gathered in intersections, maybe?' Finn muttered, the chess-player focus in his eyes. 'We're missing something, though. It doesn't tell us where the problem is.'

'Okay,' Taye said, bringing forth his inner detective. 'So, we know the giants and vaesen are waking up. We know there's something wrong with magic, and we know Aria's somehow connected to all of it—'

'We don't know that last part,' Aria interrupted quickly.

'Please.' Taye rolled his eyes. 'Giants spoke to you, you're a wildkeeper, and now ancient magic is going haywire? That's not a coincidence, that's a plot line. Ah wait...'

Taye ran to his bag, pulled out *Codex Naturalis* and sat on his bed. 'I found this in the library the other day. There was something about giants here that was interesting.' He flipped through the pages frantically. 'Here it is: "The wise völva Heidhr once wrote: *Watch the footsteps of the Jötnar*" – that's giants in Old Norse – "*for they are the first to know when magic bleeds. They feel the wound in the world before any other. Where giants tread, magic has gone awry.*"' He looked up at Aria and Finn. 'If the giants are nature's warning system... and they're showing up now...'

'Something – or someone – is disturbing the magical

system,' Finn concluded, staring at the board, looking for answers.

'Can someone manipulate magic leading to such big consequences?' Aria asked.

'Sure they can! Magic is delicate and interconnected. Tip one part too hard, and the whole thing collapses.'

'Wait!' Taye sat up, nearly knocking over his book, and stared at Aria with the most intense expression she'd ever seen on him. 'The wolf!' He smacked his forehead with his palm. 'It's obviously Fenrir! Oh my gods, my grandmother would have me murdered for being this slow to connect the dots! How did I not see it before?'

Both Finn and Aria looked at Taye, puzzled.

'Oh, come on, you never heard of Fenrir? It's connected to chaos and the end of the world. It is said that when the world trembles, it's a sign that Fenrir's bonds are weakening.'

'That doesn't sound good,' Aria said, one eyebrow arched at the wolf drawing, staring at her with yellow eyes. She tasted ash in her mouth. 'Fenrir is causing the tremors?'

'Possibly! But you don't seem to understand. This means Ragnarök – the end of gods and men.' Taye sat on his bed, looking between Aria and Finn with an expression of loss.

'Come on,' Finn said. 'Those are just stories.'

'So were giants, and yet Aria met three,' Taye said, pouting his lips.

'Who never said anything about the end of the world,' Finn said.

The words lingered in the air as they stared at each other. Aria knew her dream was a bad omen, but now it was worse than she had anticipated.

In response, the windows rattled and lamps flickered.

Another tremor shook the ground.

CHAPTER TWENTY-TWO

Stream

The Elementals classroom was quieter than ever, the empty wooden chairs worn by time and use. The vast space suffocating. Over the past few weeks, students and staff had been falling ill, one by one, by an unknown infection. Her friends were still in comas in the Healing Hall, and others were stuck in their dorms, nursing splitting migraines, too weak to sit through a lesson.

As for Aria, she didn't know why she hadn't been hit as hard. Sure, the headaches came and went, but at this stage, she was used to it. Though Finn was not himself, worn by the effects of this magical disturbance, and Taye had lost his spark and energy altogether.

There was one theory she kept circling back to: the Fox. She was certain it had been keeping her company while she slept; despite all the chaos, she'd been sleeping better than she had in months.

While the world around her was crumbling, here she was – still attending classes.

'For normalcy,' Finn had said.

Professor Kiran stood at the front, holding a piece of chalk, her arms crossed, scanning the half-empty class with her dark sharp eyes. Her jaw tightened and she turned to the blackboard and drew a diagram. Even professors were avoiding using magic at this point.

A Dog sat obediently by her feet, its fur coal-black, a tingling light reflecting on the tips of its fur. A stray dog – not what she would expect as Professor Kiran's sylvandir. The Dog's great amber eyes were alert, its pointy ears moving to the different sounds in the room – Suraya's scribblings, Kaija's sighing, and Jun's shoe tapping to the table's leg.

Staring at the blackboard, Aria was restless, tapping her fingers on the table. *It's literally doomsday. This is ridiculous.*

'Magic isn't infinite,' Professor Kiran said, the subtle reddish tone of her dark short hair reflected by the afternoon sun. 'It's just like any other resource.'

She tapped the chalk against a junction point and turned to the class. 'It flows through a series of networks, like underground rivers—' She paused with a sigh. 'Miss Beauchamp, perhaps you should visit the Healing Hall.'

Victoria was pale, her hands trembling, about to faint. A white ferret was curled around her shoulders like a scarf – her familiar, Aria assumed. By now, most wizards kept their familiars close, likely to keep their bonds from weakening as the magic continued to fade.

Kaija and Inessa stood on either side of her and carried her out. A kestrel flew after them, wings cutting through the air, while a thick-furred Russian cat padded along beside Inessa, tail flicking with quiet urgency.

Whispers echoed in the room as the door closed behind them.

Frustration rose in Aria's chest, a tide she couldn't hold back. She was supposed to be the "chosen one", wasn't she? Literal giants had spoken to her. Mythical creatures that shouldn't exist had trusted her with a message, a mission.

But what did that even mean?

She was thirteen. Thirteen and expected to fix something professors, the experts, couldn't explain. Tremors kept shaking the Academy. The magifauna were withering. People were falling ill. And no one did anything that mattered.

It was too much. Too heavy. Too impossible. And she didn't ask for any of this.

And yet, she couldn't look away. Doing nothing wasn't an option. Not when Finn looked like he hadn't slept for weeks, still tracing lines on the map beneath his textbook, trying to figure out where the source of the disturbance was. Not when Taye was thumbing through the *Codex Naturalis* on his lap like it held the last scraps of hope. Not when magifauna struggled to survive, the Great Ash was dying, and the magical system was on the verge of collapse.

Suraya sat nearby, furiously doodling with a black pen in the margins of her notebook. Her lips were pressed firmly together in tension, while her chameleon sat on the table, one eye following her pen, the other keeping an eye on her.

'Pay attention,' Professor Kiran's voice cut through the whispers, sharp as ice. 'I understand being in class while your friends are feeling unwell might feel—'

'Pointless?' Suraya finished. She put her pen down with such force that Louis jumped. She adjusted her circular glasses and narrowed her eyes. Louis flickered between concerned purple and furious red, one eye on Suraya and the other on the professor. 'Isn't it all just pointless at this stage, Professor?'

Aria blinked. Suraya challenged a professor. Not entirely surprising, as Suraya was clearly reaching her limits. For the past weeks, she had lost inspiration to paint, and nowadays, just stared at the ceiling of her box bed at night until she fell asleep. Aria was at a loss seeing her friend like this.

Another tremor rippled through the classroom, the

windows rattling as the plants curled their leaves. Aria's stomach turned, while anger bubbled inside her.

This is madness. Being forced to stay in class while the magical system collapses. Shouldn't it be all hands on deck?

Professor Kiran's lips pouted in frustration. The tremor was more of an inconvenience than a crisis.

'Knowledge is never pointless, Miss Clairmont-Ziadeh,' Professor Kiran said. 'Even if the Academy is experiencing some... issues.'

'Issues?!' Aria was on her feet before she could second-guess it. Her hands trembled by her sides; her voice rang loud and decisive.

'I am sorry, Professor, but these are not some *issues*. People are getting sick and magifauna are *dying*.' Aria's voice cracked on the last word.

'Miss Renwood, I would watch my temper, if I were you. Take a seat.'

'Or what?' Aria's challenge sliced the air, sharp as a blade.

'Or we might need to discuss your future at this institution. After all, if you find these lessons so irrelevant, perhaps the Academy isn't the right place for you.'

The temperature in the room dropped with each word. Silence stretched as the rest of class looked between them.

'*Fine*.' Aria packed her books into her satchel, each movement charged with anger. 'This is absolutely futile anyway. We are in a magical Academy and we can't use magic or else we get sick. What kind of education is that?'

She threw the satchel over her shoulder, looked at Professor Kiran in the eyes with pure hate, and slammed the door behind her with an echo that sealed her decision.

On autopilot, she walked down to the lake and sat on the edge of the deck. She took off her boots and let her feet move in the cold water. The trees in the horizon were a shade of light green as nature bloomed to spring on this warm day. Adrenaline surged through her like a plunge basin agitated by a crashing waterfall.

Being outside should have calmed her nerves, but there were too many hints of wrongness: a wilted patch in the fresh grass; a branch with prematurely yellowing leaves. Like the season itself was sick in spots.

'That was eventful,' Taye said in a calm voice, with Finn by his side moments after. 'Are you okay?'

'Okay?!' Aria snapped. 'The world around us is collapsing, and we are attending classes? What sick joke is that?'

'I know. They're avoiding the question,' Finn said, sitting next to Aria, pressing on his green robes. His shoulders slumped as he looked out at the lake. 'They're not addressing what has been happening all year. We're not blind.'

'Aria,' came a voice like frost on glass behind them.

The Fox stood there behind them, looking more agitated than she'd ever seen. Its distress made her skin prickle.

'Magic is drying up,' the Fox said.

'Can you feel what's causing it? Where?' Aria asked. 'We're trying but can't figure it out.'

'It's deliberate. We can't find the source because they're blocking us. Come, I need to show you something.'

The Fox padded swiftly along the deck, before turning right towards the Ancient Forest.

Aria slid on her boots and the three of them followed the Fox. It slipped between trees with fluid ease, leading them past the Great Ash, its leaves blazing orange in a sea of green.

They broke through a thicket and arrived by a stream that made its way to the lake, its banks lined with birches, elms, and oaks etched in runes on their trunks.

'A ritual,' Taye murmured.

'A recent one,' Finn added, reaching and touching the fresh

marks of the nearby silver birch, the carvings green.

'These runes force the path of magic,' the Fox said, voice low and tail flicking. 'Breaking what should flow freely.'

Taye moved inquisitively, fingers brushing the tree trunks. 'This is wrong,' he said, pacing between them. He dropped to his knees beside a thick knot of roots. 'Wait – something's here.'

He picked up a folded piece of paper, carefully not to tear it. The ink was smudged, the edges damp, but it was covered in diagrams, frantic, handwritten notes, and runic inscriptions.

'Looks like a ripped-out page from a book,' he said, turning it towards them. 'Calculations... diagrams... but this part's underlined: "Convergence points must be activated in sequence."'

'Convergence points?' Aria asked.

'Places where magic gathers. Sacred points,' the Fox replied.

Another tremor shook the ground. The Fox wavered violently, its distress hitting Aria like a physical wave.

'What's happening to you?' Aria asked, kneeling to the Fox's level.

'We're trying to maintain the balance, but magic drains faster than we can restore it.'

'We're running out of time,' Finn said. 'I think it's time we share our findings with a professor? This is obviously bigger than us.'

'Seriously?' Aria tilted her head in disbelief. 'The same professors that have forced us to go to class, while the world around us is collapsing? I think not!'

'They have not been the most credible people, Finn,' Taye pitched in. 'They have been giving us homework while the apocalypse is happening. That's peak delusion. That's like seeing your house on fire and worrying about watering your plants!'

'I know, but it's not safe. Maybe Professor Halvard?'

'Even though I love the man,' Taye said, 'he's an experienced timeweaver, wouldn't he have seen this and stopped it? Out of everyone, he would know what this is all about. Why isn't he doing anything?'

'I—'

'We cannot hold this much longer,' the Fox interrupted as it started to dissipate. 'Please find what breaks nature's laws before the old magic fails entirely.'

And with that, it vanished.

'Wait!' Aria called, reaching out her hand, but the Fox was gone.

They all stared at the spot where the Fox was. It was about to be the end of everything Aria held dear. And, at this point, she understood how much she actually had to lose.

CHAPTER TWENTY-THREE

North

'Let's go! We need to figure this out – right now!' Aria stormed towards the castle.

'What if there is a tool,' Finn said, hurrying beside her, 'or a simple spell that could find what is causing the magic instability? Wait, no, we can't do magic. But still, there's got to be a tool like this somewhere.'

'That's actually excellent thinking!' Taye said.

'I usually have good ideas.'

'If you're not going to be modest about it, I take it back.'

Aria walked with purpose, her quick steps causing her hair to snap behind her. The castle loomed ahead, its ancient stones dark against the spring light blue sky.

They climbed the worn steps to the Front Hall, and as Aria pushed open the heavy door, she bumped into a person coming out.

'Oh sorry!' Aria said, trying to get her footing. 'I wasn't watching.'

She looked up. Carolina was drained beyond her years. Dark circles shadowed her eyes, and her usual perfect posture was slightly hunched. Her hair was up in a messy bun.

'No, it's alright. I had my head elsewhere too,' she said,

picking up her books with haste. 'Final year's Quest of Knowledge project, you know?'

'I'll help!' Aria got down to gather the fallen books. There was an impressive mix – worn library volumes, personal notebooks filled with diagrams, and some scrolls of ancient texts. She caught glimpses of titles as she stacked them. *Historical Theories of Magical Flow* lay open on a page about pressure points, while *Advanced Applications of Crystalline Matrices* had so many paper markers sticking out, it barely closed. Carolina picked them up with trembling fingers, managing a smile that failed to light up her face.

'Thank you,' Carolina said, clutching the books to her chest. 'But I have to get going. Deadlines,' she added, then hurried out the door.

Aria lingered in the doorway, watching her rush east towards the East Garden. Or maybe the Greenhouse? Where was she going?

'Aria, come on!' Taye tugged on her sleeve.

'Right.' She shook off the strange feeling and followed them.

Magnus Nordfell stood in front of Mímir's Vault, leaning heavily on a dark wooden cane with a shiny silver dragon's head as a handle. Without magic, his hovering chair was useless – and in a castle this vast, it couldn't be easy. He wore wide-legged maroon woollen trousers, laced up boots, and a white blouse that accentuated his broad shoulders. A white rat with a circular brown spot on its side sat obediently on his shoulder.

Magnus looked tired, and it was clear that what she heard was right. He hadn't eaten or slept properly for months since the book had vanished from the records. The unsolvable puzzle was taking a toll on him.

The librarian didn't flinch as they walked past him, too

focused looking into nothing.

Finn and Aria sat at their usual table, while Taye hurried around the library, picking books that could be relevant for their investigation. He spread them on the table. One by one, they scanned pages about magical ecosystems, their disruptions, and possible tools to find them. Finn had *Signs and Portents: A Guide to Magical Disturbances*, while Aria flipped through *Historical Accounts of the Great Magic Drought*.

'Listen to this,' Taye said, pointing to a passage in *Protection of Magical Sources*. '"The signs of forced extraction are subtle at first: wilting of magiflora, fatigue, and disturbed ecosystem. By the time the larger effects manifest, the damage is often irreversible."'

'That sounds exactly like what's happening now,' Aria said.

'Here's something weird,' Finn added, eyes narrowing at his book. 'Apparently, there was a similar case in 1786 when someone tried to redirect a ley line. Everything started dying within a five-kilometre radius.'

'Wait,' Aria said to Taye. 'What was the book you found that had a missing page? Before winter break.'

'Oh, the one about energy resonance?' he said, standing up and looking through the bookcase. 'Hmm... I think it was called *Magical Current Systems* or something.'

'Is it this one?' Finn asked, picking up a large old book from under the pile of books with a leather cover, its spine cracked with age.

'Yes, yes! Didn't even realise I picked that one, too.'

'Let's see where the page is missing,' Finn said as he flipped through the pages.

'Do you have that paper we found earlier?' Aria asked Taye.

Taye picked up the piece of paper from his pocket and handed it over. 'Do you think it's the same one?'

'Here,' Finn said as he laid the book on the table and

opened it on the spot where a page had been torn out.

Aria folded out the piece of paper they found at the ritual site, smoothing its worn edges. When placed against the torn section, the ragged edges aligned perfectly. The page lit up faintly as it touched its original binding, wanting to reattach itself.

'I knew it!'

'Okay, so...' Finn said, already scanning the text. 'Listen to this: "Convergence points must never be forcefully accessed. To do so risks disrupting the natural flow of magic through established ley lines. While the power gained may seem substantial, the cost to the surrounding magical ecosystem..."' He squinted at the next part, which was stained and harder to read.

'Someone's not just studying these points, they're...' Aria said, feeling cold despite the library's warmth.

'Extracting it,' Finn finished.

A tremor shook the shelves, making dust rain from the ceiling. They stared at each other, the same realisation dawning on their faces.

'We need to find out where the magic is being redirected,' Taye said. 'Before—'

'Before someone does something that can't be undone,' Aria finished, watching the forest through the library window. Sylvandir had positioned themselves in dead spots around the grounds, their forms flickering like dying lights. And beyond was Fenrir, its yellow eyes looking straight at hers.

She shivered.

'Right, we know what. But where...?' Aria thought out loud, pacing back and forth.

'It's like finding a needle in a haystack!' Taye groaned.

'A needle...' Aria repeated, imagining a possible tool that would guide them to the right direction. Could there be a location spell with a needle and a map? Surely Sigrid would have needles in the Healing Hall. Suraya would probably know how to – or, at the very least, she would find out. Yes, that would be a good plan.

No, it isn't. We can't do magic, Aria thought.

'Oh, oh, a compass!' Taye shouted, standing proud. 'I have one in my room and—'

'Taye! Yes!' Aria interrupted, jumping from her seat. 'But not yours! The one in the Front Hall!' she added, running out of the library.

'The what?' Taye shouted back as he and Finn hurried after her.

They ran down the stairs into the Front Hall, their footsteps echoing loudly in the empty corridors. Night had arrived, and they could hear clinking in the Mead Hall where dinner was served.

Time had passed fast, and they hardly noticed it.

Aria hurried to the alcoves along the wall and stopped by the compass under the dome. A bronze circular artefact, runes etched around the border. At its centre was a frosted blue glass, glittering slightly in the candlelight. Underneath it was written *Svartálfar-Forged Compass of Freydís Himingsdóttir.*

Aria respectfully took the glass dome and picked up the old compass, cold in her hand.

'It was from one of the founders,' she said as she lifted it to eye level and looked through it. 'The dark elf in the Yule Market said the old compasses had more magic.'

They looked into the frosted glass and waited. Nothing happened.

'I didn't even know this was here!' Taye said, eyeing at the other artefacts in the alcoves, while Aria turned to the Great Staircase.

Still nothing. Was it broken?

'Do you see anything?' Finn asked, standing behind Aria trying to have a look.

'No... maybe it's not one of those special compasses.'

Aria turned around, and once facing the corridor to the western wing, a small ball of light emerged at the centre of the glass, with thin rays of light spreading from it.

'Nevermind! It's showing us the way,' Aria said with nervous excitement.

Without another word, they took off down the dimly lit corridor.

The compass led them to a door on the side; Finn tried the handle, finding it unlocked. With a shared glance, they stepped through, descending a set of worn stone stairs.

The air grew thick with dampness as they descended, the rhythmic dripping of water could be heard around them. Aria trailed her fingers along the rough walls.

'This place feels old,' she whispered.

At the bottom of the stairs, the corridor stretched out before them. The musty, earthy scent clung to the air, the passage forgotten by time.

'We should have brought a candle, maybe?' Taye said as they were engulfed in the darkness.

'Wait here,' Finn said, and he hurried back up the stairs and out of sight.

'Obviously,' Taye said. 'Where would we go? There could be a vaesen in this tunnel that would bring us straight to Valhalla. I am not moving in this darkness.'

Aria shifted uncomfortably. She did not want to see another vaesen.

Footsteps echoed in the corridor outside, fainter by every step. After a few short minutes, it echoed louder, coming closer in a hurry.

Finn emerged on the top of the stairs, his face lit by a

candle. As he descended, he picked up a torch on the wall and lit up.

'Here.' He handed the candle to Taye. 'To protect yourself against whatever comes our way.'

'Protect me from what? Spiders? I would very much prefer the torch.'

Finn rolled his eyes and stepped forward, leading the way with the torch.

The passageway lay hidden beneath the foundations of the modern Academy, undisturbed for centuries. Massive granite blocks formed the walls, their surfaces etched with faint, weathered runes.

Aria gripped the compass tightly, looking into the glass, the dot of light in its centre bigger than before.

'We must be close. Let's continue this way,' she said, her own voice lowered to match the oppressive stillness.

'Stay sharp,' Finn warned in a low whisper. 'We don't know what we might find.'

'Can you believe this has been down here all this time?' Taye whispered, his fingers tracing the uneven stonework. 'It's like stepping back through the ages.'

Aria nodded, focused ahead where all she could see was blackness. 'It feels… alive.'

Cobwebs clung to the sagging wooden beams overhead, the fire from the torch lighting them up as they walked. Spiders crawled into the cracks to escape.

'We are nearly there, I can feel it,' Aria murmured, her eyes fixed on the steady bulb of light of the ancient dark elf-forged compass.

At the far end of the passageway stood a pair of massive wooden doors, weathered and dark, engraved with runes. Above the door was the Academy crest engraved in stone, old but proud – a large oak tree. Beneath it, a runic inscription:

Taye looked up at the runes, using the candle to illuminate it. His brow furrowed. 'It says *Eikrhelgi Seiðrs ok Runagaldrs* – Oak Sanctuary of Seidr and Rune Magic – in Old Norse.' His voice was barely a whisper, his hand lingering on the door. 'This must have been the original Academy... from when it was founded 900 years ago.'

'Let's go in,' she said. Aria took a breath, steeling herself as she moved forward. The air was thicker here, like the past was waiting just behind the door.

Without hesitation, she pressed her hands to the heavy wood, feeling the slight vibration beneath her palms, and pushed, the door creaking as it slowly gave way. The ancient hinges groaned, protesting after centuries of stillness.

'What if it's dangerous?' Finn said. 'Shouldn't we discuss first what we will do?'

But Aria and Taye had already hurried through the door.

CHAPTER TWENTY-FOUR

Sunderroot

'What are they doing?' Taye's whispered as he grabbed Aria's arm, hands trembling.

The chamber beyond was large, the wooden walls stretching up into the shadows, with thick beams across the ceiling, similar to the Mead Hall. A sickly purple glow pulsed around them, making the chamber throb like a diseased heart. The smell of rotten eggs made Aria grimace. The magic here was wrong, perverted. A heavy humming echoed, but a screaming discord in her mind was louder. It made her want to cover her ears, run away, and hide.

But she couldn't. Not now.

Seven cloaked figures stood at the centre, forming a perfect circle around a crack in the stone floor. Their familiars sat obediently at their feet – among them, a furry cat with glowing yellow eyes, a golden eagle with its wings tucked close, and a bobcat with cheek ruffs and tufted ears illuminated by the purple light.

The figures chanted in a language that set Aria's teeth on edge, repeated in a loop. With each word, magic was sucked out from the crack, its movement violent, hungry. The stolen magic gathered above in a glassy sphere hovering above them.

Inside, magic moved like crude oil – thick, purple, and toxic. It sent ripples through the chamber, which made Aria's stomach lurch, while her lungs struggled to breathe in the air of sulfur.

'That's a ley line,' Finn's voice cracked with disbelief. 'They're extracting magic from a ley line. Not good. We should go back and report this.'

Finn tugged Aria's and Taye's arm to turn back, but Aria didn't budge, fixated at the sphere of light, pulsating like a dying star.

'We need to go – NOW!' Finn shouted, panic rising in his voice.

That was enough. One of the figures twitched and lifted their head. The hood fell back.

'Carolina?' Aria's heart stopped.

Carolina Valencia narrowed her eyes, searching for the source of noise that broke her trance. Her eyes glowed with that same sickly purple hue and her face looked aged past her years. It wasn't the friend Aria knew. She would never do this. This was disturbing and evil.

They locked eyes and Carolina's face twisted in shock. She gasped and the hooded figures closest to her followed her gaze and stopped chanting.

It all went sideways fast. The harvested magic from the sphere lashed out with a whip, sending purple tendrils in all directions. It caused cracks in the wooden walls, it broke the stone floor throughout the chamber, and wooden debris tumbled from the ceiling.

Aria looked in horror as a tendril whiplashed towards them with force. Her brain screamed *Run!* but her body froze, her muscles locked in panic. *This can't be happening. Not like this. Not before I've even learned the truth about my parents.* Her arms flew up, more reflex than choice, shielding her face as the tendril closed in.

But nothing happened. She peeked through her arms. The silhouette of Finn, dropped in a low stance in front of them, one foot back for balance, arms stretched with a shield he conjured – a blue concave, almost transparent barrier.

The tendril slashed into the shield again with all its might, but Finn held strong. The stone beneath him cracked around his feet, a witness to this power and force. His head turned to them slowly, and he gave them a weary smile.

In a split second, his legs buckled and gave out. Finn collapsed to the ground with a thump, the tendril wild in front of him, lashing through the chamber with the pressure of a high-pressure hose. The shield was gone.

'No, no, no, no, no!' Taye ran towards Finn and fell to his knees, his voice squeaking with panic. 'Finn! Wake up! Please wake up! You're not allowed to DIE!' His hands shook as he tried to shake him awake.

Aria's breath caught in her throat; a sharp pang shot through her chest as terror gripped her. Finn's limp body was pale and horrifyingly still, while Taye's frantic voice rang in her ears.

This couldn't be happening.

Her focus snapped to a tendril that made its way towards them like an angry cobra striking from above.

'Taye!' Aria shouted and ran at them.

A golden light illuminated the chamber and a shield materialised in front of them, just in time. The shield rippled as the tendril hit it, a dust of light fell on them.

'GET OUT!' Carolina shrieked over the chaos, her voice raw with panic.

She stood with her wand out, arm outstretched, her eyes darting between them and the writhing magic. The other hooded figures remained in the circle, chanting louder to keep the magic under control.

'What the hell, Carolina, you're FRACKING ley lines?' Aria shouted back, kneeling, her hands now pressed on Finn. 'You're destroying everything! You're hurting nature! You're hurting PEOPLE!'

'You wouldn't understand!' Carolina gestured desperately at the other cloaked figures who were scrambling to contain the magic. 'We're trying to save it! Magic is dying, and if we don't store enough of it—'

A massive crack split the floor between them. A geyser of purple energy screamed upwards.

The chanting grew even louder.

'That makes ZERO sense! Magic is dying all over Oakspire because of your fracking!' Aria shouted over the chaos. 'Carolina, *please*! Stop this!'

Carolina's face crumpled as she looked at Finn's unconscious body. Her eyes widened and stepped back into the circle of the hooded figures, pulling up her hood. She closed her eyes shut and raised her hands slightly in front of her, her palms up, joining the chanting.

The extracted magic subdued, yet the geyser still surged upwards, piercing the ceiling without leaving a trace.

Aria's stomach turned, the air around her suffocating. She wanted to yell, to run, or better yet, wake up from this nightmare. Instead, debris from the ceiling continued to fall around her.

'Taye, focus! We need to move him!' Aria shouted to Taye, still beside Finn, looking defeated.

Taye wiped the tears from his face with his sleeve and helped Aria drag Finn behind a massive wooden pillar. The chanting continued to echo in the chamber. The wild magic was contained for now, but it was clear it would not last long. Maybe this would be the moment to assess Finn, heal him even.

He looked dead. Finn was sprawled on the ground; his head limp in Taye's lap.

A tingling sensation grew in Aria's fingertips. Her trembling hands moved almost on their own accord over Finn's chest. She pressed her hands firmly and closed her eyes.

Please, let this work.

She felt nothing, heard nothing. Her heart sank with the thought of losing him. She shook her head and reached deeper, her brow frowning, focusing on Finn's grounding presence.

That's when she found him – his life force dim, like a distant star winking in the night.

'He's alive, but frail,' Aria said. She turned to the hooded figures, the sphere of magic above crawling itself out from the container. 'We can't let them continue,' Aria said, her heart pounding. 'The magic is dying, it wants to be free.' Her connection to nature was roaring in despair at her now, overwhelming her senses with the magical equivalent of a thousand withering plants.

'There's seven of them, their familiars, and two of us,' Taye called back. 'And they actually know what they're doing.'

Something snapped inside her – not fear, rage. Pure, instinctive wrath at what they were doing to the natural magic.

Behind Aria, the Fox materialised, its fur bristling with energy. A Magpie swooped down from the shadows above, wings trailing starlight, landing next to Taye, while a Bear emerged from the wall, taking form. Its massive presence radiating protective fury as it positioned itself on Finn.

With their presence, she knew what had to be done.

She pressed her hands against the pillar. The Fox closed its eyes next to her and raw magic ran through Aria's fingertips. Every vine, every speck of moss, every tiny seed dormant in the stones, awakened. Plants burst from every crack and crevice in the chamber, glowing with green, robust light. Roots burst through the floor, writhing like serpents.

The circle of wizards broke apart. The chanting stopped, replaced by shouts of surprise as vines and roots wrapped around their ankles. One fell and hit their head, staying immobile afterward. Two others struggled to get the vines loose, conjuring spells at it, but it kept creeping up onto them from behind, keeping them stuck against the wall.

The magic they pulled up wrestled to return to its natural flow. Maybe Aria could bring it back to the ley lines.

'If we can't stop them,' Taye said, 'maybe we can stop that!' he added, pointing at the crack in the floor where magic was spilling through.

'Enough of this childish nonsense!' said a wizard as they raised their wand.

A bolt of red light shot towards them.

Aria screamed, throwing her hands up instinctively. A wall of thorny brambles burst from the floor, catching the spell. The plants withered instantly.

'Cover me!' she yelled, not sure how Taye could do that, but she knew she needed to focus.

'HOW?' Taye shouted back.

More spells flew at them. Taye threw his hands up in despair and magic exploded in a shower of mirror-like surfaces, reflecting and refracting the attacks in random directions. He was creating illusions instinctively, making it impossible for the four wizards to tell where they were. Above him, the Magpie flew around the chamber, reinforcing Taye's magic.

Aria ran towards the crack in the middle of the chamber and reached out to the violated ley line with her hands. Grabbing it was like holding a fire hose, raw power burning through her as she pushed it back into the earth. Her whole body shook from the effort, and energy flowed through her with more intensity than she had ever experienced. The Fox stood beside her, amplifying her own strength.

Arms wrapped around her neck. Aria was forced to let go. She managed to turn and grab the arm that held her.

'I'm sorry, Aria,' Carolina's voice rang out amid the chaos in the room. 'We have to finish the ritual. Continue what my father started and make sure we can store magic if there is ever a shortage in the future.' Her voice cracked in desperation. 'It's the only way! You have to understand! This is for the greater good.'

Aria twisted to release herself, struggling to get air. But Carolina's grip was strong and determined.

'The greater good?' Aria called out, her voice hoarse. 'Look at what you're doing!' She jerked her chin towards the chamber, towards Finn. 'Look what you've already done!'

'I... I never meant for anyone to get hurt. They said once we managed to contain it, it would stabilise again—'

The Fox snarled at Carolina, its ethereal form crackling with fury like fire. Carolina stumbled back, her grip loosening just enough. Aria drove her elbow back and broke free, gasping as air rushed into her lungs.

Behind them, spells were being shot at Taye as he hid behind a pillar, catching his breath, peeking out to shoot light magic towards them. The Magpie swooped overhead, chasing Carolina's familiar, the golden eagle Esmeralda.

'You're wrong,' Aria said, her voice breaking. 'Your father was wrong! You can't just take magic like this. It's alive. It's connected to everything and you're killing it!'

Placing her hands on the ground, a wall of plants emerged and moved forwards like a green tide. Carolina raised her wand, deflecting them, but there were too many. A thick root caught her across the chest, knocking the air from her lungs. She stumbled backward, her head striking the stone floor with a crack.

Aria hesitated. *Is she...?*

As she was about to reach out to Carolina, a sickening high-pitched noise erupted from the crack in the stone; the ley lines wailed like the dead.

Aria refocused on the ley lines and grabbed it once more. Raw magic surged through her body like a lightning storm so powerful her teeth rattled and her vision blurred. She struggled to direct it back into the earth where it belonged.

Reflecting from Taye's swirling illusions, three wizards raised their wands in unison behind her. They were going to hit her with something big. There was no way she would survive.

A hand gripped hers. Taye knelt beside her, focused on the ley lines, sweat dripping from his curls.

Power rushed through Aria, every nerve ending ignited. Through the chaos of purple, gold, and green light, and the sound of stone cracking beneath her feet and wizards yelling, she held on.

The sphere above them shattered, exploding into a storm of purple light. Magic splattered against the walls and stone floors, glowing droplets like glittering paint. One by one, they slithered back towards the ley line in the crack, drawn to it as the tide to the moon. The earth trembled as the channel absorbed every last drop, the purple hue in the chamber subduing until only the ley line's golden current burned bright, steady and alive.

With a violent snap, the geyser reversed, plunging downwards back into the ley line with such force it sent a shockwave through the space. Wizards flew back, their spells dissolving in this wave of pure magic. Aria and Taye fell back and hit the stone floor hard, debris digging into their backs. Aria's ears rang, while magic crackled in the air around them – static after a storm.

The chamber had gone quiet except for the soft patter of disturbed dust falling from the ceiling and the groans of the scattered wizards, unable to get up. The crack in the dirt beneath the broken stone sealed itself, leaving only a thin golden line as the remnant of a new scar.

Aria's body trembled from the residual energy, her fingers tingling where she'd touched the raw magic. Beside her, Taye lay gasping, his hair standing on end as though he was struck by lightning.

Exhaustion and pain crept through her like lead, making every movement impossible. Through her heavy eyelids, a raven came into view, perched on one of the pillars, watching her, curiously. She could swear it smiled.

Everything went black after that.

CHAPTER TWENTY-FIVE

Guardian

Aria floated in a darkness that flowed like rivers, cradled in warm soil. Voices sang in a language she did not know but understood – old words, earth words, whispered by roots and streams. There was a memory trying to surface, a different song, from a time before time.

The darkness lifted, and she stood in a forest. Moonlight filtered through the green leaves, which shimmered with their own inner light. A vast tree at the centre, its branches stretching up beyond sight, disappearing into the mist above, its roots plunging into depths that held entire worlds above. Its trunk was wider than a house, deeply furrowed with ridges and valleys, with stories held in their shadows.

Before her, three women sat around a well at the tree's base, their faces unclear, with the water's reflection shifting. They weaved threads of light, natural and pure. Where the purple magic was wrong and twisted, this was ancient and true, like the heartbeat of the world itself.

The Norns' hands moved in perfect harmony without looking up at Aria or acknowledging her presence. Deities that shape the course of destinies for both gods and men. Aria didn't know of them, yet knew them well – was it from another life or from stories her mother told her?

The question lingered in her mind.

'How many times has the tree shed its leaves, only to grow them anew?' The first woman's voice rustled like autumn leaves. 'Yet the roots remember every season of drought, every storm that broke its branches.'

'Even now,' the second spoke with the sound of running water, 'you fight the current, trying to swim upstream, when the river knows its course. Nature bends but does not break.'

'The bridge is built from both shores,' the third woman spoke in a whisper of new spring growth, 'and the strongest roots grow in darkness before reaching light.'

'The balance is delicate,' they said together, their voices harmonising like wind through trees. 'The healing must be gentle. The guardian must first witness to all the voices of the earth. The old and new.'

Before Aria could respond, a raven landed on the well's edge, scattering the woven light in a spray of stardust. It turned its head to Aria, one eye clouded and blind, the other locking onto hers. In its depth, a memory that wasn't her own, or too many memories layered on top of each other, like looking through water at depths that kept changing.

'Remember,' the women's voices began to fade, 'some things must break to grow stronger. Some wounds must heal in their own time. For you, child of promise, are born from ashes. The destroyer of worlds, a cycle to end all cycles.'

The raven spread its wings and swooned towards her.

The world dissolved into darkness. Just before she woke, she heard one last whisper.

'The land remembers, guardian. And so will you.'

Aria opened her eyes to the clean wooden ceiling of the Healing Hall, the taste of soil and moonlight on her tongue. The scent of herbs filled her nostrils; water dripped from a nearby sink; and the sun warmed her skin. Beside her was a table, where a single black feather lay, though the window was closed.

'The sleeping beauty finally decides to join us!'

Taye sat on the bed beside her, propped up on several pillows and looking pale but still managing his inviting grin. A game spread on a wooden board on his lap, chess-like pieces scattered on a board – he'd been playing against himself. At the end of the bed stood a Magpie, its feathers gleaming with an otherworldly sheen, looking curiously at the pieces.

'You look awful,' Aria croaked, her throat dry and scratchy, as she tried to sit up. The Fox, curled up at the end of her bed, lifted its head at her movement, and settled back down with a soft huff. 'What happened?'

'Excuse you, I look fashionably exhausted,' Taye shot back. 'Turns out magical backlash is not great for the complexion. Who knew?' He gestured vaguely at himself and her. 'Professor Halvard came soon after we blacked out. The geyser penetrated through the ceiling into the Mead Hall above us, so they knew something was up.'

'They sure took their time. They could've come earlier.'

'Yeah... Also – guess who's joined the sylvandir club?' He pointed proudly at the Magpie. 'Meet Kevin.'

The Magpie's feathers ruffled in what could only be described as a dignified offence.

'Though I suspect he'd prefer something more majestic,' Taye added with a grin. 'Like "Lord of All Knowledge" or "Supreme Bearer of Wisdom." But he's stuck with Kevin now.'

'Of all the names in the modern tongue, you chose Kevin?' the Magpie replied in protest, its voice like stone sharpened into a blade.

The Fox looked up, amusement flickering in its amber eyes. 'Names carry power, even the unexpected ones.'

'Unexpected,' Kevin muttered. 'That's one word for it.' The Magpie hopped and propelled himself closer to the Fox, its long tail of black tingling feathers leaving a soft trail of light behind it. 'What's yours?'

'I've had many names. Though at this time, I have not yet been named.'

Aria hesitated. As her mind scrambled through names, one formed on her tongue.

'Fern,' she said.

The Fox blinked slowly.

'So be it.'

Aria chuckled, the conversation grounding her while memories flooded back into her mind.

'Finn! Where's—'

'Over there.' Taye pointed to their right. 'Still out, but Sigrid says he's stable. He used up pretty much all his energy with that shield, but he'll be fine.' He paused, fidgeting with one of the wooden game pieces – a white figurine holding a round shield.

Finn lay on the wooden-framed bed, skin nearly as white as the sheets beneath him. A bright, patterned throw offered the only splash of colour. The Bear rested by his side, head on his chest, pulsing with a soft blue light.

'The ley line,' she whispered as she put together the pieces of her memory. 'It healed and then...'

'Boom!' Taye made an explosive gesture with his hands, wincing. Kevin hopped closer to his headboard, feathers catching the afternoon light. 'Created a shockwave! Which, okay, was pretty cool, but maybe let's not do that again? I've got a strict one-near-death-experience policy.'

Aria lay back, relief settling. They were alive. Taye was making jokes, Finn was stable, they had managed to snap the ley line back and stop the wizard circle.

'And guess what! I'm an illuminator! Finn's obviously a shield mage. No one our age could do a shield of that magnitude without being naturally attuned to it. He's a natural!'

'They were trying to contain it,' she said quietly. 'The magic.' Her hands twisted in the sheets as another memory surfaced. Carolina's face in the Hall, lit by that sickly purple light.

'I can't believe Carolina did this,' Aria whispered, her voice cracking. 'She seemed so...'

'Good?' Taye finished, his usual playful tone absent. He looked down at the game pieces on his lap, arranging and rearranging them absently. 'That's what makes it worse. You think you know someone...' He trailed off, shaking his head. 'Oh, and they found the library thief. No surprise there: it was Carolina. They found the book in her room. Magnus is beyond himself, apparently whistling happily throughout the library. Everyone keeps shushing *him* now.'

'Right. But what's going to happen to her?' The sound of Carolina's head hitting the stone floor echoed in her mind. 'Is she *alive?*'

Taye's expression turned serious. 'She is. The Magic Regulation Board took them all in. Apparently, they were doing ancient forbidden magic... It's bad news. Magic that leads to droughts and famines. They thought they could control it better this time, make it perfect.' His smile didn't reach his eyes. 'Worse still is that Jonathan Thomson and Tove Bjørnstad were among them, plus four other fifth-years. Makes you trust everyone a little less. It will make voting a new Head a lot harder now, with all the trust issues.'

'Vote?'

'Each Krets picks their Head for a two-year term. With Carolina and Jonathan out before the end of year, Kiran stepped in for Fossheim and Haruki for Stenvald. Also, instead of having elections before summer, as it's usually done, they've decided to hold elections at the start of the year. No one wants to rush anything now. I mean, it's a good idea. We all need to digest this.'

Aria swallowed dry.

Flashes of last night returned in a blur: shouts, sparks, a magic so wrong it made her jaw clench. A night she deeply wanted to forget. Carolina might have saved them from one of those tendrils, but she didn't stop the ritual to protect them.

Worse. She tried to stop Aria from stopping the ritual. Tried to suffocate her.

Anger bubbled in her chest, tangled with hurt. Carolina was the closest to a big sister Aria had ever known. Carolina listened. She encouraged her. She made her feel seen. Safe.

That night, Carolina wasn't that person.

The look in her eyes, the hesitation, the fear. Carolina knew what was happening. She knew what she was doing. She saw *them*. Saw *Aria*, and yet, she turned away. Stepped back into the circle. Continued the ritual.

That look was imprinted in her mind. The moment she made the choice.

Her thoughts jumped to the Yule party, the way Carolina had opened up about her family, the warmth and joy she radiated while singing the Yule song. The first day they met, when she made Aria feel like she belonged, at a time she felt so out of place. The kind words Carolina said when she was lost.

But what kind of friend ignores friends when they are in danger? Ignored *Finn*, collapsed? Carolina could have called for help but didn't.

Maybe none of it was real. Maybe the sisterly bond Aria felt was one-sided. A true friend would *never* do that.

Aria's throat tightened.

'Hey.' Taye's voice was gentler now. 'You okay? You've got that look you get when you're overthinking things.'

'I – uh...' Aria looked around the empty Hall trying to avoid Taye's big brown eyes. 'Wait, where are the others? Fraser, Inaiê, Tenzin?'

'They've recovered!' Taye beamed, eyes wide with flair. 'Turns out our dangerously fabulous act of bravery actually worked. Magic's stable now. I mean, still recovering, wobbly at times like a newborn deer, but we'll take it.' He gestured grandly at the softly pulsating orb above them. 'Magical stabiliser. It definitely helped with the healing.'

The orb, a sphere with a blue liquid inside, turned and twisted. It emitted coolness – a soft misty sprinkler of water.

Was that...? No, it couldn't be. The one Professor Kiran got in the Yule Market was small... Though this was small, too. Could this be the sphere Aria saw? Did Professor Kiran truly want to help?

'Want me to teach you hnefatafl?' Taye gathered up his scattered game pieces, snapping Aria's focus back to him. 'It's this cool strategic board game we play at home. Excellent for distracting yourself from existential magical crises.'

CHAPTER TWENTY-SIX

Feather

They spent the next days recovering in the Healing Hall. Taye turned out to be terrible at hnefatafl, and his running commentary on the historical significance of each technique made time fly.

Astrid came by with baskets filled with home-baked goods, herbs, and teas. She often came at the end of the day to check up on them and ensure Sigrid had all she needed to treat them.

Suraya brought a get-well card that sprinkled with light when opened. Inside, she'd drawn Aria and Fern, side by side in pastels. Aria smiled at it, happy to see Suraya's creativity back.

Taye's sister, Frida, came by only once, appearing with her usual calm presence and a bag of mulberry liquorice gummies that made Taye jump in joy.

'Well, you look exactly like the aftermath of a terrible decision,' Frida said, gesturing at Taye, her light brown braids falling down her shoulders like a waterfall.

Taye placed his hand on his chest in mock insult. 'We *saved* the ley line. We saved *you*.'

'And who burned off their eyebrows in the process?'

'I didn't—' Taye raised a hand to his face and grimaced. 'No!

But only slightly. It will grow back. I bet there is a paste I can make to grow them back.' He looked up at Frida. 'There is a paste I can make to grow them back – *right?*'

Aria almost laughed, but a cough came out instead.

To everyone's relief, Finn finally woke up after five days, his life-force restored. He joined in on the hnefatafl games and was in high spirits.

'Ruadhán,' he said looking at the Bear, its smoky fur with a hint of red. 'That's what I'll name you.'

'Honourable name,' Ruadhán said with a voice like thunder on a summer's day.

At night, when the Healing Hall was silent, Aria lay awake, turning the vision of the women over in her mind. The words echoed an understanding just beyond her reach. She picked up the black feather on her side table, trying to hold onto the fading details of the vision.

Sleep came slowly, and when it did, she dreamed of broken threads and ancient stones, of magic gone wrong, and of warnings she couldn't remember in the morning.

The morning before they were due to leave the Healing Hall, Aria sat awake in her bed, watching the spring's sun rising early. She slipped out into the East Garden.

Bathed in the warm glow of dawn, Aria was caressed by the gentle rustle of leaves in the breeze now the invisible dome was lifted. The fragrance of the garden's vibrant flowers calmed her nerves, and the chirping birds soothed her. She sat on a secluded bench under a large rowan tree, holding the black feather, trying to make sense of everything that happened. Fern curled up beside her.

A flutter of wings startled her. She froze, her heart skipping a beat as a small flock of whooper swans descended onto the water in the lake beyond, their sleek bodies glowing in the morning rays of light. They landed gracefully; their soft honking carried across the still surface. Aria watched them for a moment, her breath steadying, mesmerised by their peaceful flight.

The water against the shore, rhythmic and calming, made her notice how calm the air was. Ever since she had come to Oakspire, magic was erratic and now, for the first time, she could finally breathe.

'I come here often in the early mornings,' came a quiet voice. 'Watching birds helps put things in perspective.'

She jerked back on the bench, nearly tipping over, at the sound of the voice. Professor Halvard stood a few metres away, his hands clasped behind his back as he watched the whooper swans.

'May I?' he asked with a warm smile, gesturing at the bench.

'Yes, of course.' Aria shifted uncomfortably, unsure if she was in trouble after placing her two best friend's lives at risk, expelled for the way she spoke to Professor Kiran, or about to receive a sermon for walking into the night, which almost led to her death at the hands of the Askafroa.

He sat down beside her, moving with the unhurried grace of someone who had all the time in the world. The glass bead on the tip of his white beard reflected a shade of red. He wore moss green robes that settled on his lap as he sat.

'How are you feeling, Miss Renwood?' he asked, his voice carrying the same soothing quality it had when he spoke to her on her first day.

'I'm fine,' Aria said automatically, but amended, 'I mean, better. Sigrid says we are essentially discharged today.'

'Mm.' He nodded, studying her with kind blue eyes that hinted to see more than she was saying. 'Physically, perhaps. But I think we both know there are wounds that don't show up on healing charts.' He glanced at the black feather still on her hands. 'Would you mind if I took a closer look?'

She nodded. He picked it up with careful fingers, turning it in front of him. 'Fascinating things, ravens. Did you know they're one of the few creatures that practise gift-giving?' he said, examining the feather. 'They recognise faces and form lasting relationships.'

Aria found herself relaxing slightly, despite her nervousness. 'Professor, what exactly happened? I mean, the forbidden magic? The tremors?'

'Ah, yes.' He gave her back the feather. 'Troubling business. But what troubles you most about it, I wonder? The magic itself, or the person wielding it?'

'The magic itself... I mean, all of it... Carolina,' Aria whispered, the name still painful to say. 'I don't understand how she could... She was always so good and insightful.'

Professor Halvard remained silent for a moment, letting Aria's words hang in the air. His expression softened as he glanced towards the lake, as though seeing something beyond the physical world. 'People are complicated,' he said after a pause. 'Even the ones we trust the most can surprise us, for better or worse. Miss Valencia, like many, may have found herself pulled into a situation without fully understanding its price.'

A lump in her throat made her gulp. She hadn't just lost a friend; she had lost a sense of safety, of trust in this world she was learning to navigate.

'Professor, when the ley line... When Taye and I pushed back against it, I had a strange dream. About three women around a well...' She trailed off, unsure how to describe it. At her feet, Fern's ears pricked forward, alert.

Recognition flickered in Professor Halvard's eyes. 'The mind processes trauma in curious ways, especially magical trauma. Dreams can be messages from the land itself. Some more significant than others.'

'I had a dream before, with a massive wolf,' Aria confessed. 'Taye thinks it's Fenrir.' Fern went still beside her, its silver fur bristling slightly.

'A sense of danger. You have a particular gift for hearing what the land has to tell us. For understanding the delicate balance of things.' He leant forward slightly, his blue eyes focused beneath his white bushy brows. 'Most mages spend years learning to tune in to magic, to comprehend its currents and tides. But you feel it instinctively.'

'Anyone can feel when magic is wrong, surely,' Aria protested. 'Like what Carolina was doing—'

'No,' he interrupted calmly. 'Not everyone can. Many wizards and mages see magic as a tool, a resource to be used. They might notice when something is drastically wrong, yes, but they don't feel its pain. They don't hear its whispers. They certainly don't dream of ancient powers when the balance is threatened.'

'Oh...' Aria looked down at her hands, feeling the weight of her powers, thinking about the vision. 'The women called me guardian,' she mumbled and blushed when she realised what she'd spoken aloud.

'Did they indeed?' The tone of his voice hinted at a quiet recognition. 'Compelling. What else did they say?'

'Something about remembering, but I don't know what.'

'I am sure there will be a time you will know.'

They sat in silence for a moment.

'For now, though, I think what you need most is rest.' He smiled and stood. 'And remember, my door is always open if you need to talk. About magic, about... anything at all.'

The Headmaster walked through the gates of the East Garden.

'Guardian,' she muttered to herself, holding the feather up to eye level. 'Why should it fall to me?'

CHAPTER TWENTY-SEVEN

Berserker's Ballad

Normality returned to Oakspire and, as tedious as it was, Aria enjoyed this peace and quiet to study for the exams. She read her notes under the shade of a great maple tree by the lake, listening to the water of the lake hitting the shore on that warm summer's day.

A lake swift jumped, splashing with childlike joy in water. With a sigh, Aria looked up at the green leaves dancing through the sunlight. Magic hummed like fresh air.

'I mean, why do we need to know about the Thirty Days' War in 1687?' Taye groaned, flopping back onto the grass. 'It's literally ancient history! And it was only thirty days. Like, who cares?'

'Because,' Finn said without looking up from his notes, 'it helps us understand the world of today and stops us from oversimplifying complex problems.'

'I mean, it is funny' – Aria sat up, joining the conversation – 'how a small dispute can spiral into unexpected consequences. Talk about escalation!'

'Oh my gods, can you imagine, though,' Taye said, sitting up and gesturing wildly. 'A Dane thinking he's creating these fearsome monsters out of trees and – BOOM! – they accidentally enchant every tree in the Söderåsen to sing Danish folk songs. But terribly! Super off-key! Their faces would have been priceless. Pure horror!'

'And being stuck on an old Danish drinking song for thirty days,' Finn chuckled. 'I bet the Swedish mages found it hilarious, but the local commonfolk farmers were probably less amused. They must have thought the Danes were mocking them.'

The three of them laughed. The ducks on the lake quacked, sharing their own opinion on historical magical accidents.

That was their last peaceful afternoon before exams descended upon Oakspire. The next week passed in a blur of practical assessments and written papers. Professor Haruki had them brewing complex potions which, to his amusement, led to disaster after disaster, while Professor Grünwald, who was in high spirits and more himself after the coma, tested them on identifying the calls of all magifauna in the area. Taye squealed with many of them, for this had been his hobby since he was a toddler.

Professor Kiran took the exam outside, where four stations were set up by the lake for each element.

One by one, they showed their elemental skills. Inaiê conjured fire with one hand, and moved water with the second, rolling around one another in a delicate dance, leading to applause from the first-year mages of the class. The exam had quickly turned into a competition between mages and wizards.

'Miss Renwood,' Professor Kiran said as Inaiê walked proudly back to the group. 'Please demonstrate your elemental skills.'

'You'll do fine!' Taye said, while Finn gave her a pat on the back.

Her jaw clenched and her hands tingled with barely-contained magic. Ever since they stopped the fracking, her magic had settled – a little. The slight tingle of energy at her fingertips still wanted to burst. Control was not in the cards, she knew that much.

Behind her, Kaija and Victoria whispered and laughed. Aria rolled her eyes at their constant mockery. She was determined to prove them wrong.

First was the earth station. A tall rock stood motionless, one which they were assigned to reshape into a troll. Those before her reshaped it into various interpretations of trolls. She stood in front of the rock, closed her eyes, and took a deep breath.

'Whoa!' Aria heard someone say.

Her eyes blinked open. The grass beneath her feet responded to her even before she dared to think about the assignment. It grew wildly and stretched up around the rock, making it disappear underneath it.

Professor Kiran straightened from where she'd been leaning against a tree, her dark eyes sharp with interest.

'Thank you, you can go to the next station,' she said simply.

Unsure what to make of it, for she didn't do any earth elemental magic, Aria walked slowly to the air station. Here, she was meant to create a current. Aria waved her hands and the wind whipped up, sending dust spiralling in all directions. Professor Kiran nodded and gestured for her to move on without a word.

At the water station in front of the lake, the task was to manipulate the water into a vortex on her hand. She faced the lake and concentrated on the water, but instead of a vortex, she conjured a large wave that got her completely drenched.

'I'm sorry,' Aria started, frustrated. 'I just—'

'Move to the next.' Professor Kiran's voice cut through her panic, leaving no room for arguments.

Taken aback and dripping wet, Aria stepped silently into the fire station.

Fire.

It was time to redeem herself, to show what she was capable of. She had never before conjured fire, but this was it. Aria took a deep breath and imagined flames in her mind. Her heart raced, her stomach turned, but she pushed on. And here it was, the tiniest flame floating on her hand.

Aria smiled widely and looked back at Taye and Finn, both with their thumbs up. When she looked back to her hand, the flame had fallen onto the grass and spread rapidly towards the Ancient Forest. *Oh no...* Aria ran after it, stamping on the flames, but the flames spread faster than she was able to stop them.

Professor Kiran flicked her wrist, summoning a ball of water from the lake that splashed and extinguished the flames in an instant.

'Thank you, Miss Renwood,' she said without any clear acknowledgement if Aria failed or passed the exam. 'Mr O'Heffernan, come forward.'

Aria joined the group, looking down at her feet. Kaija and Victoria tittered in the background, Inessa snorted, and Aria clenched her hands on her side. After a whole academic year, she finally managed to conjure fire, and yet, was about to burn down the Ancient Forest in the process.

Their last written exam was for Magical Ecology. Aria smiled at the first question: "Explain how the barkfox contributes to magical energy cycles in Nordic ecosystems and their importance in keeping the balance." Theoretical questions were a relief, after the year they had had.

By the end of the week, the Mead Hall buzzed as students filled their plates, laughed, and discussed the exams. Aria barely touched her food, watching Professor Halvard at the high table. He hadn't smiled once during the meal, which set her on edge.

'What do you think that's about?' she asked, her voice low as she glanced at her group of friends.

Taye shrugged, though the furrow in his brow betrayed his concern. 'Probably about the fracking. You think they'd just ignore an incident of this magnitude after the whole Academy nearly broke apart?'

Finn took a slow sip from his cup. 'I think so, too. He probably waited until everyone recovered and did the exams before making any announcements.'

'Some think the Academy might close,' Inaiê added, adjusting the piercing on her septum. 'They say the ley lines are too unstable, and the Academy's sitting right on top of them.'

'That's not what I heard,' Suraya chimed in, her round glasses reflecting the evening sun streaming into through the high windows. 'I heard Professor Kiran say the damage is superficial and fixable.'

Inaiê frowned, her fingers lightly tracing the edge of her cup. 'That doesn't sound right. I've heard the ley lines were torn. That's a lot of damage.'

The table fell silent for a moment, as the words sank in. Panic rose in Aria's chest with the thought of the Academy closing. *Where would I go?*

'The thing about ley lines,' Fraser said, oblivious to the tension, his ginger crown of tight curls bouncing as he moved his head, 'is that they've been treated like living beings – sentient. I read in *Mystical Currents Through the Ages* that Leontine Oliver, famous for—'

'Fraser,' Inaiê's voice was kind, but firm. 'Focus.'

'Oh. Right. Sorry.' Fraser nudged his glasses up his nose. 'But it is fascinating. Did you know the Academy's placement on ley lines was intentional? It was meant to have a deeper connection to the different realms. They say the ley lines are part of the root system of the Yggdrasil tree, like mycelium from mushrooms.'

'I heard someone say we're doomed,' Tenzin said casually. 'The ley lines are so damaged it may cause issues in the future.'

'They're not wrong,' Finn said, 'but the ley lines will stabilise. Magic rebounds – it always has.'

'They're saying more than that,' Inaiê added, glancing uneasily at Aria before continuing. 'Some think it's not random. That Carolina and the others were working for an underground order—'

'Oooh, Inaiê, look at you!' Taye said with a glint in his eyes. 'I never thought you, of all people, were into conspiracy theories.'

'It's not a conspiracy theory. Everyone knows there is a powerful order of magic. Centuries of reports do not lie.' Inaiê waved her hand. 'Besides, that's not the point. I heard fifth-years saying Carolina and the others were unknowingly influenced by someone who wants to harness the magic.'

'That's absurd,' Aria said. 'No one could be influenced to do these horrible things.'

'Not as absurd as you think,' Fraser said. 'Influence doesn't have to be obvious. Subtle manipulation can lead to big shifts in behaviour. You don't even need direct contact. You just need the right kind of energy to make people more susceptible. I mean, we are all natural beings, and if we can manipulate the environment, why can't we manipulate people?'

Silence.

Aria opened and closed her mouth. What if there had been someone pulling the strings all along?

Professor Halvard rose from his seat, his eyes scanning the Mead Hall with a quiet sadness. The buzz of conversation faded instantly, leaving only the occasional sound of clinking cutlery.

'I have some announcements to address before you go off to your post-exam celebrations,' he began, his voice steady but heavy.

Aria shifted in her seat. Professor Halvard's tone told her this wasn't going to be a light-hearted speech.

'It is with great regret,' he continued, 'I must address a serious matter on a celebratory evening like this. As most of you already know, some students have meddled with the core of our existence – magic itself. The balance of magic, which sustains us, has been tampered with, with little regard for the consequences. These seven individuals have already been handed over to the Magic Regulation Board, and their actions will have far-reaching consequences.'

The weight of his words sunk in. Around the Hall, several others stopped chewing, their faces frozen with a mix of concern and fear.

'May I remind you all we are living in borrowed land. The magic we use every day, the magic that flows through our veins and shapes our lives, does not belong to us,' Professor Halvard said, his voice growing more intense with each word. 'It is not ours to take, nor ours to own. We share it with the animals, the plants, the sylvandir, and realms beyond our own. It is a gift, given to us long ago, one that we have pledged to protect and safeguard.'

The silence that followed was heavy. Everyone held their breath.

'From next term onwards, we will be implementing new protective measures around our ley lines. Additionally, all students will take a mandatory course on Magical Ethics.'

A murmur rippled through the crowd, some groaning quietly. Aria could feel the tension crackling in the air.

'It is crucial you understand the responsibility that comes with your powers. We must all respect the balance that sustains us.' The Headmaster paused, his gaze sweeping over the Hall. 'That said,' he added with a warmer tone, 'we are pleased to announce that Berserker's Ballad will be performing at the End of Year Party to close out the year.' He turned to Astrid sitting at the end of the high table. 'Thank you, Astrid, for making this happen.'

Astrid nodded, her hair braided to the side. Her cheeks rosier than usual, her eyes more alert, in general – she looked healthier, happier.

The announcement shattered the tension, excited chatter and cheers cutting through it. Aria turned to Taye, puzzled.

'It's one of the biggest – no, THE biggest – bands in the Nordics!' he whispered loudly, practically bouncing in his seat. 'They're legendary! I don't know what strings Astrid had to pull to make this happen, but it will be incredible!'

Taye went on about the various times he had seen the Berserker's Ballad and sang the songs he loved the most. Aria's mind still lingered on the prospect that someone had manipulated Carolina to do this. It made her feel uncomfortable, knowing whatever this underground organisation was, it could continue to disrupt magic.

The last days of term melted away like snow in spring. Aria sat on a bench by the lake, fire dancing in sync with the Berserker's Ballad's thundering drums. Each beat sent ripples across the lake's surface, a celebration that crossed natural barriers.

In front of the stage was Taye, hands raised as he sang every word. Even from a distance, she could hear him shouting, 'This is the best day of my life!'

Aria plucked her exam results from her pocket and read them once more. Professor Haruki's neat handwriting praised her creative solutions, while Professor Grünwald drew a tiny magical creature in the margins of her near-perfect score. Only Professor Kiran's section bore a bare passing mark, without comment. She'd expected to fail, so this was a plus.

'Can you believe Taye got top marks?' Inaiê dropped onto the bench beside her, grinning. 'All that complaining about studying, and he just... breezes through?'

'He would say it is all pure talent,' Finn chipped in, amused, watching the Berserker's Ballad performance from a distance, tapping his foot on the ground to the beat.

'I failed at the practical exams,' Fraser said, pushing up his glasses nervously. 'Though Professor Haruki made a note saying he was "overjoyed by my spectacularly educational disasters."' He sighed, shoulders slumping. 'I just don't know how to tell my mums. They're going to be so disappointed.'

'Don't be so hard on yourself,' Aria said. 'The Academy is for learning, and you're learning.' Words she needed to tell herself more often.

'I suppose.'

Aria offered Fraser a sympathetic smile and shifted to the festivities, the lakeside filled with laughter and dancing. *Wait, is that...?*

'They're dating,' Fraser said following her gaze to Victoria and Jun dancing together.

'Victoria and Jun? Dating?'

'Oh! I mean... No... Urgh, they told me not to tell anyone. It's supposed to be a secret. I stumbled upon them a few weeks ago. They said they would burn my hair off if I told anyone.'

'I don't think they are being secretive anymore,' she said as the couple kissed. Aria blinked and looked away quickly – some things were better left unseen.

Oakspire Academy stood tall behind them. Majestic, witnessing the students celebrating yet another year. And what a year it had been. The Academy's leadership had failed them in so many ways, yet somehow they'd made it through. Was it surprising, though? It was the same way in the children's home, when those tormented got little support from the adults that took care of them. The only difference now is that she had her friends who have taught her what loyalty and love are.

She held her pendant, watching sparks from the bonfire spiral upward to meet the sun's last rays of light. From following a raven to North York Moors to stopping the collapse of the ecosystem. Never in her life did she imagine this to be where she would end up. They'd all changed – *she* had changed. The lost orphan who stepped through the stone portal was a person from another lifetime.

And the visions? The wolf's big yellow eyes still haunted her when she closed her own. Was Fenrir a warning of what's to come, or did it represent the danger they had already faced? And the Norns, whose messages are now fragments in her mind. What was she supposed to remember? And why did they call her "guardian"? The salmon roll on her wooden plate became unappetising.

'May I join you?' came a familiar voice. Astrid stood in front of her, a gentle smile on her face as the firelight caught the red threads in her hair.

'Yes, of course,' Aria scooted over.

'How are you?' Astrid asked as she settled beside Aria, taking in the sunset before them.

'Good, I guess.'

'Wonderful,' Astrid's voice softened. 'I was worried about all of you. What happened should never have happened. I'm only sorry we didn't find the source sooner. You were in grave danger.'

Aria looked down at her hands, unsure what to say to

Astrid's concern.

'Well, let's not dwell on the past.' Astrid's tone brightened. 'I came here with a proposal. I'm going back to Uppsala this summer, and I wanted to invite you to join me. If you don't have any plans, of course.'

Aria stared at her. She didn't even consider the summer break, having nowhere to go, and nothing arranged with her friends.

'I... don't know what to say.'

'You don't need to decide now,' Astrid said. 'It's a humble home, but Uppsala might give you some inspiration. It's a vibrant community. I have discussed this with Professor Halvard, considering your situation.'

'I would love that, actually.' Warmth spread through her chest. 'Thank you.'

Astrid's smile glowed warmer than the bonfire. She clapped her hands and stood. 'Fantastic! I'll meet you tomorrow at Eldviken.'

Aria watched her walk through the dancing crowd, appearing and disappearing as shadows danced in the firelight.

'Well, I guess I'm going to Uppsala,' she whispered to Fern who had materialised beside her.

'Uppsala is good for the soul,' Fern said, its voice like frost on glass.

CHAPTER TWENTY-EIGHT

Summer Winds

The morning sun painted Oakspire's stone walls gold as students climbed into horse wagons for the short ride to Eldviken. The clatter of hooves on the dirt path through the forest echoed the announcement of silence as students headed home for the summer break. Excitement lingered in the air.

The arrival at Eldviken was marked by the sweet scent of fresh cut grass and blooming flowers. While in winter it looked mysterious, on this summer's day, it was alive and hopeful: streets packed with students and locals; cafés bristling with movement; and various bicycles buzzing past.

The horses halted in front of a large wooden structure, its steep roofs marked by wooden dragon heads standing guard. The intricate knotwork carved through the wood was a reminder for travellers of Eldviken's Norse history. Massive timber pillars marked the large entrance through which Oakspire students entered, dragging bags or carrying large backpacks. Above the entrance was "Eldviken Train Station," its brass sign shining in the sun.

Aria jumped off the wagon, along with the friends she'd made. They stood by the entrance of the train station, unloading their bags. Aria had only her satchel, which carried books, homework, and summer clothes her wardrobe offered. She had not much else.

'Next group for Edinburgh!' called the train master through the speakers.

'Oh, that's me!' Fraser said, wide-eyed. He pushed his round glasses up. 'Well, that's goodbye then!' He gave each a hurried one-armed hug and darted inside without a backward glance, carrying a large backpack and two canvas bags with library books, one on either shoulder. He bumped into several people along the way, shouting, 'Sorry!' and 'Excuse me!' as he went.

'How is he getting to Scotland from here?' Aria asked, wondering if flying ships were a thing.

'Runestones, of course,' Finn said with a knowing smile. 'Norsemen roamed everywhere and left runestones as anchors. Step through them, and you'd arrive back in the Nordics – or elsewhere.'

'Why did I end up in the forest and not here?'

'Dramatic effect?' Finn said with a laugh. He leant in slightly. 'But here's the thing. The runestones know who you are and where you're meant to go. Two people can step through the same stone and end up in completely different places.'

'Oh, I suppose that's why they call people based on destinations?'

'Exactly. It would be messy otherwise, especially with us being underaged,' Finn said. 'Anyway, are you looking forward to Uppsala?'

Before she could answer, Taye burst between them. 'Of course she is! Uppsala is *amazing*. All those festivals and—' He broke off as the station bell rang. 'Oh shoot, that's my train.'

He pulled them both into a fierce hug, managing to ruffle Finn's hair in the process. He embraced Suraya and Inaiê and hurried into the train station, his yellow backpack bouncing with each step.

'Make sure you write!' Taye called over his shoulder as he ran.

'I don't even have your address!' Aria shouted after him.

'Honey, you don't need an address.' He grinned. 'Just ask Astrid!'

He barely dodged a cart of magical artefacts before disappearing through the crowd.

'I have to get going, too,' Suraya said, Louis chilling on her head, his eyes darting in every direction. 'I need to go to the souvenir shop first and get a gift for my parents. I know they would love anything magical. Maybe a magiflower that sings lullabies... though they'd probably want to study it, rather than enjoy it. Perhaps something less organic.'

'I'm sure you'll find something nice,' Aria said, embracing her roommate.

Suraya hugged Finn and Inaiê and rolled her massive suitcase behind her, which was packed with notebooks. Aria helped her pack them, each one with observations recorded during the year for her parents' curiosity.

Tenzin stepped beside them. Aria gave them a small wave, now accustomed to Tenzin's tardiness.

'Finally!' Inaiê said to Tenzin, squinting at the schedule board. 'We thought you'd miss the stones for Gyantse. How did you even manage to miss the wagon?'

'There was a moose wandering the grounds,' Tenzin said, beaming as they pushed their green fringe out of their eyes. 'I've never seen one before. They're enormous. And majestic. I couldn't just leave.'

'I saw a ghost moose,' Aria said. 'First day here. It was quite a welcome.'

'Aren't they great?' Tenzin agreed, glancing over at Eldviken's square. 'I'm going for a short walk. Might as well enjoy the warmth before heading home.'

'I'll join you,' Inaiê said, tugging at her black top. 'My stone to Paraytã isn't till later, and the Amazon's basically a wet furnace right now. I'll take all the mild air I can get.'

'Let's go then!' Tenzin said as they waved at Aria and Finn with enthusiasm. Tenzin walked away with their colourful backpack; they clearly had less things to carry than even Aria did.

Inaiê tipped her head, her index finger brushing her fringe in a lazy salute. She fell into step beside Tenzin, hands tucked into her shorts' pockets, a duffel bag of woven natural fibres slung casually over one shoulder.

'Good. This way Tenzin doesn't miss their ride home,' Finn said, chuckling.

'Next group for Dublin!' called the station master.

'That's me!' Finn said cheerfully. 'Write to me too, I want to know all about Uppsala!'

'Sure, if I figure out the mailing system. Can't I just write you a letter?'

'That works for me, too! But I think you'll appreciate the magical mailing system better.'

Aria raised an eyebrow, imagining magical pigeons flying at the speed of light.

Finn hugged her and walked inside to the runestones as the sun reflected his blond hair, a leather travel bag on one hand.

How strange it was that just months ago, they'd all been strangers.

'Ready?' said Astrid behind her.

'Yeah, I think I am.'

The station bell rang, its deep tone echoing through the building. Once inside, the Grand Hall was lighter than the building's exterior. White walls, illuminated by the sun coming in from the high windows above, reflected the stone floor below. Rows of benches were occupied by travellers, waiting for their train or runestone. The aroma of coffee made her turn to the long queue at the café, where people sat and chatted with ease.

They stepped into a simple old train on Platform One. The inside looked modern and spacious, the ceiling reflected the weather outside, the light beige benches looked comfortable, and the light wooden floorboards made it all look so fresh.

As the train pulled away from the station, Aria pressed her forehead against the cool glass. Eldviken shrank into the distance until there were only forests and occasional lakes.

'Tea?' Astrid asked, pulling out a thermos. Steam curled from the cup she poured, carrying the scent of birch and meadowsweet. 'An old recipe,' she added, when she caught Aria watching.

Aria wrapped her hands around the warm cup. 'I keep thinking about them,' she admitted. 'Taye and Finn. If I wasn't so... if I just... they could have...'

'They chose to stand by you,' Astrid said, her voice gentle but firm. 'That's what friendship is – not just the easy moments but choosing to face the hard ones together. They knew the risks.' She paused, a soft smile touching her lips. 'What a change for a girl who arrived with nothing but a backpack with a bag of crisps, isn't it?'

The mention of the crisps startled a laugh from Aria. 'You knew about that?'

'There are many things that I know, Aria Renwood,' Astrid said simply, with a twinkle in her eyes. She looked out the window where the landscape had changed to rolling farmland dotted with red wooden houses.

'Sometimes it scares me,' Aria admitted quietly. 'The magic. It's like... like it has its own ideas about things.'

'Magic always does. It's wild. It takes time to learn its ways.'

She reached into her bag and pulled out a small package wrapped in brown paper and gave Aria some cookies that smelled of cardamom.

'Uppsala has old magic,' Astrid said. 'Well, it's different from what you've known at Oakspire. Older. More settled into its ways.'

'Is that why you're taking me there? Because of the old magic?'

Astrid was silent for a moment, watching the countryside roll past. 'I wanted to take you there because everyone needs somewhere to belong,' she said finally. 'And Uppsala has a way of showing people where they're meant to be.'

'Is that where you are from?'

'Yes, born and raised.' She paused. Astrid looked Aria straight in the eyes with a small smile. 'My parents have since passed, and my sister, well, she's lost. Doesn't live in Uppsala anymore. So, I call Oakspire home now.'

'Have you looked for her?'

'I have. But there's nothing that can be done.' Her eyes tingled in the light and she turned to face the window.

Aria didn't want to ask any more questions. It was clear this was a tragic story.

The train curved around a lake. For a moment, Aria could have sworn there were figures moving by the water, echoes of ancient gatherings still playing out across time.

Finally, as the evening fell, Uppsala drew closer. After months being in the wilderness, the sight of an ordinary city was almost dreamlike. The cathedral towers came into view, rising above the town – watchers of the land, the sun high in the sky, illuminating the brickwork.

When the train pulled into Uppsala's central station, she might as well have stepped into another world. People walked hurriedly to their trains, holding paper coffee cups, and office workers in pressed shirts checked their phones while waiting for their bus. A university student lumbered past them with an overstuffed backpack, heading home for the summer break.

No one glanced twice at the large tracks that glittered faintly in the station's shadow, or the ravens that seemed too knowledgeable as they watched from the rooftops. Would Aria have noticed these things herself a year ago? Could there have been magical things hidden in plain sight in York that she never took notice of?

Astrid's cottage sat on the outskirts of Uppsala, where city gardens turned into a landscape of hills with a mosaic of grassland and forests.

It was smaller than Aria had imagined: a small red house with white frames around the windows, a herb garden wrapped around one side, flowers dancing to the summer's breeze. Inside, the white-painted walls and light wooden beams reminded her of illustrations from fairy tales.

'Home sweet home,' Astrid said, pushing open the door. 'It's where I grew up, though now I only come here in the summer, sometimes during winter break.'

Aria followed Astrid up the narrow stairs to one of the rooms upstairs. A bed with a patchwork quilt sat under a window that looked out over the garden and the woods beyond. A vase of wildflowers stood on the windowsill.

'I know it's not much—' Astrid started.

'It's perfect.' Aria meant it. After everything – the children's home, struggling with magic, the fracking – this cottage was a place where she could breathe.

They spent the night in a comfortable quiet, recovering from their travels. Astrid showed her where everything was, explained about the temperamental kettle that only boiled if you sang to it, pointed out which herbs in the garden were for cooking and which were for healing. It felt almost normal, except for moments when Aria caught Astrid watching her with an expression she couldn't read.

As she settled for the night, the cathedral bells tolled in the distance and wind rustled through the trees, carrying new scents. She looked out, mesmerised by the light when it was supposed to be dark.

A soft gronk made her look up. There, perched on a gnarled branch of the apple tree, sat a raven. But unlike the one she had met that day in York, this raven had only one black eye open, the other blinded white.

The raven called once more and spread its wings. It launched itself towards the distant woods, where the old gods once roamed.

Aria's pendant was enclosed tight in her hand, no longer a chain to her past but a root binding her to the present. Her heart swelled as she took in the warm fresh air.

Home at last.

Acknowledgments and Author's Note

The idea for Sunderroot, and the rest of the Threads of the World Tree series, was born during a summer of fieldwork surveying invasive species. Witnessing damaged ecosystems left me longing for healthier ones, and from that contrast grew a world where magic, like nature itself, is not infinite. This series has since become a mirror of the environmental crisis we face today. I wanted to tell a story that helps a generation understand the complexity of our natural world, while also inviting them into a place of magic, mystery, and fantasy.

I once imagined writing my debut in solitude, in the drawing room of an English manor, watching birds splash in a sunlit birdbath. That, of course, was not how it happened. Instead, this book was written in my apartment in Sweden, often in the evenings, and it was anything but solitary. This book would not exist without the help of many people.

To my developmental editor, Nej Steer, whose insightful wisdom helped shape this story; to my line and copy editor, Nicole Evans, who made the words shine; and to my proofreader, Wren L. Helgren, whose keen eye ensured a polished manuscript. Your dedication and brilliant suggestions transformed this work into something I am truly proud to share. Thank you.

To my beta readers who volunteered to read my unpolished work and somehow chose to remain my friends. Your honest feedback and constructive criticism strengthened every part of this story, and I am so thankful for your contagious enthusiasm.

This book would not be complete without the exceptional artistic talent of Zoe Badini, whose incredible skill brought a single description to life in a breathtaking cover.

To the online community of writers and artists who inspired and supported me in ways they may never realise. Your encouragement carried me through the toughest moments. And to those who personally guided me through the challenges of being an indie author, thank you.

To my friends and family who have cheered me on. It means a lot to be able to do this journey with all your support.

To my wife who helped me navigate plot holes despite not being a fantasy reader, who served as my alpha reader and in-house line editor, and who was my cheerleader and rock during moments of self-doubt. I could not have done this without you.

To my father my literary accomplice, whose bookshelves prepared me for this journey. Our early brainstorming helped shape the series, and your unwavering belief in me carried me through.

To my son who unknowingly sparked this entire adventure. You taught me more about magic and wonder in your first year of life than all the fantasy novels I have ever read.

And finally, to the readers who embark on this adventure with me. Thank you for giving these characters a home in your imagination.

Keep the magic alive

The adventure isn't over!

Join me online to peek behind the curtain of this world, discover secrets that didn't make it into the book, and be the first to know about the next book in the series.

Sign up at **christinajuhlin.se/newsletter**
or scan the QR-code:

About the author

Christina Juhlin is a fantasy author whose storytelling grew out of countless unfinished drafts, until the quiet hours of their newborn's contact naps sparked a new creative focus. Drawing from a background in conservation biology, they weave themes of nature, magic, and social justice into richly imagined worlds grounded in science, mythology, and folklore. They live in Sweden with their family, and when they're not writing, they can often be found hiking, birdwatching, or photographing the natural world. Sunderroot is their debut.

www.ingramcontent.com/pod-product-compliance
Lightning Source LLC
LaVergne TN
LVHW091029080826
845145LV00002B/415

* 9 7 8 9 1 9 9 0 6 7 0 0 1 *